The Vigil of Rain
Amanda Taylor

Published by Northern Heritage Publications
an imprint of D & M Heritage Press

Dunn & Mills Business Park
Red Doles Lane
Huddersfield
West Yorkshire HD2 1YE

www.dandmheritage.co.uk

First published 2016
Text © Amanda Taylor

ISBN 978–1–911148–02–9

"There is no faith which has never yet been broken, except that of a truly faithful dog."

Konrad Lorenz (7 November 1903 – 27 February 1989)

The Vigil of Rain Population Census 1901

Name	Occupation
ASHBERRY HALL	
Lord Frederick Hambleton	Gentleman
Andrew Ashberry	Gentleman
Gerard Ashberry	Gentleman
Stephen Ashberry	Gentleman
BROADSHAW FARM	
Reginald Bowden	Farmer
Mary Bowden	Wife
Lydia Bowden	Daughter
Malcolm Bowden	Son (Farmer)
THE CITY OF YORK	
James Cairn	Barrister-at-Law
Martin Trotter	Barristers Clerk
Winifred Holbrook	Scholar
John Beardsley	Member of Parliament
Louis Chatterton	Architect
Charnley Lodge	Private Secretary
Robert Brown	Solicitor
Digby West	Barrister-at-Law
THE CITY OF LEEDS	
Benjamin Levi	Kings Counsel
THIRSK	
Timon White	Police Inspector in The North Yorkshire Constabulary

Age	Status	Birthplace
68	Widowed	Ashberry
40	Unmarried	Ashberry
35	Unmarried	Ashberry
18	Unmarried	Ashberry
56	Married	Rievaulx
53	Married	Rievaulx
22	Unmarried	Rievaulx
20	Unmarried	Rievaulx
36	Unmarried	London
44	Unmarried	Poole-in-Wharfedale
24	Unmarried	Sligo, Ireland
39	Unmarried	York
26	Unmarried	York
34	Unmarried	York
39	Widowed	Dublin, Ireland
37	Unmarried	Northampton
40	Married	London
36	Married	Northallerton

Chapter One

1901 – The Queen is dead, long live the King – but no one was expecting very much from the new King: the erstwhile, *bon vivant* Prince of Wales, lover of Mrs Langtry and others.

However, Edward VII had set a trend and I was about to join the ranks of good livers myself. A legal colleague, Robert Brown, had invited me to accompany him to a weekend house party at Ashberry Hall deep in the Yorkshire Wolds. As things were to turn out it would be a weekend I would never forget, none of us would.

Set in its own parkland, the Hall was not the easiest place to reach from York. Although main carriage routes had improved in our region on the backs of the previous century's pioneering road builders, such as the partially blind local man John Metcalf of Knaresborough, nonetheless rural travel left a lot to be desired with rutted lanes traversing the country like arthritic limbs. It was a great relief when we eventually spilt from our carriage at journey's end, clutching our luggage for dear life.

'Feel like a shaken up bag of beans dumped by a Midwestern tornado,' said Brown.

I made no effort to reply – he had expressed my own Wild West sentiments exactly – we had obviously been reading the same literature.

'Ashberry Hall,' he announced, waving his hand exuberantly towards the Doric pile as if this would be compensation for our journey.

I stubbornly refused to be jolted out of my weariness – I had already been jolted enough – as some polished flunky insisted on tugging the Gladstone out of my hand.

'Wait until you see inside the house,' enthused Brown.

Robert Brown, affectionately known as Bob to his intimates, had told me the party was to celebrate an old friend's betrothal to a local girl. Brown and I had become close friends owing to our professional interests crossing more than once, he as solicitor and I as a barrister. At the eleventh hour Brown had invited me to escort him – be it reluctantly on my part – to this grand affair.

'My father and the patriarch of Ashberry Hall have been friends for almost a lifetime as they were at Trinity College, Dublin, together. It only followed that I would be chums with Lord Hambleton's son, Andrew,' he explained.

'That's not always the case,' I replied. 'I intensely disliked most of the sons of my father's army pals.'

'That's you all over, James,' retorted Brown. 'Relax, man, forget your cynicism for once and simply enjoy yourself.'

Brown was at least right about our current setting: the forty foot high hall within the building was truly magnificent with its Corinthian pilasters and baroque panels of female figures. Speaking of which, he and I were led into first one heavily oak panelled obviously bachelor suite and then into a second a little way down the long corridor. Both suites would be, at a guess, well away from the single ladies' rooms.

'You have first choice, James,' said Brown magnanimously.

'I do believe, Mr Brown, the Marquess designated this room for you,' came the liveried footman's down the nose assertion.

Shrugging, I told Brown a couple of nights stay was nothing to me and bounced back into the original room next door. Which, on closer inspection, was equally richly draped with a fine view overlooking the deer park.

A little later, watching the sunset turning the leaves of autumn to a translucent orange, I wondered if my role of accompanying "wallflower" to the already established Ashberry intimate, Bob Brown, might not turn out to be so bad after all.

'Mr Robert Brown and Mr James Cairn,' announced the butler.

Washed and groomed we entered the salon where that evening's ball was to take place. It was the Marquess of Hambleton himself who stepped forward to greet us.

'So glad you could come, Brown, and ...' he hesitated looking at me.

'My good friend, James Cairn,' introduced Brown.

'Ah, Cairn, the celebrated barrister. Your reputation goes before you, sir.'

'Lord Hambleton,' I acknowledged with a curt bow, before Brown and I quickly moved on deeper into the room.

'That's Gerard Ashberry, the Marquess' second son. See, he's standing over there talking to that elderly matron with the fan,' said Brown.

Unlike his father who was stoutly built, Gerard was extremely tall and lean. His hair was wispy and had seen better days but he made up for his bald crown with an elaborate moustache. He wasn't making the slightest effort to disguise that he was totally uninterested in the matron's company. He kept twisting one side of his moustache and looking about him with the nervous stretched neck of a threatened peacock.

'Was he a guard's officer?' I asked Brown.

'Yes, I believe he was and still is. He's just returned from fighting Kruger in the Transvaal. Do you know him?'

'I know the type,' I replied caustically.

'James, do try,' sighed Brown.

'Is there a Lady Hambleton?'

'Died years ago having their third child.'

'And the child?'

'The child lived. Stephen, the youngest brother, he's over there by the wall on his own watching on. Looks as if he's propping up that Corinthian column, doesn't he? Stephen's an affable enough chap but not a great one for company.'

'I have something in common with the youngest Ashberry then.' I looked to where Brown was pointing. Stephen Ashberry looked nothing like the rotund Marquess or thin Gerard. He was small with a beard – Abraham Lincoln in miniature.

'And that's the eldest Ashberry son, Andrew, Earl of Fadmoor, see over there. Come, I'll introduce you.'

Our boots beat a passage across the wooden floor. We sounded like two charging musk oxen. There was nothing to dampen our embarrassment. No one had started dancing yet, the guests spoke in the hushed modulated tones of the well-bred.

Andrew Ashberry immediately broke off what appeared to be an animated conversation at our approach.

'Brown, so glad you could make it,' he said.

'James Cairn, Lord Fadmoor,' introduced Brown.

'Thought you would have had a lovely lady on your arm by now, Robert, rather than a boy,' said Fadmoor, glancing at me with a rather disturbing appraisal.

'Boy? I am thirty-six,' I exploded.

'Well, I must say you don't look it,' said Fadmoor, winking at Brown.

'At a guess, sir, you yourself are not much older than I.'

Fadmoor, who looked to be in his early forties, refused to rise to my challenge. He had a confident air that the aristocracy – the super rich – all had. A presence that we minions lacked. I envied the peerage that.

'Gentlemen,' he announced, indicating a young bespectacled chap. 'Allow me to introduce you to Louis Chatterton, student of the history of art and architecture.'

'You're interested in architecture too, aren't you, James?' said Brown.

'Well, perhaps you'll be interested in Ashberry Hall then, Cairn, as Louis here is. Plans are already underway to restore much of William Wakefield's original building, that's if the old man will agree to foot the bill,' roared Fadmoor.

'William Wakefield? The same William Wakefield who was the architect of the Debtor's Prison in York?' I asked.

'The same,' confirmed Fadmoor.

'I'm not sure about Wakefield, but the baroque splendour of your home is very much in keeping with the style of Vanburgh.'

'Sir John Vanburgh was an associate of Wakefield's, I believe,' said Fadmoor.

'The Hall is eclectic to say the least, don't you think, Cairn?' asked Chatterton.

'Sorry?' interrupted Fadmoor, looking at Chatterton askance, saving me from having to give an answer.

'Well its styles are multiplex, Corinthian, Doric and this salon itself has a positively Ionic feel to it.'

'But eclectic? Is that such a bad thing?' asked a still perplexed Fadmoor.

'No, no,' muttered Chatterton. 'It is usual for the age.'

'Has the Marquess come round to the idea of your betrothal to Lydia yet, Lord Fadmoor?' cut in Brown, rather rudely I thought.

'No, no, he hasn't. Pa says I could have done much better than bring a village girl to foal,' smirked Fadmoor. 'Beautiful though she is.'

Speak of the devil or in this case an angel: a catch of breath – a breath taking moment – the room parted that Friday night as the most voluptuous creature I had ever seen entered the room, accompanied by an older but extremely fine looking woman whom I took to be her mother.

The angel's Saxon hair flowed freely and her unfashionable high colour was enhanced by a flowing almond green satin dress. A diamond cross pendant flashed against her neck. But forget fashion, she had the country freshness of youth that put the rest of the room into shade. Though not svelte, she appeared to glide across the floor as if on air. Some female guests released a collective sigh at this perfection in one of their own, the envious merely looked on tight-lipped. But it was the intensity of the men's appraisal that was disquieting – I was put in mind of Darwinian primates about to pounce. Even Gerard stopped toying with his moustache, his eyes fixed on the girl's every move. But Lydia Bowden seemed innocently unaware of the effect she was having on the gathered company. Ripe with the health and happiness of harvest fields, she swayed across to us – across to Andrew her fiancé – across to a fiancé who appeared to be the least affected by her beauty, preferring to smile affably at Chatterton instead.

'What a lovely ring, my dear,' said Brown, taking Lydia's hand in his. 'An emerald in a diamond cluster. It matches your dress perfectly.'

'According to the ancient Hindu writings of Veda, an emerald is the gemstone of good luck and improves one's personal well-being,' said Lydia.

Not the utterance of a village girl brought to foal, I noted.

'I believe emeralds were favoured by Cleopatra,' offered Chatterton somewhat obscurely.

'Let's dance,' said Fadmoor, offering his arm to Lydia.

'Quite an age difference,' whispered Brown.

'Twenty years, give or take a year or two,' I suggested.

'Yes, Fadmoor has taken some catching. I hope it works out for him this time.'

'Might I say he made a similar observation regarding you,' I reminded him.

'I have already been married. I intend to go to my grave a widower. No one could ever replace my late wife,' retorted Brown.

The floorboards began to rumble as most of the party took to the floor. Even the multi-layered chandeliers overhead tinkled from the energy in the room.

'Shall we dance?' I gestured to Brown. Brown creased over laughing. Chatterton frowned his disapproval.

Indeed the whole evening began to feel strange, unreal. Tension was in the air. Lord Hambleton glowered at his son and heir, as he and Lydia danced on. The penguin-suited Earl of Fadmoor moved rather stiffly compared to the flowing woman in his arms. I could see she was totally enamoured with him though. His feelings were not so transparent.

Then Gerard cut in on the betrothed couple. Fadmoor appeared to easily, too easily, relinquish his future bride. Stephen, still propping up his column, watched his brothers with superior sarcasm as Gerard scooped up Lydia with all the *joie de vivre* of a man recently relieved from action at Mafeking. Whereas Lydia had seemed beguiled by the older Ashberry, she now pulled an expression of mild distaste while dancing with enthusiastic Gerard – a guard's officer transformed.

Mopping his brow, Fadmoor gratefully returned to our small bachelor huddle.

'Do you think anything much will come of this Fawcett woman's commission?' he asked Brown.

Brown shook his head. He seemed unsure how to answer. We all sensed that the Boer War was nearing its end. No one in the legal profession was expecting very much government action regarding Millicent Fawcett's investigation into the disturbing allegations made in June by a Cornish woman, Emily Hobhouse. Hobhouse was a member of the Adult Suffrage Society, she visited Africa and sent word back about the appalling conditions in Lord Kitchener's concentration camps. We were not holding our breath either for the speedy disbandment of the camps, despite the Fawcett Commission beginning to send back reports confirming many of Hobhouse's findings.

'I have heard that the conditions in the Brandfort camp are particularly inhuman,' said Brown, finally finding his voice, a low measured voice at that.

'Yes, but having these bloody suffragists poking their noses into African affairs,' objected Fadmoor. 'What do they know about anything?'

'They know about oppression,' cut in Chatterton surprisingly.

'Well, Gerard's just back from being bombarded by the pom-pom. I think he would have a word or two to say about oppression,' snapped

Fadmoor. 'Any rate, he says improvements in administration have already begun in the camps.'

'A bit late in the day,' I piped up. 'Thousands of Boer women and children, mainly children, have perished in our "care", and no one has even troubled to investigate mortality in the black native camps. We considered ourselves to be triumphant, but I always question the validity of a victory conducted in an enemy's backyard.'

'Look at Afghanistan,' agreed Brown. 'Nationals keep on fighting to the last man while all invading armies eventually go home.'

'Are you two white feather men or what?' jeered Fadmoor. We did not respond to the taunt. 'Fancy a little partridge shooting in the park tomorrow?' he asked; abruptly lowering the temperature as he turned to watch his fiancée still dancing with his brother. 'Pa's got it all arranged, dogs, guns, beaters and keepers.'

'Will Gerard be leading the way, Lord Fadmoor?' enquired Brown.

'Please, gentlemen, no need for all this formality, call me Andrew.'

'So will Gerard be showing us all how it's done again,' persisted Brown.

'Ah, you are referring to the seventy-seven pheasants he bagged with only eighty shots last season,' sighed Fadmoor. 'Put us all to shame. He might be persuaded to lower his sights and make an appearance.'

'And Stephen, will Stephen be joining us this time?' asked Brown politely.

'Stephen?' frowned Fadmoor.

'Stephen doesn't like killing things,' interjected Chatterton.

Chapter Two

"Stephen doesn't like killing things," well neither did I. I had once spent a week some years ago stalking the deer in Sutherland with my friend Digby West. Although I had evolved into a reasonable shot, once had been enough. I had sworn then that I would never take part in field sports again, and the rapid firing technique required to bring down small birds was totally alien to me.

However after a sumptuous breakfast, throughout which Brown had pressured me to give the partridge shoot a try, we took to the outdoors.

Grey clouds hung low in the sky like leaden weights. Brown confessed he had been on numerous shoots before. I had no idea of what to do or the new terminology being bandied about either: driving; walking up; pointers; flushing dogs; retrievers; brace and bags. I felt ill at ease in this new rarefied sporting environment and extremely ignorant.

We walked across the parkland to a wilder more open landscape of rounded hills and steep valleys. Andrew and Gerard Ashberry strode out a yard or two ahead, their expensive looking guns breeched. I could not help noticing that Gerard had a tic in his left cheek, and his hand was shaking as he smoothed back his hair. Perhaps his aim wouldn't be quite as steady after the stresses of the Transvaal.

'The Wolds proper,' announced Brown with glee.

Cloth-capped Thomas, a highly experienced instructor and loader, had been appointed to me by the Ashberrys as they judged me to be a relatively novice gun. He explained that we were about to embark on a driven grey partridge shoot know as a battue – the beating of woods and bushes to flush out game – first introduced to this country by the Prince Consort in the 1840s.

I was told to stand in line with the other eight guns, two of which to my surprise were women. Thomas presented me with an unloaded shotgun. He advised me how to handle it, feel the weight of it, before sighting and pressing the weapon against my shoulder.

Suddenly I heard a distant shriek. Thomas pressed his binoculars into his eyeballs.

'A covey of birds are heading our way,' he said, dragging the gun from me to load. 'Be bold and focused, sir. Instead of waiting for the inevitable you must go out to meet them birds, choke barrel first. My advice is to point the gun's muzzle into the mass of birds, before one individual pops up as being the right one for you. Go for it and take your shot, keeping your cheek firmly on the stock until you see the bird fall to ground.'

I did as he said, conscious of the amusement around me.

'*Bang.*' The gun jumped against my shoulder. I saw a formless black shape tumbling out of the threatening sky to earth.

I would have felt sorry for the bird if it had not been for Brown. He was staring at me in paralytic disbelief. This was to be his moment, his accomplishment, his area of expertise and I had stolen it from him.

'*Bang. Bang.*' The other guns had no time to applaud me with their own kills to make.

'*Bang.*' My next shot missed as a second flight of birds flew over.

Brown had not moved, missed his chance of a prize, and it began to rain heavily.

'Just a lucky first shot,' I reassured him. I turned to Thomas asking, 'Can we go back to the Hall now it's raining?'

My instructor shook his head wryly. 'We've a few more drives to make yet before lunch, sir.'

During the next passage of birds, Brown shot two. I was too excited to hit anything else, and due to my nervousness the kedgeree I had enjoyed for breakfast was beginning to repeat. Altogether our party shot thirty brace of partridges before the morning ended.

I was glad of a rest and the protection of the shooting lodge as I tucked into the prepared packed lunch. But in truth, apart from being famished, cold and wet, I was becoming emotionally uncomfortable. Shooting down birds for sport and enjoyment wasn't quite my style. Now hunting for food, that was a different matter, that made a lot more sense to me. Certainly the birds we shot that day would be eaten but the "sport" seemed the most important thing to the guns. These rather pretentious types gathered round the plank table weren't quite my thing either. Their wealth had mainly come from inheritance rather than brains and industry. There was a distinct class division involved in field sports too. The beaters, who had walked miles in military formation to flush out the birds, sat someway off in their humble turfed hut.

Still, the Ashberrys were my hosts for the weekend, and I felt it would have been churlish of me to express my class sensitivities at this juncture. But then the Ashberrys were not at the plank table. Andrew and Gerard were nowhere to be seen. I guessed they certainly would not have been breaking bread with the beaters.

'What do you do for a living?' asked one of the toffs, struggling to place me.

'I'm a barrister,' I said.

He bit into his beef sandwich lost for further comment.

Brown looked at home amid all this. In our professional life I would never have put him down as a sportsman.

'I saw you shoot two partridges down in one covey.' The lady next to Brown was full of praise for him. 'Would you like a piece of my Battenberg cake?' she asked him, adjusting her fox fur stole. 'Watching my figure, you know.'

Brown scoffed his second helping of pink and yellow chequered sponge down in two mouthfuls to my disgust. I could see he was revelling in his reputation of being a useful shot. At that point I left, eager to escape and take the air, hating my weakness for agreeing to participate in this event.

'Are you sure you've never used a gun before?' the Head Keeper asked me out in the yard: a slim, extremely fit looking countryman, his peaked cap failing to contain a mass of blond hair.

'He's a natural,' quipped Thomas.

'Just beginner's luck,' I reiterated, before admitting that I had once stalked the deer.

'But partridges are particularly difficult customers to hunt. They are the most unpredictable intelligent birds,' said the Head Keeper.

'You must come again, Cairn,' said Andrew, striding up to us.

'Yes,' tee-heed Chatterton in his wake.

'Are you part of the shoot?' I asked Chatterton. I had not seen him during the morning drives.

'No, no, I've better things to do with my time,' he jeered.

'You should see His Lordship shoot,' countered the Head Keeper, obviously offended. 'The Marquess is one of the finest guns in the land.'

'Yes, even now,' sighed Andrew. 'Pa's one of the quickest men I've ever seen to get his shots off.'

In the afternoon, I managed to wing another two birds; Brown shot six outright; our party as a whole shot forty brace of partridges and eighty-five pheasants. I wondered if we would be given any game birds to take home the next day. I was getting hungry from exercise and country air. My stomach growled at the thought of partridge, shallots and lean ham sweetened by a generous splash of Madeira. However we had the night to come, and the events of the night were about to obliterate all thoughts of *salmi de perdrix*.

* * * * *

'For what we are about to receive ...' The Marquess said grace and we fell on the turtle soup like savages. It appeared to be a dinner for gentlemen only.

'Nothing like a day's shooting to stimulate a man's appetite,' murmured Chatterton, placed on my left.

'How would you know, you didn't shoot?' I retorted more sharply than intended.

'Oh, I know,' he replied smiling.

'Who planned this seating arrangement?' I whispered my complaint to Brown.

'Andrew, I expect.'

Following the poached salmon and *confit de canard*, Andrew proposed the first toast of the evening.

'"Drink to her that each loves best, and if you nurse a flame that's told but to her mutual breast, we will not ask her name".'

'A strange toast for an Englishman to make,' I muttered.

'Yes, Thomas Campbell,' slurred Brown, already well in his cups.

Peering over his eyeglass the Marquess cast his gaze at Andrew, then at us, then down the rest of table.

'Where's that bloody whelp of a son, Stephen?' he growled.

'He wasn't on the shoot, Pa,' replied Andrew.

'Neither was Chatterton but he seems to be here already flushed with wine.' His Lordship didn't wait for a reply, perhaps expecting none. 'Where's

Gerard then? I'll not have guests late for dinner, least of all my own sons.'

'He was feeling unwell at lunchtime, Pa, and left the shoot to return home,' explained Andrew.

'Well, where is he now?' demanded the old man. The shooting party at the table shook their heads. 'Has anyone seen him?' His next appeal was made to the servants.

'I'll send a man up to Mr Gerard's room right away, Your Lordship,' replied the butler. Smethers was a decrepit looking character, bent towards the earth, who looked for all the world as if he had just stepped out of Dracula's castle in Transylvania.

Irrespective of the missing Gerard we tucked into our sirloin of beef with chateau potatoes as if there was no tomorrow.

The slick haired manservant soon reappeared and whispered something to the butler. The butler's already creased brow furrowed deeper as he in turn addressed His Lordship's ear.

'His bed's unused?' shouted the Marquess. 'So where the hell is the bugger? I'll not have it, I tell you, I'll not tolerate discourtesy in my house.'

The Marquess' temper abated somewhat with the coolness of peaches in jelly. But I saw that Andrew was beginning to look rather worried regarding his absent brother, and had distanced himself from the rest of us. He didn't even laugh at Chatterton's dry jokes as he normally did.

'Pa, maybe we should send some of the men out into the park. Maybe Gerard was taken badly on the way back here this afternoon and is laid up somewhere.'

'Do as you please,' snapped the Marquess. 'Drunk somewhere is probably more the truth of it with your brother. He's not been the same since returning from Africa.'

'Right,' said Andrew, springing up followed by Chatterton.

'I'll come too,' slurred Brown.

'Me, also,' offered another man.

By the time the shooting party had joined up with workers rallied from across the estate there must have been twenty or more of us. The Marquess was left alone to wallow in his jelly dessert at the head of the table, and level insults against the characters of his younger sons to indifferent household servants.

The evening had drawn in but it was a full moon. I hardly needed my borrowed lantern as I struggled up the grassed terrace and along to the Ionic Temple, which, like the Hall, was built in the style of Vanburgh in the 1730s. The building was an open rotunda with ten fluteless columns supporting a frieze and cornice. The architecture reminded me of the Temple of Vesta, which I had visited during a trip to Rome in my youth. I looked up to the lead domed roof – a perfect protection against the weather – and wondered if a sick Gerard might have sought shelter here. Shining the lantern carefully round each pillar, I was relieved to find no one.

I began to walk along the half-mile grassed terrace between temples, swinging my lantern this way and that.

'Over here.' A strident male voice hollered through the darkness. 'My God! He's over here.'

My heart dropped. Fifty/fifty – I had chosen my temple well. The accented Yorkshire voice was not coming from my Ionic Temple but from its balancing twin, the Doric Temple, south from me. The door was flung back on its hinges. Chatterton stood transfixed in the entrance as if not daring to venture further.

More men, many men had reached the building before me. They buzzed like angry excited wasps beneath the dome – their agitated cries enhanced by the acoustics.

'Is he all right?' yelled Andrew.

The estate worker who found him was now speechless. I could see the man's pallor even in the poor lighting. Andrew pushed him aside and inched through the now silent colony, his evening pumps sliding in the mess of blood emanating from his supine brother. He knelt next to him, feeling his neck for a pulse.

'He's cold. Cold.' Andrew looked up at us in bewilderment.

I could see Gerard's chest was opened up and bloody. Yet his face was untouched and perfectly still, the colour of marble. His mouth gaped a little as if in surprise. A shotgun rested across his trunk.

'How can I tell the old man?' asked his brother in a plaintive moan. 'What will I tell him?'

'Obviously an accident,' said the Head Keeper calmly. 'You'll tell your father it was a shooting accident, Master Andrew. These things 'appen.' He gestured to another man to lead both Lord Fadmoor and the anguished estate worker away from the scene.

The corpse was wrapped up in a cloak and several of us helped to carry it back to the Hall. How easily Gerard had become an *it*. How eventually we all do.

As we passed, I noticed Chatterton remained in the same position leaning in the doorway. His face was expressionless. He had not moved a muscle, not even to support his friend Andrew Ashberry.

Gerard's body was laid out on a chaise longue in the great hall. The Marquess was beside himself. Andrew had fallen silent. Amid the furore the outside doorbell rang followed by loud impatient knocking. An in-shock footman staggered forward to open the door, only to be thrust aside by a muscular young man bursting into the hall.

'What on earth do you want, Malcolm?' demanded Andrew.

'Where's Lydia? Where is my sister, Ashberry? You said she would return home in the morning before the shoot. It's eleven o'clock at night now.'

'Is it?' said Andrew indifferently.

'Yes. Is Lydia still here with you?' asked her brother, looking round the hall askance. It was then that he focused on the chaise longue – on the draped marble corpse of Gerard – and his mouth fell open.

'Lydia told me last night she intended to walk back to the village early this morning. She insisted that she would be all right alone, taking the air was good for her,' mumbled wooden Andrew.

'Well, she's not arrived. Our mother is frantic with worry, says she is convinced something has happened to …' Lydia's brother's voice trailed away. He looked across at Gerard again as if trying to make some connection with the dead body and his missing sister.

The connection wasn't made, would not be made for a long time. There was to be no Sunday roast the next day and there was no gift of game birds to take home for Brown and me. All social niceties had vanished at Ashberry Hall following Gerard's death and Lydia's disappearance. Our appetite gone. We left without breakfast.

Chapter Three

A month or two later, I was looking out of my office window down onto Bootham. It was one of those December twilights when night comes in early and cities throw their own magic. Above the pavement entrapped spirits flickered within their glass cages while escaping house light splashed more robust illumination across the street. I blinked – whom should I see passing below. I blinked again – was I mistaken? No, it was definitely Andrew Ashberry and Chatterton. Then, to my amazement, I saw a third man who appeared to be trailing them. He was darting behind basement railings, pulling into doorways with great athleticism. Though he wore a cloth cap pulled down over his eyes from his superb muscular physique I could have sworn it was Lydia's brother, Malcolm Bowden.

'Trotter! Trotter!' I screamed for my clerk Martin Trotter. If not actually at a trot, he came at a fast walk. He must have thought I was having a heart attack. 'See those two men walking in the direction of Bootham Bar with a third slinking behind them, do you think you could follow them? You are not known to any of them but they are known to me and I would be recognised.'

'Leave it to me.' Without further ado, I could hear Trotter's feet bounding down the stairway towards street level.

It was some time, perhaps an hour, before a coatless, shivering, all in the line of duty Trotter returned.

'Well?' I asked.

'Well, indeed,' he retorted.

'Did you keep up with them?'

'I did. I shadowed the three of them.'

'Where were they going?'

'All the way to Coney Street. The first two men stood outside a jeweller's there, James Inglis'. They seemed uncertain what to do. Eventually the taller of the two remained outside while the slighter man went inside the premises.'

'And the third man?'

'The third man remained skulking in a doorway across from the shop. When the first two men walked off together he went into Inglis'.'

'What did you do then?'

'I decided to follow the original pair. They got into a waiting carriage outside the Three Cranes in St Sampson's Square.'

'I think I will pay a call on Mr James Brown Inglis myself before the trail runs cold.'

'Do you know him then, sir?'

'Mr Inglis is well known to me. He is an upstanding citizen of York. Our paths have crossed on occasions more through his political interests than through trade.'

'Can I come with you?' Trotter asked.

'If you like. I think all our other business is finished for the day.'

'Here, you'd better put this on until you warm up.' I threw him his sack coat before reaching down my Chesterfield from the stand.

Coney Street was once the road which ran along the boundary of a Roman fortress. Its present name derives from Cuningstreta, Konungra and straet, the Viking for King's Street. In 1200 this was the Jewish quarter of the city with its own synagogue. Aaron of York had his residence here. Aaron, fil Josce, moneylender and arch presbyter of the Jewish community in England, was reputed to be one of the richest Jews in the realm. For taxation purposes his estate was worth £40,000 in 1241. Between that year and 1255, Henry III and royal taxation began to bleed him dry. Henry imposed the indignity of confiscating Aaron's prize black palfrey, presenting it as a gift to Bishop Passelewe. Aaron died in 1268 in penury.

Brushing away thoughts of the humiliations and thefts meted out to my fellow citizens in the past, Trotter and I pushed through the doorway of Number 4, Coney Street, to be greeted by a middle-aged Arian rather than a medieval Jewish retailer. The bell still clunking in our ears, the shop's proprietor regarded us quizzically from behind the boundary of his counter – this was a jeweller's after all and his wares were expensive.

'I was just about to close,' he announced.

'Mr Inglis?' I asked.

'Indeed.'

'Perhaps you don't remember me.'

'Mr Cairn, isn't it?' James Inglis seemed surprised. 'I believe I've not had the pleasure of welcoming you onto my premises before.'

'No, sir, our last meeting was outside the council chamber.'

'That's right. I do remember now. So, how can I be of service?'

'I am searching for an unusual ring for a very special young lady,' I explained.

Trotter cleared his throat and glared at me in astonishment.

'And as your reputation in the jewellery trade is second to none ...' I rushed on.

'I am sure we will be able to find something that will please the young lady.' Inglis was in no mood for flattery with an evening meal awaiting him at home.

'Something expensive,' I told him.

He pulled out a tray of exquisite rings.

'More expensive,' I insisted.

'Well, I ...' Inglis' monocle dropped down from his eye. Wrinkles began to form all the way up to his receding hairline.

'The ring doesn't have to be new but it does have to be expensive,' I added, as if trying to be helpful. 'My lady friend is particularly found of emeralds.'

'That's a strange coincidence,' said Inglis. 'No more than an hour ago a gentleman brought in a diamond cluster ring for sale whose centre piece is one of the most magnificent emeralds I have ever seen.'

'And have you got that ring to show me?'

Inglis hesitated. His bushy moustache twitched as if sensing something was awry. Born in Edinburgh this canny Scot was one of the finest gold and silver engravers of our time. He was nobody's fool, least of all mine.

'I have only just bought it from the gentleman but already I have a customer in mind,' he said.

'Nevertheless, might I take a peek?'

Inglis turned on his heels and disappeared into a backroom.

'What's this about a young lady?' queried Trotter, afraid that our chummy bachelor allegiance was under threat.

I answered with a finger to my lips and steel in my expression.

'Here we are,' said the returning Inglis; his native accent growing more pronounced and ready for business. He placed the emerald and diamond cluster ring on a black cloth on the counter between us.

My heart skipped a beat. Even Trotter gasped at the brilliance of the gems. There was no mistake: this was the same ring I had seen on Lydia

Bowden's finger the night of her engagement party at Ashberry Hall.

'And what, sir, is the asking price for this ring?' I enquired.

'Although strictly secondhand, this ring has hardly ever been worn,' prevaricated Inglis.

'The price, sir,' I insisted.

'Two hundred and eleven pounds.'

Trotter whistled and I sighed.

'As I thought way beyond my means. But who I wonder is willing to sell this extraordinary piece?' I asked.

'I cannot tell you that, Mr Cairn, client confidentiality.'

'Of course you can't but a word of caution, Mr Inglis, you cannot sell this ring either at present.'

The mouth beneath the moustache gaped open. 'What are you saying, Mr Cairn? You aren't saying this ring has been stolen? Why the gentleman who brought it in works for one of the most respectable county families. I know him well.'

'I know him too,' I admitted. 'Louis Chatterton. At present he is working over at Ashberry Hall.'

'I glimpsed the Earl of Fadmoor, himself, waiting for his man outside,' admitted Inglis.

'So, did I,' let out Trotter. I could have killed him.

'What happened after they left?' I asked Inglis.

'Another young man came in. He was asking the same questions as you,' replied Inglis; his frown deepening. 'He asked what Mr Chatterton was doing in my shop. Perhaps unwisely I revealed he had been trying to sell jewellery, a ring.'

'Did you show him the ring?' I asked.

'No, no, of course not. I didn't know him from Adam and he didn't look the type to be able to afford such a piece.'

'Not a word to anyone about this, Mr Inglis. Not until I've had a chance to look into the matter further.'

'Please, reassure me, Mr Cairn, unless you do I'll not sleep a wink tonight. I'm not about to be accused of dealing in stolen property, am I?'

'Sleep soundly, Mr Inglis, you've not sold anything yet. Rest assured, it is not you who has done anything wrong.'

'But will I be recompensed for my purchase?'

'That I cannot say. But what is a loss of earning to a loss of freedom.'

With that we left the jeweller to ponder his afternoon's innocent, if possibly costly, transaction.

Trotter and I parted at St Martin's Church beneath the famous double-sided clock with its jaunty admiral atop scanning the horizon with a sextant. This iconic figure's mind and thoughts appear to be far above the petty cares and woes of generations of York citizens, including mine at that moment. What impulse had directed me to have my clerk follow those men to Mr Inglis'? What was I getting involved in? I needed time to think, time to myself.

Fortunately, York is blessed with many quiet churches for contemplation. I crossed over the river Ouse to North Street and the Parish Church of All Saints. Originally a site of worship since the 11th century, here was a small oasis away from the hustle and bustle of the streets. Its beautiful stained glass windows fascinated me, particularly the Corporal Acts of Mercy Window with its glimpse into medieval life through panels depicting feeding the hungry; clothing the naked; supplying drink to the thirsty; visiting the sick; offering strangers hospitality, and finally visiting and relieving three prisoners who appeared to be in the stocks. Stocks like the 18th century one I had recently seen in the churchyard of Holy Trinity on Micklegate, a reminder of the punishments dispensed to the mainly unfortunate by a populace hungry for cruelty. What justice this? Did not Lydia Bowden, a good living country lass, deserve her day of truth and justice? Whatever viper's nest I had to dig out to get there and however long it took, I swore on that late afternoon in All Saints Church that I would find out what happened to Lydia Bowden.

Chapter Four

'Trotter, who is Thomas Hill's successor in the North Riding Constabulary?' I asked my clerk the next morning.

'I believe a Major Bower is now acting Chief Constable, sir.'

'Pity, I enjoyed a good relationship with Hill.'

'I know you did, sir. Wasn't it Captain Hill who originally led the old North York Militia?' asked Trotter. I nodded. 'Unfortunately, I believe Captain Hill passed away over two years ago.'

'As always I bow to your encyclopedic knowledge, Trotter.'

'Would you like me to contact Major Bower for you, sir?'

'No, not yet, Trotter. This situation is very delicate, particularly with the Ashberrys being involved. We need more information. Better to get word to Mr Robert Brown first and ask him if he would be good enough to attend chambers as soon as possible.

'Where's the lovely Emma?' asked Bob Brown that afternoon, as our new middle-aged acquisition, Mrs Perdue, set a tea tray down before us. Mrs Perdue had the look of a woman who had suffered some great disappointment in life; her mouth forever set against the slightest suspicion of a smile.

'Emma has left us in the shambles,' I whispered to Brown, as soon as Mrs Perdue was out of the door.

'"In the shambles"?'

'Yes, she is going to marry a chap called Lawrence who owns a butcher's shop down in the Shambles.'

'Ah! I see,' laughed Brown. 'A great loss indeed to *Bingham, Leacock, Fawcett and Cairn*. And more to the point where are the macaroons?'

'I don't believe Mrs Perdue runs to macaroons. Anyway, haven't you just had lunch?'

'I could always find a place for Emma's almond macaroons. Now tell me, James, why have you got me here with such urgency? With no appointments scheduled, I thought I might get in a spot of Christmas shopping this afternoon.'

'A very delicate matter has arisen. Seriously, Bob, as well as your friendship with the Ashberrys do you act as their solicitor?'

'Of course I do. I thought you knew that, James.'

'Do you remember that spectacular engagement ring the missing Lydia Bowden was wearing the night of the ball at Ashberry Hall?' I felt nothing would be gained by subtlety and launched in.

'Yes, I think I complimented her on it at the time.'

'Well, we've discovered that Louis Chatterton, accompanied by Andrew Ashberry, sold that same ring to a jeweller in Coney Street.'

Brown's expression froze.

'Are you sure?' he asked.

'Yes, Trotter followed them to the shop. I later saw the ring for myself. An even more perplexing angle to this situation is that I believe Lydia's brother, Malcolm Bowden, was following them too.'

'Did Bowden know that Chatterton and Andrew were selling Lydia's ring?'

'I don't believe so. At least he never gained conclusive affirmation it was that particular ring involved as the jeweller refused to show it to him.'

'But the jeweller showed it to you?'

'He knows me and I pointed out that it might be stolen.'

'Stolen?' exclaimed Brown. 'Surely it is too early to make that inference when Andrew bought that ring for Lydia in the first place.'

'But as you will be aware, in law, unless she was the one to break off the engagement and gave the ring back to him willingly that property remains hers.'

'Then perhaps she did. Perhaps she didn't want to go ahead with the wedding and felt morally obliged to return Andrew's ring.'

'From her disposition at the ball I don't think that likely, do you?'

'Perhaps the ring was a family heirloom.'

'It was not.'

'Or given on condition that it would be returned if the marriage failed to take place.'

'Just suppose it had been Andrew who had decided to call the wedding off, a breach of promise suit could quickly have followed, and irrespective of any ensuing litigation I am sure that engagement ring would still have been deemed to be Lydia's.'

'Yes, although would she have wanted to keep it under those circumstances. But this is all conjecture on our part, James. I didn't get the impression anything was amiss between the couple that weekend, did you?'

'Perhaps not. But you have to admit the fact that she is missing and Ashberry sold her engagement ring looks very suspicious.'

'What are you going to do about this?'

'Before contacting the police, I wondered if you might be able to elicit a reasonable explanation from your client.'

'But what if something untoward has occurred? Wouldn't that put Andrew on his guard?'

'That being the case he will already be on his guard.'

'This is all very irregular,' fussed Brown. 'But in the circumstances, I could try.'

* * * * *

A week later Bob Brown returned to Bootham Chambers with a rather sullen looking client in tow. Chatterton was not with them which caused me little regret.

'Please,' I indicated the two chairs at the other side of the table. 'You don't mind if my clerk, Martin Trotter, sits in on our discussion, do you?'

'I've nothing to hide,' blustered Ashberry. 'Now what's this all about, Cairn? Brown here tells me you have had your man spying on me.'

Trotter, seated across the way at his own desk, scowled at being dismissively referred to as my "man".

'I was concerned, Lord Fadmoor,' I said, doing my best to avoid Trotter's hostility. 'I saw you and Mr Chatterton walk below my window and realised you were being followed by a third party.'

'Followed, followed by whom?' Taking off his fashionable grey Homburg – made fashionable by Bertie, when Prince of Wales – Ashberry slid the hat on the table between us like a barrier.

'I could not identify the man with any certainty,' I prevaricated; glad that Brown had not furnished His Lordship with too many details. 'Whoever he was he looked a roughneck and I feared for both your and Mr Chatterton's safety. My clerk was merely making sure you reached your destination unmolested.'

'Well, I expect I should thank you for that,' conceded Ashberry with a sulky reluctance.

'Now tell me, Lord Fadmoor, have you had any word from your missing ex-fiancée?'

'No, not as yet.'

'That must be of some concern to you.'

'For me, not for you,' snapped Ashberry.

'Can you tell me, My Lord, why you sold a ring to a jeweller in Coney Street late last Wednesday afternoon?'

'So, you had your man snoop into that shop after we'd gone,' objected Ashberry turning pale.

'No, it was I, personally, who visited the shop.'

'Why, for heaven's sake?'

'Because, Lord Fadmoor, I learnt from my clerk that was exactly what the shadowing third party had done. Once you had left, he went into Mr Inglis' shop.' I felt nothing could be gained now from protecting James Brown Inglis' partial cooperation with us. 'We feared he was set on compromising either you or the jeweller in some way.'

'I see,' said Ashberry. I wasn't sure he saw at all. I wasn't convinced he realised the difficult position he was in.

'Why, sir, were you selling your fiancée's ring?'

'I ...' Ashberry hesitated, looked flustered, cornered even.

Brown shuffled uncomfortably in his squeaking leather chair.

'You don't have to answer any of Mr Cairn's questions, Andrew,' he instructed his client. 'But if there is a simple explanation, matters need not go any further than this room.'

'"Matters"?' exploded Ashberry. 'My private matters.'

'No, police matters,' retorted Brown.

'How was it that you had that ring in your possession?' I asked. 'Had Lydia Bowden broken off your betrothal?'

'No, no, as far as I was concerned our wedding was going ahead as planned.'

'So how did you come to be selling her engagement ring?' I was determined to get an answer.

Ashberry took a deep gulp of air. 'I don't exactly know why myself.'

'You don't?'

'If I tell you the truth, I'm not sure you'll believe me.'

'Try me,' I said.

'You remember how after the shoot dinner we found my brother's body in the Doric Temple.'

'We are hardly likely to forget,' muttered Brown.

'We then laid him to rest on the chaise longue back at the Hall.' Ignoring Brown, Ashberry gulped again over his own more personal memory.

'Please go on,' I encouraged.

'Well,' sighed Ashberry. 'After everyone else had gone to bed, I found Lydia's ring in Gerard's waistcoat pocket.'

* * * * *

What are you going to do about this? Bob Brown had asked me before my interview with Andrew Ashberry.

'What are you going to do about this?' Martin Trotter asked the same question as soon as Ashberry and Brown had left.

'Did you think his story credible?' I bounced the question back to him.

'It's not for me to say, sir.'

'Proof, we need more proof one way or the other.'

'But if Lord Fadmoor was telling the truth perhaps the key to Gerard Ashberry's death and his fiancée's disappearance is that the engagement ring was found on his brother's person. Then again if he is lying, and people do, why was he selling the ring of a girl who has only been missing for a few months?'

'That is the mystery, Trotter.'

'Would you still like me to contact Chief Constable Bower, sir?'

'No, no, take this note round to James Brown Inglis and ask him to confirm in writing that an emerald and diamond cluster ring was sold to him last Wednesday by Chatterton. If he is in possession of a bill of sale that would be even better. And Trotter, tell Inglis he is free to sell the ring on now to his prospective customer.'

It wasn't long before Trotter arrived back in a state of great excitement. He waved the bill of sale in his right hand like a referee's handkerchief.

'Sir, sir,' he shouted. 'Mr Inglis realised as soon as we left the other day that he had failed to mention, he was the one who had originally sold the ring from new to Andrew Ashberry six months earlier.'

'Thank you, Trotter,' I told him, locking the bill of sale in my desk drawer. 'Maybe one day this might be a piece of important evidence.'

But with Ashberry involvement I knew we would need a lot more than that.

Chapter Five

"Everything flows and nothing stays", said the Greek, Heraclitus, around 475 BC.

1905. Four years on in my own era.

Are you going to Scarborough Fair – for you'll find no pier there. At the very beginning of the year East Coast gales washed away Scarborough Pier and flooded Great Yarmouth. *Parsley, sage, rosemary and thyme* – a simple pagan love charm but perhaps the world has become far too complex for things to be so easily warded off. If anything can be conceived as more important than Scarborough's misfortune, then I have seen it in this morning's newspaper – a day or two old image that reflects a world which will never be the same. But I digress ...

I ran across my old friend Bob Brown in the County Court House earlier today. He was there on behalf of a farmer who had shot at a trespassing dog on his land. Unfortunately the dog was still on a lead and, instead of the dog, the farmer shot its owner in the foot – whether accidentally or deliberately has not yet been determined.

Meeting Brown and hearing about his agricultural client's predicament, I was reminded of the tragic shooting incident at Ashberry Hall. Brown told me there had been no more developments regarding the affair – it remained a mystery. Andrew's fiancée was never seen again after the night of the ball. She never reappeared to alleviate her family's suffering. Lydia Bowden has been missing for well over three years now.

Many rumours and counter rumours continued to follow in the wake of her disappearance. Surely Gerard's death and her fate must have been linked in someway. Had he fallen in love with her? – murdered her rather than let his brother marry her? Had he then killed himself? But, if true, why was Lydia's ring in his pocket? Poor Lydia had been so reassured that her emerald engagement ring denoted good luck and well-being. Where was that luck now? – missing and presumed dead.

Back at Bootham Chambers, I could not help reflecting on the eerie similarities to Gerard's death and that of Francis Archibald Douglas, Viscount Drumlanrig: both men were put down as victims of "accidental death" by a coroner. Drumlanrig had been found shot in the head in a ditch some eleven years before Gerard's fatal shooting in the Doric Temple. Drumlanrig had been Rosebery's private secretary, and gossip had been rife down the corridors of Westminster that they had enjoyed a love affair at one time. Due to the termination of the two men's relationship, perhaps because of fear of exposure by Drumlanrig's father, Lord Queensbury, it was speculated that the young nobleman might have taken his own life – murder was even suggested. Queensbury was famous for his ruthless pursuit of Oscar Wilde because of Wilde's homosexual relationship with Drumlanrig's younger brother, Lord Alfred Douglas, better known as Bosie. Coincidence upon coincidence, Lord Hambleton must have known both Drumlanrig and Lord Rosebery as he had served in Rosebery's 1894 liberal ministry.

Had Gerard really taken his own life? Was it simply a shooting accident or could someone have murdered him? I remember thinking at the time it would have been a difficult manoeuvre to shoot oneself in the chest with a double barrelled shotgun at close range. Although Gerard must have had the muzzle against his skin for the type of injury he sustained, otherwise there would have been a greater spread of pitted shot marks.

Guns, guns, are everywhere, the bane of a civilised society. The world moves on and still more and more people are shooting each other. On Sunday, 22nd January – four years exactly to the day of Queen Victoria's death – something momentous has happened abroad. I quote from my newspaper's vivid eye-witness account: led by a Father Georgy Apollonovich Gapon, thousands of people marched towards the Tsar's Winter Palace in St Petersburg to deliver a petition calling for better working conditions. A low sun hung in a cloudless sky. At the head of the demonstration, long coated men's breath formed warning smoke signals in the crisp air. Scarfed women hugged their bareheaded children close to their sides as they swarmed over two bridges spanning the river Neva. All faces were set in that Russian way of grim determination. Though the intention was to hold a peaceful demonstration in Palace Square, the elite soldiers of the Preobrazhensky regiment opened fire without warning killing many unarmed protesters. Soon the hated Cossacks joined the slaughter, discharging musketry into the terrified mob from every direction. It was reported that the soldiers deliberately aimed at people's heads to cause terrible disfigurement. Blood was everywhere.

Below the article, the photograph of an eight year old child lying in the sepia snow. Its face was no longer human. Its mother knelt in tears over its lifeless corpse. My gut feeling was that this one evocative image could change the course of history.

All this worthy of only an inside page in the British Press.

'Unless Russia disengages from her costly war with Japan and starts feeding her people there will be revolution,' I sighed across to Trotter.

'Really, sir,' he replied, hardly listening.

'A revolution that will make the French one look like a skirmish.'

'Indeed, sir.'

'A revolution that will change the world.'

'I'm sure you are right, sir.'

'Trotter, are you listening to me at all?'

'Of course, sir. You are saying there is about to be a revolution in Russia. But I believe the Tsar will never allow things to go that far. He'll put a stop to matters before it gets to that.'

'Then tell me, where was Nicholas II when his troops opened fire on his unarmed subjects in St Petersburg's Palace Square?'

'I've no idea,' replied Trotter, making not the slightest attempt to conceal his indifference. 'First I've heard of any of this.'

'Instead of placating his people, Nicholas was safely ensconced in his favourite quarters, Alexander Palace, some twenty-five miles south of St. Petersburg. Alexander Palace makes Buckingham Palace look like a shooting lodge.'

'I can hardly believe that, Mr Cairn sir.'

'I have seen pictures of it. Never seen anything like it in my life. A palace sumptuously decorated in the neoclassical style.'

'Forget the Russkies and their architecture, we have the greatest empire the world has ever known.'

'But the Russians frequent a huge continent and have a population more than two thirds greater than ours. Their future industrial potential is massive.'

'Then why turn against their figurehead, their leader?'

'They didn't. Those peaceful demonstrators bore the Tsar himself no ill will. Indeed they carried banners and sang songs in praise of him.'

'So why did the Tsar's soldiers open fire on them?'

'Through fear or perhaps because it was easy. Guns are remote weapons to bring down prey, and with that same sense of arm's length detachment they can end the life of anyone who gets in our way or whom we choose to regard as an enemy.'

'Sir, you are still fretting about that unfortunate business at Ashberry Hall,' said Trotter.

'Am I? How did you guess that?'

'I didn't guess,' admitted Trotter smiling. 'I could not help overhearing you discussing it with Mr Brown this morning at the Court House.'

'One day, Trotter, you'll earwig something that is personally detrimental.'

'When that day comes, you'll be the first to know, Mr Cairn sir.'

'My question is why do we need guns in the world at all?'

'I am afraid we haven't reached that point of emotional sophistication in our civilisation, sir. I doubt we ever will.'

'That being the case, Trotter, would you be kind enough to bring this mundane affidavit to the attention of Mr Carlton-Bingham?'

Trotter nodded, taking the document out of my hand, leaving me to my own thoughts.

Did someone regard Gerard Ashberry as their enemy back in the September of 1901 and if so who, I wondered. Did that same person or persons unknown dispatch Andrew Ashberry's fiancée? – or had she simply got cold feet about marrying him, run away, and Gerard's death was a coincidence? I usually find that if a crime has been committed and is failed to be solved within weeks, then usually it never gets solved at all. With the passage of time memories and evidence become faded and distorted, and it was increasingly unlikely that the Ashberry Hall mystery would ever be unravelled. Pity! I hated unresolved mysteries and hadn't I made that promise to myself, a few years ago in All Saints Church, to find out what happened to Lydia Bowden.

* * * * *

Trotter arrived to work the next morning on a bicycle. His new purchase was a Sunbeam Royal Roadster with a two-speed chain wheel gear. He insisted on showing me every detail of the gleaming black machine which was to be kept in the downstairs entrance hall. He was particularly proud of the Lucas candle lamp and the leather carrier box dangling from the handlebars. York, he assured me, was eminently suited for this form of transport.

Bob Brown, however, arrived a few minutes later on foot and unannounced. Luckily, I wasn't expecting anyone else until eleven-thirty.

'Some anonymous person has sent me this.' A rather outmoded folded letter shook in his hand. 'Please, please,' he said, handing it across to me in disgust.

I opened it out carefully on my table. The paper was flimsy, creased and had seen better days but the hand wasn't bad and the composition educated I would say.

Dear Sir,

I understand that you are the legal man who acts for the Marquess of Hambleton and his brood. Let me tell you, sir, you are representing a hornet's nest. At best the Ashberrys are driven by avarice. The Marquess plans to rob many of his tenant farmers of their livelihoods by selling off land to quarry for stone. But more than this, he is culpable in the gross crime of filicide, not just a son but a daughter too. Take my advice, sir, and withdraw your services before it is too late.

Yours faithfully,

A Well Wisher

'What am I to make of this, James?' asked Brown.

'You must take it to the police,' I told him, 'without a moment's hesitation.'

'But what about client confidentiality?'

'Have you been called to advise the Ashberrys on any of the matters mentioned here?' I asked, picking up the letter and passing it back to him.

'No, no, I know nothing of a proposed quarry or murder, God forbid.'

'So, you have nothing to worry about.'

'But what do you make of this reference to filicide?'

'I am as much in the dark as you, Bob.'

'The writer couldn't be suggesting that the Marquess was implicated in Gerard's death, could they? And what's this about "a daughter too"?'

'A daughter-in-law to be,' I suggested.

'Lydia, you mean?' Brown looked horrified.

I nodded, somehow I knew even then that good old Bob Brown was going to look much worse over the coming months as things started to implode.

'Trotter! Trotter!' I screamed for my clerk. 'Trotter, there's a good fellow, would you be kind enough to get Major Robert Lister Bower's address for Mr Brown here.'

'What, you think I should contact the Chief Constable over this matter?' asked Brown.

'I would when dealing with aristocrats. The higher authority the better.'

'Here it is,' announced Trotter triumphantly. 'Yatton House, Thirsk, now known as The West House, I believe.'

Chapter Six

In light of the anonymous note and the delicacy of the situation, Brown sent word through Trotter at the courts that Major Bower was putting his best man on to reinvestigate Lydia Bowden's disappearance.

'"Delicacy of the situation". Puh! That means because the Ashberrys are implicated,' I exploded.

'An Inspector White.' Trotter ignored my outburst.

'White, I see.'

'Robert Brown and Timon White, Brown and White, like bread,' laughed Trotter.

'That amusing association has not escaped me, Trotter.' I smiled back, with little real enthusiasm, as I abstractedly shuffled papers one way and the other over the leather desk top surface.

As I was at Ashberry Hall for the ball and the discovery of Gerard's body the next day, Brown has told Trotter that I should expect a visit from the police too. After all this time, despite my self-imposed promise in the Church of All Saints, I felt I could do without any extra burdens with my present full diary. I was about to represent a seventy-seven year old farm labourer accused of bestiality with an ass in a field at Market Weighton; a nineteen year old man accused of stealing a cow and a hog off common ground near Easingwold, and a twenty year old Kirk Hammerton woman accused of poisoning her fifty-five year old husband of one year.

'Mr Brown feels he is in a precarious position being the Ashberry's family solicitor,' Trotter's voice cut into thoughts of my baleful future.

'He isn't the only one with problems,' I muttered back.

* * * * *

'Mr Cairn, I am conducting an investigation into the disappearance of Miss Lydia Bowden,' announced White; his six foot plus physique dominating my office. 'And I would like to ask you a few questions.'

'Please,' I indicated a chair. The aquiline nose twitched, undecided. 'Please,' I insisted once more.

'I believe you attended a ball at Ashberry Hall in September, 1901, and the next day joined a shooting party on the estate?'

I reached into my desk drawer for my diary of that year, and began leafing through it. Neither of us spoke as the pages crackled in the silence. My forefinger traced down columns of information referring to what now seemed to be a far distant year let alone month. 'Yes, here's the entry. It was the last long weekend in September beginning Friday, the twenty-seventh, to Sunday, the twenty-ninth.'

'And what occasioned you to be at Ashberry Hall?' asked White.

'I was invited by Mr Robert Brown to accompany him there for an engagement party and ball.'

'Between?'

'Between Miss Lydia Bowden and Andrew Ashberry.'

'Did you notice anything unusual during the party?'

I hesitated, I wasn't used to this: it was usually me doing the interrogation.

'"Unusual"?' I hummed and hawed.

'Yes, was anyone acting abnormally, suspiciously?'

'Well, I ...'

'Come on, Mr Cairn sir, I would imagine nothing would escape the notice of a man in your profession.'

'It was a long time ago.'

'But a man with your powers of recollection.'

'Now look here, officer.'

'Inspector,' White quickly corrected.

I felt I knew White from somewhere. I had encountered this rugged handsome face before at close quarters. I racked my brains for a time and place.

Apart from being a police officer, White was obviously a mind reader: 'Remember the Nathaniel Briggs case, stole some Galloways up Northallerton way. You got him off,' he filled in accusingly. 'He went on to steal many more until one night a Thirsk farmer shot him dead in his yard.'

'And you were the arresting constable ...'

'Sergeant,' corrected White again.

'Sorry Sergeant, Inspector, dealing with that original allegation of theft made out against Briggs,' I persevered. The arrogant lift of the chin was beginning to rankle.

'"Allegation" that's rich. And you got him off.'

'Alas, Inspector, I am sure during the course of my professional career I have unknowingly got many guilty men off.'

'And now, sir, you are in the dock.'

'Not quite the dock.'

'But it is your turn to answer my questions.' White licked his perfect lips with relish.

'Of course, if I can.'

'Now back to the night of the ball at Ashberry Hall. Did you notice anything out of the ordinary? Did you notice anyone acting peculiarly?'

'Perhaps Mr Brown is more suited to answer such questions, he was far more familiar with the gathered company than I.'

'Mr Brown has already been interviewed. We would welcome your unbiased opinion.'

'Meaning Mr Brown is biased?'

'Meaning nothing.'

'Well,' I sighed. 'In truth I found quite a few of the guests to be a little odd that night.'

'And the family?'

'More so. There seemed to be a strained atmosphere especially between Ashberry family members. There was no attempt to conceal the Marquess' displeasure over his eldest son's engagement.'

'That being again Andrew Ashberry, the Earl of Fadmoor, his heir?'

'The same.'

'Why do you think the Marquess was unhappy with the match?'

'This is pure hearsay but the Earl expressed the opinion that his father was unhappy that he had already got Lydia pregnant.'

'"Pregnant", you say?' verified White with raised eyebrows: this, it appeared, was news to him.

'Yes, and I believe the Marquess considered a country girl to be very much beneath their aristocratic status.'

'Anything else? How did say Major Ashberry appear to get on with his future sister-in-law?'

I paused: wondering how ethical it was to voice an impression.

'Mr Cairn?' prompted White.

'Well, I'd say the Major seemed somewhat enamoured,' I reluctantly admitted.

'Are you saying that he was attracted to his brother's fiancée?'

'From the way he danced with her, I would say "yes".'

'How did he dance with her exactly?'

'Enthusiastically. I didn't see him dance with anyone else the whole evening.'

'How did Lord Fadmoor respond to his brother monopolising his intended?'

'With indifference.'

'Well, perhaps he knew his brother's attentions were merely a soldier's frivolity.'

'Perhaps.'

'Did you see anything of Lydia Bowden the next day?'

'No, nothing.'

'And Major Ashberry?'

'Briefly, in the morning on the shoot.'

'Lord Fadmoor?' enquired White.

'I saw Andrew Ashberry in the morning, and passed the time of day with him after lunch.'

'How did he seem then?'

'Perfectly normal. He was accompanied by his architect, Louis Chatterton.'

'Have you any idea who might have sent that libelous note to your friend, Mr Brown?'

'No.'

'It was you, Mr Cairn, was it not, who first saw Malcolm Bowden following Mr Chatterton and Lord Fadmoor here in York?'

'Yes, from that window.' I pointed to the window that looked out onto Bootham. White scraped back his chair, got up and strode across to the window to take a look for himself.

'A good view,' he acknowledged.

'You don't think Malcolm Bowden wrote that letter to Mr Brown?' I asked, puzzled.

'No, we've already checked his writing.'

'What reason did he give for following Lord Fadmoor and Louis Chatterton that day?'

'He said he simply chanced upon them while visiting his mother. Unfortunately, Mary Bowden had to be admitted to Bootham Park Asylum suffering from a breakdown due to the distress of her daughter's disappearance. Malcolm told us he had decided to follow Lord Fadmoor and Mr Chatterton on a whim to see what they were up to.'

'And have you asked Andrew why he was selling his fiancée's ring so soon after her disappearance?'

'Not yet,' replied White curtly. 'Although I am sure he will give me the same explanation that he gave to you. He decided to get rid of the ring to cover up the fact that he found it in his brother's pocket.'

'Mr Brown told you that?' I asked, surprised.

'No, no,' laughed White, shaking his head. 'He cited client confidentiality, legal professional privilege, that sort of thing.'

'Who then?'

'That would be telling.'

'Louis Chatterton. It could only have been him. You've already interviewed him while skirting round the Ashberrys.'

'The law moves in subtle ways, Mr Cairn, you should know that.'

'Sometimes it does and at other times it is rapid and explicit.'

'Explicit, eh? I like that. Am I right in thinking that you were among the party of men who discovered Major Ashberry's body in the Doric summer house?'

'I was.'

'Can you remember who else was there?'

'Mr Brown, Andrew, the Head Keeper. I believe it was an estate worker who was first to find poor Gerard. There were many men off the estate helping to search that night.'

'How did the man who first found the body react?'

'He was in a state of shock.'

'And Lord Fadmoor?'

'Extremely upset. Oh, I forgot to mention that Louis Chatterton was also there in the Temple. He was so affected, he appeared to be paralysed.'

'I expect the Marquess was overcome too with grief being confronted with his son's body.'

'Indeed, he was. It was a harrowing scene there in the great hall. Fathers do not expect to outlive their sons.'

'I fear my old father will outlive me,' laughed White.

'Mine will not.'

White made no reply to this but offered his hand instead, saying, 'You have been a great help, Mr Cairn.'

'Lydia Bowden was one of the most beautiful women I ever set eyes on.'

'I might need to call on you again, now we are on the same side.'

'Are we?' I asked doubtfully.

'Of course, you sound as if you want to know what happened to the young lady as much as I do.'

I watched from my window as Inspector White evaporated into the masses going home along Bootham – and although White was tall and extremely handsome he did have that enviable quality for a policeman of blending in – I called for my clerk who was equally gifted in disappearing, usually when I most wanted him.

'Trotter! Where are you, dammit! Ah, there you are.'

'Your visitor has gone.' Trotter was a great one for stating the obvious too. 'I trust the interview went well.'

'Tell me, weren't you once friendly with a nurse on the female wards at Bootham Park?' I asked, ignoring the pleasantries.

'You mean the County Lunatic Asylum?'

'No, I mean Bootham Park. You know as well as I do the asylum was renamed last year.'

'Whatever it's called, it comes to the same thing,' replied Trotter off-handedly.

'So are you still friendly with a nurse there or not?'

'No, sir, certainly not, sir. Nothing like that.'

'Like what?'

'Like the inference you are making.'

'I am doing no such thing, Trotter. I am merely asking if you know or knew a nurse on the female wards of the hospital down the road.'

'I do know such a person as a matter of fact,' he finally admitted.

'It's like getting blood from a stone,' I cursed under my breath.

'She is the daughter of a neighbour.'

'Do you think you could ask this neighbour's daughter if she has ever encountered a patient called Mary Bowden, and if she has is Mrs Bowden still a resident of Bootham Park?'

'I'll try,' said Trotter without much conviction.

Chapter Seven

La crème de la crème – the cream of the crop – was about to take on a new meaning for me.

The stolen cow and hog in the Vale of York and the bestiality case on the edge of the Wolds would have to wait. For the moment my interest in Lydia Bowden's disappearance had to be postponed. Both my leisure and working hours were taken up with preparations for the defence of the twenty year old Kirk Hammerton woman accused of poisoning her husband with strychnine. The victim in this case, Brian Tiplady, had obviously been a popular man and through his passing was sorely missed in the old city and its surrounding countryside. True enough his final hours had been dreadful but the innuendo and vitriol in the York newspapers did not bode well for my young client receiving a fair trial. In short, emotions were running high in the immediate area, forcing me to plead in the magistrate's court before a specifically designated judge, Bruce Pendleton, for a change of venue from York Assizes to a more neutral setting in the interests of justice.

I quoted to Judge Pendleton the words of Lord Mansfield citing *Mylock v. Saladine* in 1764: "'A juror should be as white paper, and know neither plaintiff nor defendant, but judge the issue merely as an abstract proposition, upon the evidence produced before him".'

Pendleton's mouth twitched with what I took to be wry amusement though it could have been annoyance.

'Lord Mansfield made that observation a long time ago, Mr Cairn,' he responded grudgingly. 'However as the parish of Kirk Hammerton straddles both the Ainsty of York and the West Riding of Yorkshire, I am more than willing to grant your request.

Ultimately, despite his initial response, Pendleton wasn't prepared to contradict such an eminent 18th century source as Mansfield – that was the real reason Catherine Tiplady now languished in Leeds Prison, rather than in Northallerton Gaol, awaiting trial at this flourishing woollen city's local assizes.

I acknowledged that Leeds might prove to be a logistic difficulty should any urgent consultations be required with the defendant as I was based in

York. But then with the closure of York's Castle Prison, my clients were often distributed across the three ridings.

There had been two highly publicised strychnine murder cases towards the end of the previous century. Both committed by medical men – a far cry from a simple Lower Nidderdale farm lass – and it was through these reference notes that I now trawled in the quiet of my chambers.

A cherubic looking Staffordshire doctor, William Palmer, was accused of poisoning his horse owning gambling friend, John Parsons Cook, on the 21st November, 1855. Known as the Rugeley Poisoner, Palmer was suspected of killing many others including family members. He was hanged in Stafford Prison on 14th June, 1856. A customary death mask was made following his execution. This gruesome relic I believe can be viewed today.

Now back to *la crème de la crème* of habitual killers – Dr Thomas Neill Cream, a Scottish-Canadian, who became known as the Lambeth Poisoner after murdering four prostitutes in the 1890s. An arrogant man, the really strange thing about Cream is that unlike other murderers he didn't hang around to enjoy his kill. He slipped his victims a dose of strychnine in pill form, usually under the pretext of a deterrent against the clap, and went on his merry way. There is evidence that the good doctor had grown to hate women, blaming them for all his previous misfortunes which included a spell in Joliet Jail, Illinois, for the murder conviction of a Mr Stott, the husband of his mistress. Mrs Stott turned state's evidence to avoid imprisonment implicating Cream alone instead. After serving a ten year gaol sentence, Cream's brother somehow managed to secure his release. Joliet's loss was London's gain – Cream fled to 103 Lambeth Palace Road to renew his taste for the low life. Despite his conceit, Thomas Cream was an extremely foolish man. A New York detective friend of his was in London and was fascinated by the Lambeth poisonings. Cream offered to take him on a tour of the murder locations. The detective soon realised that his host had astonishing detailed knowledge of the offences and reported him to Scotland Yard. Cream believed he had murdered a woman called Lou Harvey, also known as Louisa Harris. Unfortunately, or fortunately for her, the streetwise Lou was suspicious of her medical punter and had thrown away the pills he had prescribed to put a little more colour in her cheeks. Only the murderer would have been surprised to be confronted by the living intended victim in court. Miss Harvey/Harris's evidence was fundamental in convicting Cream and he was hanged on the 16th November, 1892.

Poison is often the chosen weapon of women and doctors, I had to reluctantly admit. How I hoped it wasn't so in the case of Mrs Tiplady.

*****

We are living in the age of the train. The train has changed all of our lives – speeded life up, shortened the miles that divide. I was about to embark on a new challenge.

Leeds Borough Gaol, known locally as "Armley Gaol", was opened in 1847 at a cost of £43,000. It is probably one of the best examples of an archetypal Victorian prison in the north of England. Built on the lines of the Pentonville model, it has four wings radiating in a semicircle from a central hall, or so Catherine Tiplady's solicitor, Mr Arthur Hewlett, informed me on the journey there.

Hewlett and I alighted at the local station in mists of steam from our train, from other trains, and smoke from surrounding mills. Though the choking mill smoke remained, the trains moved on and the mist cleared a little. I blinked – the town of Armley was a cultural shock from York, to say Armley was industrial did not do it justice. Slabs of row upon row of terrace houses defined work rather than poverty here, work was all. Phallic chimneys slashed across the picture – masculine and ever present – with only the occasional blot of gentle green, an overlooked remnant of an agrarian past.

'There's the gaol,' pointed Hewlett in excitement or was it apprehension.

The building appeared to have been constructed from local quarried stone like many of the mills surrounding it. Now entirely soot blackened, it stood on a slight elevation above everything. I had thought the now defunct York Castle Prison was bad enough but this was a monster. Enclosed by a high wall, Armley Gaol was something between a medieval fortress and a slave factory.

'Perkins and Backhouse designed it in the style of Windsor Castle,' said Hewlett.

'I don't think they were very successful in their objective.'

'See, there in the wall, that's the hangman's tunnel.'

'The what?'

'That blocked arched tunnel was where the condemned were led to their public execution. James Sargisson and Joseph Myers must have walked through there, theirs was the only public execution to take place outside this gaol. Myers beat his wife to death and Sargisson murdered a man for his watch. At least eighty thousand people waited to see the spectacle. The two men mounted the scaffold. Sargisson asked Myers "Are thou happy lad?" to which Myers responded "Indeed I am." Myers died quickly from the drop although an earlier self-inflicted throat wound opened up, Sargisson however struggled violently for two or three minutes before he succumbed to strangulation.'

'A man after my own heart, Arthur, I see you've done your research.'

'I always do my research,' he retorted dryly.

The inside of the prison was as grim, if not grimmer than the outside.

'Catherine Tiplady?' I enquired through the reception grill. 'We are her legal representatives,' I added for good measure. A wardress was called. The stony faced woman escorted Hewlett and me along one of the radial wings to our client's cell which was offset at the very end. She lifted her chinking chain of keys, selected one and still without so much as a "how do you do?" turned the lock.

Catherine was seated on the edge of a cot bed. She was flaxen-haired and her cheeks still retained the high colour of the fields. Her eye rims were red too, she had obviously been crying a great deal. And who could blame her, the future ahead was difficult and her present situation was stark. The room was little more than a cubicle and struck me as particularly austere: apart from the cot and a bench running down the opposite wall, a bucket and wash basin waited in a recess beneath the barred Gothic window. Cold water, cold cell, was the phrase that came to mind.

'This is Mr Cairn,' introduced Hewlett. 'He is the gentleman I suggested might represent you in court.'

'I didn't do it, sir. They said I did it but I didn't.' Catherine's blue eyes settled on mine before falling to the ground. 'I didn't do anything and they've locked me up in here and taken my bairn from me.'

'Tell Mr Cairn exactly what happened,' invited Hewlett.

'One of the wardresses keeps telling me they hanged a woman called Swann only a year since for murdering her husband.' Catherine rambled on, ignoring Hewlett.

'Emily Swann,' Hewlett interrupted, 'and her lodger, possibly lover, John Gallagher murdered her husband, William, who had a history of violence against her.'

'Your knowledge is impressive, Arthur,' I told him.

Catherine meanwhile looked me up and down blankly, seemingly unimpressed.

'When he was in drink and I couldn't stop our bairn crying, Brian would sometimes beat me up,' she announced.

'Brian, being your husband?' I asked.

'My late husband,' she replied with precision.

'The fact that he occasionally knocked you about is no grounds for mounting a defence as Emily Swann found out,' I told her. 'Not yet, not in this age. And whoever this wardress is chastising you with that piece of macabre information about Swann, give me her name and I will have her immediately removed from your proximity.'

'Normal rules don't apply in here,' said Catherine. 'It's not taken me long to find that out.'

'In the nineteenth century the "silent system" was used in this gaol. Perhaps it should be reinstated for wardresses,' I suggested. For the first time I saw the hint of a smile forming on the pastoral lips. For the first time I realised that country girl Catherine Tiplady was nobody's fool. Sitting down on the narrow bench, I took out my pen and notebook from my brief case precariously balancing them on my knees. Hewlett, who was an extremely large man, remained standing.

'I really didn't do it, sir,' reiterated Catherine.

'So tell me what happened.'

'Brian came home late one afternoon. He said he did not feel himself and was very fitful. I made him a bowl of broth with bread and he washed it down with a tankard of small beer.'

'What date are we actually talking about?' I looked to Hewlett who checked his working diary.

'Friday, twenty-third of December, 1904,' he informed me.

'My husband's last day on earth,' sniffled Catherine. 'Just before Christmas. Who would murder a husband two days before Christmas?'

'Please go on,' I told her.

'Soon after his meal he began twitching, became fitful, then he said his whole body had gone stiff. Said he couldn't move his jaw. I struggled with him to bed. A quarter of an hour later, it cannot have been more, I looked in on him. He was arching his neck and back in agony, froth was spilling from his mouth and he was blue in the face. He looked terrible and I sent my mother, who lives next door, for the doctor.'

'How long before the doctor came?'

'Another half hour.'

'By then Brian was struggling for breath. The doctor was obviously shaken by his condition but there was nothing he could do. He died in my arms a few minutes later.'

'It must have been an extremely harrowing experience for you.'

'I wouldn't wish to see a dog suffer like that, sir.'

'Mr Hewlett, here, tells me Mr Tiplady was an agricultural labourer.'

'Brian would turn his hand to anything, work in the fields was often seasonal. Between November and the end of June he usually travelled between farms and estates as a wanter.'

'"A wanter"?'

'A mole catcher,' explained Hewlett.

'And had he been employed catching moles on the day of his death?' I asked Catherine.

'I believe so. I was told there wasn't a mowdiwarp safe in the countryside when James Wright and my husband were abroad.'

'"James Wright"?'

'Aye, he was a young lad Brian worked with.'

'How old is Mr Wright?'

'Early twenties.'

'About your age then?' I asked. Catherine did not answer. 'And where were your husband and James Wright working that Friday?'

'Snaith Farm, I believe, a mile or two from our cottage.'

Chapter Eight

Catherine was due to appear at Leeds Assizes in March, known as the Lent Assizes in the old legal calendar, but thankfully her case was moved to the Summer Assizes at the end of May. Until then I had a lot of people to interview and a lot of depositions to read in preparation for her defence. In addition, I had my two other local cases pending at York regarding a cow, a hog and an irresistible ass.

The nineteen year old man accused of stealing the two domestic animals off common ground near Easingwold had been caught red-handed by their owner. Philip Cubitt pleaded guilty as charged. Nevertheless, his sentence was harsh: ten years hard labour, five for the bovine, five for the pig. I had to remind myself that my client would have hanged for the same offence less than a hundred years ago.

Trotter, always the conservative, was adamant that I should not take the case of the Market Weighton grandfather accused of fornication with a donkey.

'You really are getting a reputation for defending oddities, sir,' he complained 'They read about your defence of the cross-dressing priest and all the freaks of nature make for your door.'

'Young Philip Cubitt was ordinary enough,' I objected.

'He was a thief.'

'An ordinary thief,' I pointed out, reasonably I thought. Trotter scowled unimpressed. 'Unfortunately, it often falls to my lot to represent the indefensible. Anyway, I thought you had grown to like the Reverend George Hobb.'

'Felt sorry for him.' Trotter pouted.

'And we won that case.'

'Yes, but this Edwin Holroyd's crime is even more ridiculous, more disgusting,' shuddered Trotter.

'But what if he is innocent?'

'It's your reputation, sir,' shrugged Trotter. 'Not mine.'

'Innocent until proved guilty,' I reminded my long-suffering clerk. 'And Holroyd has assured me of his innocence.'

'Puh!' scoffed Trotter.

* * * * *

Through the roof's domed window, winter daylight shone on the court. There was a full house for the bestiality trial. A practice not entirely unknown in rural communities though such cases were uncommon in court and devilishly difficult to prosecute. The public gallery waited with bated breath for the performance to begin. The sound of moans, groans and creaking boards broke the silence as my client wheezed his way up into the dock. "Innocent until proved guilty" was solicitously aided by a warder on one arm and a walking stick in his other hand, two warders had obviously been deemed unnecessary.

The case was to be heard before the newly appointed His Honour Judge Humphrey. An old adversary of mine when a QC – known disrespectfully then as Humpty Dumpty Humphrey because of his peculiar egg shaped body – always a groveller, it had been no surprise to me when Reginald Humphrey moved onto the bench.

'All stand.' The clerk of court announced Humphrey's ponderous entrance soon after that of the defendant's.

Like an overfed, if ever hungry, black crow, Humphrey stared across at the dock. I turned to follow his line of vision. Edwin Holroyd was nowhere to be seen.

Humphrey looked askance at the usher saying, 'We appear not to have a defendant.' He waved imperiously for something to be done. This was not court etiquette at all: beneath the dignity of a judge to be kept waiting by the accused man.

Before the usher could reach the dock, the warder – guarding or was it nursing Holroyd? – heaved him up so his little white head eventually peeked over the balustrade.

'Is this man a midget?' asked Humphrey.

'No, your honour, my client is so feeble he appears to have sagged under the strain of his present situation,' I apologised with undisguised mirth. 'As you can see, Mr Holroyd is hardly able to stand let alone mount a female donkey.'

'Was the animal his?'

'The jennet was and still is indeed his, your honour.'

'And I suppose you have medical evidence to substantiate this man's physical infirmities at the time the alleged offence took place, Mr Cairn,' grunted Humphrey.

'Of course, your honour.' I bowed.

Prosecuting counsel's face dropped. The judge's eyes burned with indignation at this waste of his and the court's time.

'Mr Parker anything to add?' Humphrey turned to the KC.

'In light of …' Parker faltered. How could he justify the prosecution of a cripple for a crime that would have required the athleticism of a Cretan bull-leaper?

'Case dismissed.' Humphrey tapped his hand in frustration across the top of the bench like a headmaster spanking a naughty boy. My client sank to the floor again but this time from relief rather than disability or fear.

'Thank you, thank you, sir.' The invisible Holroyd's voice rose from the cavity of dock. 'Thank you, thank you, sir,' he reiterated in the holding cell below the court, shaking my hand wildly. His rheumy eyes encompassing me, Trotter and Charles Besant, his solicitor, with eternal gratitude. Trotter looked to the floor, he could not bear to meet Holroyd's loving gaze.

'A free man, aye, Mr Holroyd,' he sniffed instead. He had been proved wrong yet again regarding a client's guilt.

'That Northallerton Gaol was a terrible place,' complained Holroyd.

And not a female ass in sight, I cruelly thought.

'You might smile, Mr Cairn, but the food … the food was something awful. I would have rather died than go back there.'

'Well, you'll not have to,' I reassured him.

'This was all my wife's sister's doing. 'Twas her that spread that malicious rumour,' he explained. 'She'd always had a fancy for me and when my Vera died last year she thought I'd wed her, but I wouldn't. I would rather have wed the donkey.'

'Don't let anyone else hear you saying that,' Besant warned him.

I laughed. I laughed all the way back to the robing room.

* * * * *

'One day you'll get it right.' I gave Trotter's back a patronising little pat the following morning in chambers.

'Get what right, sir?'

'Our clients' innocence.'

'You think so?'

'You don't still feel decrepit old Edwin Holroyd was capable of such depravity?'

'Who am I to judge,' shrugged Trotter. 'By the way, sir, my neighbour's daughter, the nurse who works in York's madhouse ...'

'Trotter,' I reprimanded.

'She says should you wish to visit, visits are usually conducted in the afternoons,' concluded Trotter, who appeared to consider himself above all censure. But he was wrong about that, I would make him see that he was wrong.

'Wasn't there some rumour of misappropriation of funds in the past regarding that institution?' I asked.

'Yes, sir. There was an inquiry held at the beginning of the previous century. I believe we have a copy of that report.'

'Please be good enough to find it for me.'

The report into the running of the lunatic asylum was disturbing. My instinct had always been to avoid the place. I had occasion to visit the more progressive Retreat, just outside York, several times but you can understand my reluctance to interview Mary Bowden at the establishment round the corner. And, anyway, I had heard nothing from Inspector White, things had gone ominously quiet on that front. Quite frankly I was beginning to feel relieved about putting the Ashberry affair and its complications behind me.

Coincidentally, just as I had begun to dip into the dubious accounting methods and containment practices at York Lunatic Asylum, Trotter again knocked on my door to say that our head of chambers, Mr Carlton-Bingham, wished to discuss finances over tea and biscuits forthwith.

Our boardroom table was so highly polished, it mirrored any nervous hands. Carlton-Bingham's performance was usually highly polished too. *Bingham, Leacock, Fawcett & Cairn* was not doing badly financially but could do better. Thomas Leacock's hands were fidgeting more than most, indeed sweat pooled on the impermeable polished surface beneath them. Without actually naming poor old Thomas, Carlton-Bingham said we all needed to take on more prominent cases, and – though a lovely man – we all knew that Thomas, in particular, had failed to appear in any notable cases for many years.

'Saw something that might interest you, Cairn, in the announcements of the *Yorkshire Evening Press*,' said my bête noire, Gerald Fawcett, just as the meeting was concluding. While Thomas Leacock was extremely pleasant but professionally unsuccessful, Fawcett was disagreeable and highly successful.

'Thought you were a *Herald* man,' I threw back at him.

'It was about a girl I seem to remember you walked out with at one time,' continued Fawcett; suddenly the rest of the boardroom was all ears too.

'Oh, and who might that be?'

'Miss Holbrook,' stirred Fawcett. 'She's got engaged to The Right Honourable John Beardsley, MP.'

'Really,' I said feeling numb. All I could think of was how unfitting for Winifred to marry a Tory MP. 'Well, good luck to her,' I added, struggling to collect myself. I could see from the horrified looks on the faces of my other partners down the table that they had also seen the same announcement but had been too kind to draw my attention to it. 'By the way, I never actually walked out with her,' I told Fawcett, striding out of the room as best I could on rubber legs.

* * * * *

The second Wednesday in February. Far away a cyclone devastated Tahiti and its neighbouring islands killing ten thousand people as Bob Brown's father, Mr Brown senior, fell gravely ill in his bleak terrace house along Coppergate. A wheelchair invalid, he had suffered from heart failure for sometime. Now in the final stages of his illness, the sick man had recently exploded in size due to water retention caused by his faulty pump. Whenever I chanced upon Bob, he had complained that his father hardly ate; nevertheless, he was forced to buy him garments, pyjamas and suchlike, that would fit an elephant. Then one day Bob stopped complaining but expressed the fear that unless I visited the old chap soon it would be too late.

Immediately, on my arrival at Coppergate that evening, I could see Bob's warning had been appropriately urgent. Twilight had dimmed the intelligent sparkle in Mr Brown senior's eyes, and his breathing was extremely laboured. However, he managed to raise his usual gappy smile on seeing me – slower now, more ponderous but still there. There was something else there too – something out of reach – as if he was already preparing himself for that other world where we mortals could not yet follow.

The smile faded and Mr Brown became thoughtful. His bony hand grasped for mine. His words did not flow but came out in small spurts.

'You well, James?'

'Yes, thank you, sir. And yourself?'

'We are like branches on a tree. When we are young and supple we bounce back from the storms that bend us. When we are old we become taut, stiff and lose that capacity to bounce back but break instead.'

'But surely there's hope,' I began.

Mr Brown waved aside my denial with a corpse-like arm.

'I never believed that Ashberry thing would come off,' he panted.

'"Thing"? Do you mean Andrew's marriage, Pa?' asked Bob.

'Freddy hinted as much to me. I feared for that young girl's safety then ... ,' the old man faltered.

'Who? Lydia Bowden's?' My jaw clenched on the question.

The old man's head nodded on its feeble neck. 'The aristocracy can be ruthless when it comes to inheritance and titles. Remember me telling you, James, about the unusual inclinations of Percy Jocelyn, Anglican Bishop of Clogher. Well, from a young age Freddy always believed his eldest son might share the same bent. Possibly homosexual, possibly undecided.'

'How could the Marquess have known that?' Bob sounded dismissive.

'Easy, my boy, Andrew was always forming passionate friendships with other fellows as far back as his prep school.'

'A stage,' offered Bob. 'Merely a stage he was going through.'

'It's only because you feel your own nose was put out of joint because he didn't fall in love with you,' cackled the old man.

'But all the more reason for the Marquess being happy to see Andrew married, the line of succession continued?' I suggested.

'But not with that girl. There were other reasons,' Mr Brown told us hoarsely before promptly falling asleep.

When death comes slowly, it is never easy. It was not easy for my uncle with tongue cancer; it was not easy for Mr Brown senior with his rasping breaths; it is perhaps most difficult for those watching helplessly on.

Mr Brown opened his eyes and stared transfixed at the ceiling as if he had seen a vision. Like birth he had begun a journey that he had to take alone. He was leaving us.

'What shall we do?' asked Bob, turning desperately to me. I thought at first he meant with his dying father until he added, 'With the information?'

'Nothing. Put it away in our mental repositories for a rainy day. Unfortunately, this is mere hearsay.'

'Hearsay, of a dying man,' whispered Bob.

'I've not gone yet, son,' responded Mr Brown senior with sudden and surprising verve. His head rotated a fraction to fix his gaze on his son.

But the next day he had gone – he died as the first dry northerly gales struck our landscape, a fitting drum roll for the old Classics scholar. And I was left wondering ever after what vision had so arrested the old man's attention there on the ceiling.

Chapter Nine

My Gillygate widow box was blazing with *Couleur Cardinal* tulips bought in Amsterdam many years ago. Rather as my favourite Farndale walk's daffodils nodded towards Easter, the tulips proclaimed spring for me.

It was Saturday and I had given Kate, my maid, the morning off allowing me the freedom to enjoy the delights of the York Coffee House. 16 to 18 Lendal was a fairly new venture for me but both their coffee and breakfast were perfection. From time to time I dropped my defensive newspaper to sip, chew and observe. Occasionally nodding, like the Farndale daffodils, to one or two regulars who like me were destined to eat alone. The *Times* announced that yesterday Emmeline Pankhurst had led her first protest outside the Parliament building in London, following the filibustering of the women's suffrage bill. On that score I had a feeling that things were about to get much uglier before they'd get better. I was reminded of Winifred Holbrook and her dedication to the suffrage cause. I could not help wondering if her political fiancé shared her views.

'Good morning,' I took my leave of the coffee house's proprietor – nodding ridiculously again – how self-conscious we become regarding our every action when alone.

Ten a.m. – I checked the time on Lendal Bridge's toll house clock and decided to walk my breakfast off. Of all the bridges in York, Lendal is the most impressive, although the river Ouse, flowing beneath it, never smells at its best in the city and is prone to flooding. In 1892 the sewerage works itself overflowed into the Ouse when the river reached eleven feet above its usual level. The Foss too was overwhelmed. But the bridge, the bridge is magnificent. Built of iron by Thomas Page in 1863, it has all the Gothic details popular during the previous century. The parapet is adorned with decorative metalwork: white roses of York, the crossed keys of the Diocese of York and the lions of England. York's coat of arms and the initials V & A, for Queen Victoria and Prince Albert, complete its ornamentation.

I must be imagining it – I was almost midway across the bridge when whom should I see springing from the bank below into one of J. Todd's pleasure boats but Winifred Holbrook. I had not set eyes on her for years but I was sure it was her from the positive flow of her body, nobody else moved like that. It was as if thinking about her back at the cafe had willed her into existence. My heart missed a beat and then missed another. I felt that old dizzy sensation of electricity whenever I was in her presence. Then my spirits fell to my boots – a tall dark fellow, already waterborne, offered his hand to steady her. They were laughing as she fell into his arms, they looked very happy. I continued with my crossing, eager to wipe this image of relationship bliss from my mind, when something else caught my eye walking along the opposite bank. Another duo, a decidedly more edgy coupling, was making towards the bridge from the direction of Wellington Row. Ridiculously, I attempted to duck behind a sculptured white rose. It would have taken only a glance down the bridge from one of the pair, and I would have been spotted rooted in this farcical pose.

Andrew Ashberry and Chatterton thankfully passed by the bridge end. They appeared not to have seen me. Chatterton had linked his arm in Ashberry's. Ashberry swayed a little uncomfortably as if at any moment he was about to break free. It was then that I began to seriously entertain Mr Brown senior's insinuation.

Winifred Holbrook's and friend's craft had moved from the pontoon and was floating beneath me. Unseen, still crouching, I looked down on their heads. Winifred's luxuriant locks blew in the river breeze. Her male companion's hair thinned over a small circle of scalp, he was moving to baldness. Seated together, not quite together, they looked more hesitant in each other's company than they first had done getting into the boat. I wondered how Winifred felt navigating the waters that had taken her stepfather's life.

On the day the spy and courtesan Mata Hari made her stage debut in Paris, I encountered Winifred Holbrook in the company of another man. Can my memory of the perfect woman ever be trusted?

* * * * *

End of May, the Summer Assizes at Leeds. I headed for the south fronted main entrance off Victoria Square rather than creeping in at the side door off Calverley Street. Climbing the town hall steps, I saw the four guarding lions which I had the doubtful privilege of encountering once before. Far from my previous impression of them as fierce snarling creatures, they appeared to be a benign sleepy bunch in the morning light. Their Portland stone bodies, sculpted by William Day Keyworth, cost the city fathers a mere five hundred and fifty pounds in 1867. I have heard tales that when the town hall clock inaccurately strikes an extra note after midnight, they stretch up and prowl the city circumference while Leeds sleeps, sometimes returning to scramble back onto their plinths in a slightly different position.

I have always had a healthy respect for big cats. I can have been no more than six or seven when I was first taken to a circus. It was just after Christmas and the New Year's Day holiday. My military father, who was on leave, took me by train from our home in London up to Bolton where his brother, William, traded in cotton. The same brother who was to die of tongue cancer only two decades later.

I can remember now the smells of the beasts, the caravans, the ragged children who frequented the world of Manders' Menagerie. Massarti, the lion tamer, opened his act by introducing the audience of some five hundred people to a few exotic animals – a long thick serpent and a gorilla particularly captured my imagination. It was getting late, must have been well past ten, when the menagerie decided to put on an extra performance as they were leaving for Bury the next day. Massarti, now dressed as a gladiator, entered the lions' den. I stood at the front, my father and uncle pressed behind. I grabbed the rails, my hands aching with excitement, when the faint whiff of alcohol passed in a belch from our hero of Rome.

'MacCarte's the worse for wear,' muttered Uncle William.

'"MacCarte"?' asked my father.

'Aye, Thomas MacCarte is Massarti's real name,' explained my uncle, fixing the lion tamer's jabbing sword with a hint of disapproval.

Massarti had already lost his left arm to a lion in Liverpool some years before. Some spectators around us began to whisper that only the previous Monday he had been bitten by the black-maned African lion which was now prowling its ground restively. As part of his act, Massarti would often adopt the risky pose of turning his back on the beasts but that night his attention was firmly fixed on the restive lion. Perhaps too much so, disregarding the danger from the other four animals.

I remember thinking even as a child that Massarti's space looked very reduced as he jabbed his sword towards the wild creatures. His stern face began to sweat with tension. Then somehow he slipped. Struggling to regain control, find his footing and re-sheath his sword, one of the lions crept behind him and sank its teeth into his right hip spinning him back down onto his side. At first the public was spell-bound, thinking this was all part of a daring act, until the blood started to flow and the rest of the pack joined in tearing at Massarti's theatrical garments, tearing at his flesh down to the bone. Women screamed, men rushed to get pitchforks and brooms or any other available weapon. Unfortunately audience panic prevented the approach of the proper handlers, and the crush prevented the three of us from moving back.

'Let us out,' implored my father. 'We have a child here.'

But we were not allowed to move back, not before I had seen poor Massarti dragged from one end of the cage to the other, one lion almost scalping him. I was told later that a quarter of an hour had elapsed from the beginning of the attack until they could extricate Massarti through a sliding door, which had to be broken down, as his growling oppressors were corralled by glowing iron bars. Bars that had only just been heated, which were usually heated and available before the performance, a prearranged task that for some reason had been neglected on this occasion. Each minute of that horror remained in my developing mind.

It is said Massarti told his helpers that he was beyond medical treatment: "I'm done for" were his exact words. But I heard none of this carried on that dank northern night as we walked away from the circus. Only the memory of Massarti's cries, women's screams, the crack of impotent blank cartridges fired by the police at the attacking lions from toy rifles, hurriedly gathered from nearby stallholders, rang in my ears.

Massarti died a few minutes after reaching the infirmary. He was thirty-four.

Only recently I came across an old report on the inquest verdict. It made interesting reading in light of my own childhood experience of the attack. Mrs Manders, widow of the late William Manders, said that during training lions were given a territorial line, known as the office, a barrier beyond which the performer must not trespass. She suggested that the primary cause of this tragedy was that Massarti possibly had crossed that line.

I am reminded of my own professional line – the bar table – from where we English barristers are not allowed to venture forth to wander the court like our American counterparts.

Onwards and upwards through the mirroring town hall's Ashberry Hall Corinthian columns – my own lion's cage awaited.

The law courts, a massive social hall and the city's basement lock up, known as the Bridewell, together with a police office were all housed under the same roof. This civic enclave was designed by Cuthbert Brodrick and opened by Queen Victoria in 1858. Indeed as I walked into the vestibule, I broke the gaze of the old queen staring across at her consort: two giant statues sculpted by the short-lived Matthew Noble who, I believe, was originally a native of Yorkshire.

Once wigged and gowned – the Leeds Assizes' robing room was palatial compared to that in York – I was summoned by a court official to visit my client in the cells below. She was, I was told, in an extremely volatile state.

The spiked barred gate creaked as the gaoler took me though into the cell area beneath the town hall steps. The ceiling was vaulted and the white washed walls smelt musty. This was more a cave than a prison.

Catherine Tiplady was sitting hunched forward on a wooden bench that ran down one of the walls. She was dressed in a black crepe dress with a matching coat that had seen better days. Though not shackled there was an iron ring on both the bench near her thigh and on the wall above her bowed head. There was no window, a single gas lamp provided minimal light. A plumbed, cream toilet bowl rested in the corner. Male or female, there is no dignity left once a prisoner.

'Catherine,' I said.

She did not look up, seemed hardly aware of my presence. She had lost weight over the months since I had visited her in Armley Gaol. Her hair was unkempt and when she did eventually lift her head there was a wildness in her eyes. Her widow's clothing enhanced her prison pallor all the more.

'Listen,' she said, a hand dramatically to her ear. 'I can hear the feet of free folk walking into the town hall above. It is as if they are already walking over my grave.'

'Catherine,' I repeated, in a desperate bid to draw her towards some rationality.

'They are going to hang me,' she finally mumbled. 'They are going to hang me like they hanged Emily Swann. I know they are, Mr Cairn.'

'Nonsense,' I reassured her.

'Yes, they are going to hang me and I haven't done anything wrong. I didn't poison Brian.'

'Then we will prove it.' I reached for her hand but she withdrew it straightaway to hide beneath her coat.

My old college friend, Dick Tate, who had assisted me in a previous case was waiting for me outside the crown court. Dick had become an eminent Leeds pathologist. He was engrossed in conversation with another gentleman whom I did not recognise.

'James, James, let me introduce you to Doctor Friederich Eurich,' he announced with all his usual enthusiasm.

A little surprised, I took Eurich's hand. I suspected he was a couple of years my junior but with his moustache and side parting he looked much older than his years.

'Pleased to meet you.' Eurich had a pronounced German accent.

'Friederich has agreed to appear for us,' said Dick

'But I thought Henry Johnson Campbell was to be our expert witness.' I could not hide my disappointment as I turned to Dick.

'HJ recommended Friederich here as better suited to the task.'

'Yes, yes,' said Eurich. 'The professor knows me well, I am his class assistant at the medical school.'

'"Class assistant"? A woman's life hangs in the balance here today and any forensic evidence could be vital to our case. It needs to be delivered by a person of standing to give it extra weight.'

'James, James,' appealed Dick, pulling me to one side. 'Please trust me. Eurich is a better bet than the professor regarding the testimony you are requiring. He is both a toxicologist and bacteriologist. His research into cutaneous anthrax at Bradford is second to none.'

'"Cutaneous anthrax"?'

'Woolsorter's disease,' explained Dick.

'I know what it is, but what has anthrax got to do with strychnine poisoning?'

'I looked over the notes you gave to Doctor Tate,' cut in Eurich. 'And I definitely think I can help your case. But if you don't feel I am qualified to do so, don't require me ... well.' He began to move off down the corridor of decorative tiles more reminiscent of a bathhouse than a house of justice.

'You're not going to let him go. The man's a brilliant scientist.'

'So why isn't he a professor?' I asked.

'He's Jewish,' said Dick.

I looked around for inspiration. There was nobody else about, no other expert witness to be had.

'Doctor Eurich! Doctor Eurich! Please come back,' I shouted after the disappearing back.

Eurich slowly turned round and for the first time he smiled.

'You'll not regret this,' said Dick.

'I was sorry to hear of the death of Mr Scattergood,' I told him.

'Thomas is sadly missed by us all at the Infirmary. Dead some four or five years now and there's not a day goes by that I don't think of him. Friederich's character is much more complex than Thomas' but he is equally analytical and gifted, just you see.'

'So, Doctor Eurich, how shall we present our evidence?' I asked, pushing back my wig which had slipped forward a fraction.

Chapter Ten

I walked through the east entrance beneath a fine carving of the royal coat of arms. Despite the town hall's beckoning cherubs and Victorian grandeur, the crown court itself was a rather plain and austere room. My assisting junior counsel, Harold Scott-Davis, greeted me with a perfunctory 'good morning, sir'. Catherine stood in the dock. Her face now concealed by a half veil: a nice touch this, I thought, no doubt on the advice of her solicitor.

I gave Arthur Hewlett, who was sitting behind me, an appreciative nod before smiling reassurance at my client the grieving widow. Catherine's head jerked momentary recognition. At least it seemed I had managed to calm her nerves a little.

It was going to be a tough one this. My old friend and adversary, Benjamin Levi KC, was acting for the prosecution. He was to be assisted by a young barrister called George Blackburn who was unknown to me. Levi smiled before giving me the briefest of bows. He was one of those men who whatever he wore it finished up looking like a crumpled sack on him. As now the bands about his neck were all over the place and his black court gown seemed to entirely engulf his small unathletic frame. But appearances can be deceptive, they certainly were in Levi's case, he was regarded as one of the most gifted counsels on the North Eastern Circuit.

'All rise,' instructed the clerk of assize as the red-faced and appropriately named Mr Justice Mulberry took his preliminary bow.

There was much clearing of throats, rustling of papers, adjustments of seats in the well of the court before the performance proper began.

'Catherine Tiplady, you are indicted and the charge against you is murder in that on the twenty-third day of December, 1904, at Kirk Hammerton near York, you murdered Brian Tiplady,' announced the clerk of assize. 'How say you, Catherine Tiplady, are you guilty or not guilty?'

A hush fell over the court. Catherine sank in the dock. Not as far as my previous donkey loving client, Edwin Holroyd, but far enough.

'Not guilty,' she finally whispered; conquering her buckling legs and pulling herself to attention.

I watched on as the business of empanelling and swearing in the jury began.

'Members of the jury,' the clerk of assize's voice boomed out again. 'The prisoner at the bar, Catherine Tiplady, is indicted and the charge against her is murder in that on the twenty-third day of December, 1904, at Kirk Hammerton near York, she murdered Brian Tiplady. Upon this indictment she has been arraigned. Upon this arraignment she has pleaded that she is not guilty and has put herself upon her country, which country you are. It is for you to inquire whether she be guilty or not and to hearken to the evidence.'

'May it please your lordship, members of the jury.' Levi unfurled to all of his five feet two inches. 'Brian and Catherine Tiplady lived as man and wife in a tithe cottage in the rural location of Kirk Hammerton. Though there was a disparity in their ages – he was fifty-five, the prisoner only twenty – during their first and only year of marriage to all intents and purposes to the outside world they seemed happy. However, the Crown intends to bring forward witnesses who will dispute this superficial appearance of harmony to the reality of unhappiness and squabbles that took place within the Tipladys' four walls. That is ... ' Levi lifted his forefinger as if to silence the whole court. 'That is ... ' he repeated theatrically, finger still raised, 'until the night of the twenty-third of December when Brian Tiplady had to endure the most horrific and unimaginable death. We have the testimony of the doctor who visited this poor dying man that all his symptoms fitted with that of strychnine ingestion. We have confirmation from the pathologist who conducted the post-mortem that particles of strychnine were indeed found in Brian Tiplady's system. We have the testimony of a York chemist who sold the prisoner two packets of strychnine only weeks before her husband's death.'

Scott-Davis' mouth fell open. This was the first we had heard of such a purchase. I glanced back at my client. Her head fell to her chest, she would not meet my questioning stare.

'I have spared you a great deal of detail,' continued Levi smoothly, 'which soon it will be necessary to call before you. But there you have the briefest of outlines on which the prosecution in this case will ask you to say that the prisoner is guilty of the murder of her husband of one year, Mr Brian Tiplady.

'Brief indeed,' muttered Scott-Davis.

'Short, sweet and lethal is more the way of it,' I muttered back.

'With the assistance of my learned friend, Mr George Blackburn, I will call the evidence before you,' concluded Levi, regaining his seat with a flourish.

'Call Joseph Penworthy!' cried the clerk of assize. 'Call Joseph Penworthy,' reverberated down the tiled corridor outside.

A large rotund figure rumbled up into the witness box. An ostentatious watch chain attempted unsuccessfully to swing the girth of his stomach. A ringed finger supported the bible as he read, 'The evidence I shall give ...'

'Are you, sir, the landlord of the Bay Horse Inn, Green Hammerton?' began George Blackburn.

'I am.' Penworthy's chest expanded with pride; a chest developed no doubt from hauling barrels.

'Tell me was the deceased Brian Tiplady known to you?'

'He was. Well known to me. He was a regular on my premises come Saturday night.'

'Did his wife, Catherine Tiplady, enjoy your hospitality as well?'

'Never. She's never set foot in the place to the best of my knowledge.'

'And why do you think that was?' asked Blackburn.

'My lord,' I was on my feet in a trice.

'Mr Blackburn, please keep to the facts and away from opinions,' reprimanded Mulberry.

'Mr Penworthy, did Brian Tiplady ever indicate to you that his marriage was not going well?' asked Blackburn.

'My lord,' I appealed again.

'Aye, Brian told everybody with an ear to listen, said they fought like cat and dog all the time,' began Penworthy undaunted. 'He admitted he'd made a mistake, she was far too young for him.'

'This is simply taproom talk, hearsay, my lord,' I managed to splutter. Too late, far too late, the damage had already been done.

'Mr Blackburn, although I realise you are new to the bar, you should know better than to try my patience this far. Facts are needed here. This court is only interested in facts. Mr Tiplady is no longer with us to corroborate what he told this witness or did not tell him. This line of questioning is both speculative and inflammatory,' reprimanded Mulberry.

Blackburn compressed his bloodless lips and flounced back into his seat like a petulant teen.

The judge looked to our table with a raised brow. Scott-Davis sprang to his feet.

'A right pennyworth this,' he muttered down into his bands, before asking loudly, 'Mr Penworthy how often did you say Mr Tiplady drank in your public house?'

'Saturday night,' offered Penworthy guardedly.

'Only Saturday night?'

'Occasionally Monday, maybe Tuesday.'

'Maybe Wednesday, Thursday, even Friday,' put in counsel sarcastically. 'And how much did the deceased drink on these occasions?'

'A pint or two,' responded Penworthy sullenly.

'Or three or four?'

'Sometimes.'

'Thank you, Mr Penworthy.'

Beaming victory Scott-Davis retired as a demoralised Penworthy left the witness box.

Dr Jasper Rigg was the next to take the box. A thin young man wearing spectacles, he looked very nervous. Then who wouldn't be about to be examined by my honourable friend, Mr Benjamin Levi.

'Doctor Rigg, were you called to Brian Tiplady's house on Friday, twenty-third of December, last year?'

'I was.'

'Who called for you?'

'Mrs Eileen Porter, the mother-in-law of Mr Tiplady.'

'About what time was this, Doctor?'

'Fortunately, I had just finished evening surgery so it must have been around a quarter to seven.'

'And what did you find, Doctor, on your arrival at the Tipladys' cottage, known I believe as Tithe Barn Cottage?'

'Brian Tiplady was gravely ill. He was having tetanic convulsions.'

'"Tetanic"?' asked Mulberry.

'Convulsions, your lordship, where both the flexor and extensor muscles participate. However, the latter predominate and the limbs are rigidly extended, throwing the head back and opisthotonos occurs.'

'"Opisthotonos"?' queried Mulberry again.

'Yes, your lordship, a spastic condition where the head, neck and back contort into an arching position.'

'And you found Mr Tiplady in this state?'

'Yes, your lordship.'

'How terrible,' said Mulberry. 'But please try and use terms that are accessible to the jury and the rest of us poor uninformed laymen, Doctor Rigg.'

Rigg nodded as Levi, obviously relishing every graphic description of suffering, resumed his examination.

'Then tell the court what happened?' he asked.

'The angles of the patient's mouth were drawn back, risus sardonicus,' show-off Rigg could not help adding. 'His face cyanosed from respiratory stoppage, then thirty seconds later tremors occurred, and after some more spasmodic contractions the muscles relaxed from the fatigue of their motor cells. Reflex irritability increased again and another convulsion began. There was nothing I could do for him. Mr Tiplady died a few minutes later from asphyxia due to respiratory failure and exhaustion.'

The silence of the court was only broken by the low sound of weeping from the dock.

'And would you say, Doctor, that Mr Tiplady's symptoms were compatible with a diagnosis of strychnine poisoning?' asked Levi.

'I would, sir.'

'Doctor Rigg,' I said, resuming centre stage. 'Would you be kind enough to tell the court at what time precisely you pronounced Mr Tiplady dead?'

'Twenty minutes past seven exactly. I remember checking my timepiece.'

'Doctor, you have painted a very vivid and dramatic picture of Mr Tiplady's final suffering. Do you agree it would take someone of a totally amoral and wicked nature to kill another person in such a way?'

'Undoubtedly.'

'Doctor Rigg had you ever been called to Tithe Barn Cottage before?'

'No, never.'

'So this was an unprecedented occurrence?'

'Yes.'

'Did you realise straight away that strychnine was involved?'

'No, not until the toxicology results confirmed it. However, I did suspect it was some form of poisoning, possibly strychnine.'

'Could you tell us how Catherine Tiplady reacted faced with her husband's dying?'

Rigg pushed his glasses back up onto the bridge of his nose. He pondered a moment or two. 'Normally,' he finally said.

'"Normally"?'

'She was normally upset, I would say.'

'Thank you, Doctor Rigg. I have no more questions for this witness, my lord,' I announced with a bow.

'Doctor Rigg,' Levi bounced back to re-examine. 'Would you say you are qualified to make a judgement as to whether or not the prisoner's attitude was normal regarding her husband's *excruciating* death?'

'Only so far as I have seen many people die and witnessed many grieving relatives. Mrs Tiplady was extremely distressed as we all were.'

'Good for Rigg,' whispered Scott-Davis. 'He's become a witness for the defence.'

'Anymore questions?' asked Mulberry. 'No, then I think we will adjourn for lunch.' His lordship rose – his red gown fluttering out of the high-backed red chair.

'Have you noticed everything about Mulberry is red, even his cheeks,' observed Scott-Davis as I had done.

'Let that be a warning,' I told him.

Chapter Eleven

'The evidence I shall give ... ' The bible shook in the uniformed man's hand. Clearly this servant of the public was unused to court appearances.

'Derek Horsfall, you are a police constable in the North Riding of Yorkshire Constabulary, are you not?' asked Blackburn, hand on lapel.

'I am, sir,' replied the constable; a big man with a booming voice despite his nervousness.

'And you look after the villages of Kirk and Green Hammerton, do you not?'

'I do, sir.'

'Would you be so good as to tell us what happened on the evening of the twenty-third of December last?'

The constable's trembling hands struggled for the page.

'I was called to a property, Tithe Barn Cottage, on the edge of the village of Kirk Hammerton at about seven-forty p.m. A doctor there told me he had pronounced Brian Tiplady dead about twenty minutes before.'

'That doctor being Doctor Rigg?'

'Yes, sir.'

'Was Doctor Rigg happy with the manner of Mr Tiplady's dying?'

'No, he wasn't.'

'Did he express the opinion that he feared it wasn't due to natural causes, that foul play might be involved.'

'He did, sir. He felt this was an unexpected death in an apparently healthy man and that the body must be referred for post-mortem.'

'Had you ever had occasion to visit Tithe Barn Cottage before, Constable?'

'I had, sir, the previous October.'

'Why was that?'

'A loud domestic dispute had arisen between husband and wife. A worried neighbour sent for me fearing the outcome.'

'Are you telling this court and the gentlemen of the jury that Catherine and Brian Tiplady were involved in a physical altercation?' Blackburn licked his milk lips like a satisfied cat.

'I am. Though they had stopped fighting by the time I arrived.'

'Were any injuries visible to you?'

'The accused had two black eyes and Brian complained that she had bitten him on the arm.'

'So you weren't entirely surprised to find Mr Tiplady dead two months later?' slipped in Blackburn mischievously.

'My lord,' I objected, grudgingly forced onto my feet again.

'Upheld. As I have already informed you the court requires facts not opinions, Mr Blackburn,' sighed Mulberry; a headmaster with a tiresome boy.

'Did you find out the cause of disharmony within the Tiplady household?' asked Blackburn unabashed.

'Brian believed his wife was too familiar with James Wright,' replied Horsfall.

'"James Wright"?' enquired Blackburn.

'Aye, Wright was a young lad that Brian worked with around and about the local farms.'

'Doing what?'

'Catching moles, harvesting, that sort of thing.'

'General labouring duties then?'

'Yes.'

'Tell me,' pondered Blackburn. 'How old is James Wright?'

'Twenty years or so.'

'A contemporary of the prisoner unlike her husband.' With that Blackburn slouched back into his seat.

'Constable Horsfall, would you say Brian Tiplady was drunk at the time of the October altercation?' I asked.

'Brian might have had one or two but he wasn't drunk.'

'I cannot help noticing that you refer to the deceased as Brian. Did you know Mr Tiplady well?'

'Aye, I saw him about the village from time to time.'

'And in the Bay Horse?'

'Aye, occasionally in the Bay Horse when I was off duty.'

'Thank you, Constable Horsfall.'

'Professor Anderson, you are a pathologist working at York County Hospital, are you not?' I could see Levi was up for this, rubbing his hands at the prospect.

'I am, sir,' said the shaven professor, brushing away the mop of black hair that had fallen across his eyes.

'Why bother with a beard when you've so much hair,' sniggered Scott-Davis, whose cryptic asides were beginning to get on my nerves. 'You'd think it would get in the way of his work.'

'And it was you who performed a post-mortem on the agricultural labourer, Brian Tiplady?' asked Levi.

'I did, sir, on the Thursday, twenty-ninth of December, following the Christmas holiday,' replied Anderson, checking his notes.

'Did you find any indication as to the cause of death?'

'Not at first, sir. I found no obvious tumour or haemorrhage. Although the deceased was a rather overweight individual, his heart, stomach, spleen and kidneys seemed free of disease. I did however find fatty deposits in his liver indicative of a heavy drinker.'

'Are you saying alcohol might have brought about Mr Tiplady's demise?'

'No, sir, in my opinion the damage to his liver wasn't sufficient to bring about death.'

'So what had?'

'I proceeded to remove the brain, stomach, liver, both kidneys, heart, upper part of the duodenum and half a pint of bodily fluid. I found the lungs to be congested and oedematous. With regard to the family practitioner's reservations, I decided to employ Mandelin's reagent.'

'And what pray is Mandelin's reagent?'

'An ammonium vanadate-sulphuric acid solution to test for strychnine. When the poison is treated with Mandelin's reagent a violet-blue colouration results, which then changes to orange-red and finally to yellow.'

'And did you find any strychnine in the body of Mr Tiplady, Professor?'

'I did, sir. I found some crystal powder in the back of his throat though nothing much from the stomach contents themselves.'

'How many grains, would you say?'

'Three to four grains.'

'And how many grains does it take to kill a man?'

'It only takes two to three grains to cause death even in a heavy man like Brian Tiplady.'

'Thank you, Professor Anderson,' Levi nodded reverentially. He was well pleased as he joined George Blackburn at the bar table.

'Professor Anderson.' My turn now. 'You would have the court believe that strychnine is so lethal that only a few grains can kill a man the size of Brian Tiplady.'

'It only takes the tip of a teaspoon for death to ensue in one to two hours in most human beings.'

'Indeed, indeed, and you found all of that in the deceased man.'

'I did.'

'Tell me, Professor Anderson, did you find any strychnine crystals in his nasal cavity?'

Silence. The professor looked perplexed, started rummaging about in his notes.

'I did, as a matter of fact,' he admitted.

'And what about his hair, skin and clothing?'

'Yes, I actually tested his skin and hair and found a small residue of powder on them.'

'Were you surprised?'

'Not really. I suspected they could have become contaminated from other parts of the body during its removal.'

'No more questions, my lord.' My briefest of smiles gave nothing away.

'Mr Levi?' enquired Mulberry. 'Do you wish to re-examine this witness?'

'No, my lord, though we would like to call our final witness.'

'You are Mr Edmund Lawrence, chemist, the Market Place, Knaresborough, are you not?' asked Levi.

'I am, sir.'

'Did you dispense an amount of strychnine to Mr Brian Tiplady at a date just before the twenty-third of December last?'

'No, sir, although I had in the past.'

'Did you dispense strychnine to any other member of the Tiplady household just before that date?'

The court held its breath. A dropping pin would have sounded like a loud explosion.'

'Yes, sir. I have an entry in the register book for the previous month, the twenty-eighth of November, a Monday afternoon I believe it was.'

'And who made that purchase?'

'Why Mrs Tiplady.'

'And how much strychnine did she order?'

'Twelve grains.'

'"Twelve grains",' you say,' emphasised Levi. 'What purpose did the prisoner give for wanting twelve grains of strychnine?'

'She said her husband had sent her for it.'

'Why? What use would Mr Tiplady have for strychnine?'

'For agricultural purposes. He was a mole catcher.'

'But on this occasion it was Mrs Tiplady herself who purchased the poison?'

'Yes, sir.'

'No more questions, my lord,' announced Levi; bowing away, bowing his way towards victory.

'Mr Lawrence, before Mrs Tiplady made her purchase, you told the court that you had occasion to sell strychnine directly to Brian Tiplady himself, is that not so?' I asked.

'Oh yes, quite often. He was a fairly regular customer.'

'How regular?'

'Maybe three or four times a year.'

'Can you tell the court exactly why Mr Tiplady needed so much strychnine?'

'To eradicate moles. He would roll worms in the stuff and push them down into the moles' chambers. The moles would eat the worms and voila,' the chemist tittered over something he considered to be so self-evident.

'And this is a new method of killing vermin?'

'Oh, yes, fairly new.'

'No more questions, my lord.'

'Mr Levi,' asked Mulberry.

'The Crown rests its case, my lord,' replied Levi.

'Then we'll take this opportunity to adjourn for the day,' said Mulberry.

'I am sorry, Doctor Eurich, you'll have to come back tomorrow,' I apologised to my star witness waiting outside in the corridor.

'Not to worry, Mr Cairn, I will not let you down,' sighed Eurich.

'Perhaps this is why Professor Campbell chose to send you rather than appear himself. Anyone familiar with court procedure knows there is a lot of wasted time and inactivity involved.'

'Again you are correct, this is all a new experience for me.'

Immediately I regretted my lack of tact as Eurich strode stiffly away.

Chapter Twelve

'Despite its strong bitter taste strychnine has been successfully employed by a few poisoners in recent years,' I opened the case for the defence the next morning. 'I am well aware that poisoning is often regarded as a female crime. However, the most infamous strychnine poisoners of late have been men – medical men – Doctor William Palmer and Doctor Thomas Cream. Strychnine is a poison whose purchase and sale must be registered by law, as my learned friend, Mr Levi, has already demonstrated. But it is in fact both regularly and easily obtained. Why only last year in the Olympic Games in St. Louis, Missouri, one sixtieth of a grain with brandy was given as a stimulant to Anglo-American athlete Thomas Hicks towards winning the marathon. When Hicks began to flag near the end of the race, he was given yet another dose of the same resulting in the Olympic champion's collapse soon after crossing the finishing line. The defence has no argument with the findings that the deceased was poisoned by strychnine, nor that on at least one occasion Mrs Tiplady purchased this pesticide. What we do dispute is the manner in which that strychnine was administered. My lord, I call the prisoner.'

'Mrs Tiplady, is it true that you obtained twelve grains of strychnine poison from a Knaresborough chemist, Mr Edmund Lawrence, on the twenty-eighth of November last?'

'I did but it was at the behest of my husband.'

'I understand Mr Tiplady used it in his work?'

'He did, sir.'

'Sparingly, would you say?'

'Yes, sir, Brian was well aware of its dangers.'

'Now can you tell the court what happened on Friday evening, the twenty-third of December?'

'Brian arrived home at six o'clock for his supper. He had been working on a nearby farm.'

'Would that be Snaith Farm?' I asked fingering my notes.

'Yes, sir.'

'Did he usually work locally?'

'No, not always, he occasionally travelled further afield.'

'How far afield?'

'He sometimes went west to work on the Allerton Mauleverer Estate, or further west to work at Scriven Park, or north to work on the Ashberry Estate.'

'Did he indeed?' The mention of the Ashberry Estate caused me a raised eyebrow. 'He was well thought of as a mole catcher then?'

'Mole catching was in his blood.'

'Strychnine too.' Blackburn's cynical comment floated across to me.

'Mr Blackburn, I heard that. No more,' warned Mulberry.

'Since his father and grandfather afore him,' concluded Catherine, hearing nothing but her heartbeat.

'Was Mr Tiplady in good health on his arrival home from Snaith Farm?' I asked.

'He said his eyes were burning something terrible, and he could scratch the skin off his arms they were itching so. He said he wasn't very hungry.'

'But you made him a bowl of broth and poured him a tankard of small beer, isn't that right?'

'Yes, sir. Brian seemed to have difficulty swallowing it though.'

'Then what happened?'

'He became very troubled, said he was poorly, insisted I send my mother for the doctor.'

'What were the symptoms of your husband's illness?'

'"Symptoms", sir?'

'What was your husband complaining of?'

'He said his jaw felt as if it was locking up, then that he could hardly breathe. I managed to get him to bed. I thought whatever it was he would just sleep it off. A short while later, hearing noise, I went back to him. One minute he was stiff, the next jumping up like a jack-in-a-box so as I couldn't hold him down. Then he said nothing for the foam coming out of his mouth. I can't tell you how glad I was when Doctor Rigg arrived with my mother.' A hovering tear splashed down onto the witness box.

'Would you say you enjoyed a good married life with Mr Tiplady?' cross-examined Levi.

'We managed.'

'But he drank, didn't he? As alluded to by your own counsel, Mr Cairn.'
Catherine looked lost, frightened at this.'

'Mrs Tiplady, please answer the question,' instructed Mulberry.

'A little,' pouted Catherine.

'He drank a little and knocked you about a lot, didn't he?' pressed Levi.

'Mrs Tiplady?' prompted Mulberry again.

'Yes,' she finally admitted, eyes downcast.

'Enough for you to kill him?'

'My lord, my learned friend is badgering Mrs Tiplady,' I shouted.

'A fair enough question I would have thought, Mr Cairn, in the circumstances,' responded Mulberry.

'No more questions, my lord,' a smirking Levi quickly interjected.

I thought of lodging some further objection but decided to call Mrs Eileen Porter, mother of the accused, instead.

'You are Mrs Eileen Porter of Kirk Hammerton?' I asked.

'I am,' said forthright Mrs Porter, heaving up her ample bosom with crossed arms.

'And you are the widowed mother of Catherine Tiplady and live next door to your daughter?'

'I do.'

'Can you give the court an account of what happened on Friday, the twenty-third of December last?'

'I was baking bread, hands covered in flour, when our Catherine bursts in all of a dither saying Brian had been taken really badly and would I fetch the doctor straightaway.'

'Which you did?'

'I did.'

'At what time did you arrive back to the Tiplady house with the doctor?'

'About a quarter to the hour of seven. Perhaps a little later.'

'Would you say your daughter was happy in her marriage?'

'It's not for me to say.'

'Mrs Porter,' I insisted before Mulberry had a chance to intervene.

'Brian was not good to her, despite her carrying his bairn.'

'Are you telling the court that your daughter was with child at the time her husband fell ill?'

'Aye, what woman in her right mind would kill the father of her coming bairn?'

'That's just it, my lord, is the prisoner in her right mind?' shrieked Blackburn, jumping to his feet.

The judged scowled at this, he didn't like this at all.

'Mr Blackburn there has been no mitigating plea of insanity raised here, and if there had been it would have been made by counsel for the defence at the beginning of this trial, not by you now. One wonders whose sanity is in question here,' muttered Mulberry.

'But Mrs Tiplady is not pregnant now?' I resumed calmly.

'No, she's lost it since in prison,' replied Mrs Porter with bitter resentment.

'The Crown has hinted that Catherine might have been having an adulterous affair with James Wright, do you know if that is so?'

I could see pencils balanced in readiness in the journalists' box.

'No, no, never,' said Mrs Porter appalled. 'What could an unworldly youngster like Wright do for our Catherine with a bairn already in her belly?'

Unworldly or not, James Wright was my next witness.

'Were you working with Brian Tiplady on the twenty-third of December last, the day of his death, at Snaith Farm near Kirk Hammerton?' I asked the willowy six-footer. Indeed he looked so asymmetric in the witness box, he appeared as if he would tumble from it.

'Aye.'

'Please reply "yes" or "no" to counsel's questions,' instructed Mulberry.

'Yes, your honour. We was catching the mowdiwarps.'

'Mowdi ... what?' asked Mulberry.

'Colloquially known as mowdiwarps, my lord. *Talpa europaea* – the European mole,' I explained.

'Well, that's a new one on me,' proclaimed Mulberry.

'Did you know Mr Tiplady's wife?' I asked Wright.

'A little,' he mumbled.

'Did you indulge in any illegal congress with her?'

'Eh?'

'Did you fornicate with Catherine Tiplady?'

'You mean did I ever bed her?' asked Wright, wriggling his nose in disbelief.

'That is what I mean.'

'No, certainly not.'

'As suggested by another witness.'

'No.'

'How many moles did you catch that day, the day of Brian Tiplady's death?' I asked Wright.

'Difficult to tell, we was using the baited worms. The mowdiwarps usually die underground after eating 'em.'

'Are you telling the court that you use worms laced with poison to kill moles?'

'Aye, we roll the worms with poison afore dropping 'em down t' tunnels.'

'What sort of poison?'

'Couldn't rightly say, Mister. I always left that sort of thing to Brian.'

'Did Mr Tiplady do the worm preparation by himself then?'

'Always, sir.'

'Did anything unusual happen in that preparation on the day of Mr Tiplady's death.'

'Nothing in the preparation, sir. But Brian told me he had spilt one of them little parcels of poison in Farmer Harper's barn just as we was leaving.'

'Farmer Harper being William Harper owner of Snaith Farm?'

'Aye, that's him. Brian said he'd done his best to clear up the stuff, it being dangerous like.'

'"It being dangerous like", you could certainly say that,' I concluded.

A drip-white Levi reluctantly got to his feet.

'But surely Mr Tiplady was used to doing this poisoning process, wasn't he? He must have become slick at it,' he added lamely.

'Oh, he was, sir,' agreed Wright. 'But accidents 'appen, even to the best of us.'

'Indeed,' agreed Levi, sounding satirical. Then again perhaps there was no irony intended. 'No more questions,' he said, slumping back down into his seat.

I was flowing now – surely nothing could go wrong – I would show Levi how to develop a case. Bring on the owner of Snaith Farm, Bill Harper.

'You are William Harper of Snaith Farm, near Kirk Hammerton, are you not?' I asked.

'I am, sir,' replied Harper; his legs adorned in canvas leggings.

'And you employed Brian Tiplady on the twenty-third of December last to clear your land of moles?'

'I did, sir.'

'Did you know Mr Tiplady was using strychnine?'

'I did, sir.'

'Did you approve?'

'Not really. From Roman times right through to medieval days, mole catchers used earthenware pots filled with water as traps. Then we had wooden traps, steel traps and now we have poison.'

'Nevertheless you employed Brian Tiplady to catch these pests the best way he could?'

'I did. It's the modern way.'

'Was he good at his job?'

'He was, sir. The young lad working with him was good at it too.'

'That would be Mr. Wright?'

'Yes.'

'Thank you, Mr Harper, no more questions.'

I had hardly resumed my seat before Levi was asking, 'Farmer Harper did you find the remains of any strychnine powder on the floor of your barn?'

'Unfortunately not, sir.'

'Why not? Surely you couldn't afford to leave a trace of such a dangerous poison near to livestock?'

'Brian never told me about the spill. Perhaps he didn't want to, perhaps he died before he could. By the time young Wright told me about it, it was too late, I had mucked out the cow stalls. I must have placed a pile of ...'

'Thank you, Farmer Harper,' cut in Levi.

'Right on t' spot.' Harper's voice trailed off.

'So James Wright and Catherine Tiplady are the only two people who can verify the story of Mr Tiplady's mishandling of this highly toxic substance? A substance, I hasten to add, that Mr Tiplady handled daily without incident.'

'Possibly,' replied Harper hesitantly.

'My lord, how can the witness be expected to know how many people knew of the spillage?' I was irate, annoyed, not at Levi personally but because he had cleverly sown the seed in the jury's mind back to some sort of collaboration between Catherine and James Wright.

'Damn,' said Scott-Davis.

'Damn,' I agreed.

Chapter Thirteen

Friederich Eurich stood before me in the witness box after lunch. His stiff winged collar and beautifully knotted silk tie were the only statements of confidence about the man. Otherwise, he appeared to be "ever so 'umble" – not in the creeping, fawning Uriah Heep sense – humble as in modest.

'Doctor Friederich Wilhelm Eurich, you are a physician, bacteriologist, as well as holding a position in the Department of Forensic Medicine at Leeds, is that not so?'

'I do, sir. I currently hold all three positions.' Eurich expressed his agreement with a surprising Germanic precision that took me back a little.

'Now what can you tell the court about strychnine poison, Doctor Eurich?'

'Strychnine is a colourless crystalline powder with an exceptionally bitter taste.'

'So you would expect a person to detect it in their food? Say if they had been given it in broth or small beer?'

'Certainly in broth or weak beer.'

'Can you tell us where strychnine comes from, what it is obtained from?'

'It is obtained from the bark and seed of *Strychnos nux-vomica*.'

'"*Strychnos nux-vomica*"?'

'Indeed, otherwise known as the strychnine tree or the poison nut tree. I believe it can also be found in the Ignatius bean, whose plant is a close relative of the strychnine tree.'

'How much would have to be ingested, Doctor, to kill a grown man?'

'Very little,' shrugged Eurich. 'Two to three grains.'

'But he would still taste it in his food?'

'Yes.'

'Could a man die from strychnine inhalation, say if a bag was dropped and burst open as it is alleged happened to Mr Tiplady at Snaith Farm, near Kirk Hammerton?'

'Yes, I believe it is possible to absorb strychnine through membranes in the nose, mouth or eyes. Especially if a cloud of the powder has suddenly been released into the air.'

I checked my notes.

'Professor Anderson has told us that he found some crystal powder in the back of Mr Tiplady's throat though nothing much in his stomach contents,' I informed Eurich. 'Would that, in your opinion, be consistent with death from strychnine inhalation rather than ingestion?'

'It would, sir.'

'I have no more questions for this witness, my lord.' I took my seat with a dramatic flourish.

Levi unfurled like a cat piqued from sleep.

'What actual post do you hold in the Department of Forensic Medicine at Leeds, Doctor Eurich?' he asked, obviously having done his homework.

'I am a class assistant to Professor H. J. Campbell.'

'"Class assistant",' sneered Levi. 'And you "a class assistant" feel yourself qualified to disagree with the conclusions of someone as eminent as Professor Anderson.'

My spirits fell. I had feared this all along.

'I do not disagree with Professor Anderson's post-mortem findings, indeed I endorse their thoroughness,' replied Eurich, stroking his moustache thoughtfully. 'They confirm my own diagnosis.'

'And what is that?' sniffed Levi.

'That the deceased died of strychnine inhalation rather than ingestion.'

'Isn't there a small possibility that you might be mistaken?'

'I don't think so,' wound up Eurich.

Benjamin Levi sank back defeated.

I saw the expressions on the jurymen's faces. Their backsides shuffling uncomfortably in their seats. They cast pitying glances across to the dock. Friederich Wilhelm Eurich had held his nerve. He had remained steadfast under fire from Levi. He had proved to be an excellent witness, and he might have just saved my client's life. Still, you can never be a hundred per cent sure with a jury until that first word of those two exuberant words are expressed by their foreman.

They returned from their consideration in less than an hour.

'Members of the jury, are you all agreed upon your verdict?' asked the clerk of assize.

'Yes,' replied the foreman with slow deliberation.

'Do you find Catherine Tiplady guilty of murder, or not guilty.

'Not guilty,' pronounced the foreman.

'You find Catherine Tiplady not guilty of murder, and that is the verdict of you all?'

'Yes,' said the foreman, delivering the word into the drop dead silence.

However Catherine, who had just learnt she was to live, sank her head with a clonk onto the dock railings in relief.

Levi, on my left, let out a heavy sigh. Despite losing, good barristers like Levi always prefer getting to the truth than gaining an unjust conviction.

'It takes one son of Abraham to defeat another,' he muttered. 'Where on earth did you dig up Eurich from anyway?'

'The classroom,' I laughed. 'You can't win them all, Benjamin.'

'No, you can't. A robust defence, James. I congratulate you.'

* * * * *

I visited Catherine in the cavernous charge room beneath the town hall. Arthur Hewlett was already there. But no other friends or well-wishers were present to compliment Catherine on her wriggling escape from the shadow of the gallows. Not even her mother, Eileen Porter, was there to celebrate or merely acknowledge her daughter's freedom. True enough, Mrs Porter had given my hand a manly shake in the corridor outside the court. Then she was gone.

'How can I begin to thank you, both of you,' said Catherine, turning to include her solicitor in the praise, seemingly unperturbed by the lack of familial support.

'Think nothing of it. You are innocent,' I told her.

'Yes,' agreed Hewlett.

'Yes,' said Catherine, as if hardly daring to believe in her own innocence.

James Wright appeared, red faced and gushing with delight. A look passed between him and Catherine, and for the first time I wondered if there was some truth in the accusation that they were lovers.

Well, what of it, I thought, Catherine had been unhappily married.

'You said back in court that your husband had been employed moling on the Ashberry estate,' I ventured.

'Aye, he was for a few seasons,' replied Catherine. 'Along with James here.'

'The Marquess' youngest was a strange lad,' offered Wright.

'How strange?' I asked.

'Well, it's funny in the light of all that has 'appened since.'

'What exactly is funny?'

'I remember the Marquess' youngest, Stephen I think he was called, begging a bag of strychnine off Brian.'

'He what?' I asked in disbelief.

'Yes, he then proceeded to poison two of the gamekeeper's dogs we found out later. Nothing was ever proved for sure, the whole thing was hushed up, but Brian believed it to be so from hearing of the appalling manner of the dogs' deaths.'

'Which is extremely poignant in light of his own dying, don't you think, James?' put in Hewlett.

A cold shudder travelled the length of my spine. I remembered Brown had referred to Stephen as an "affable enough chap". He didn't sound very affable to me. Even here and now in Leeds, the bizarre behaviour of the inhabitants of Ashberry Hall was closing in on me like a visceral web.

'How ghastly, perhaps Mr Tiplady likewise recognised the terror that had accidently befallen him,' added Hewlett.

He and I watched in silence as Catherine walked out through the Bridewell's iron gate on the arm of James Wright.

'Do you think there could be any truth ... ?' began Hewlett, staring uneasily after the couple.

'What, that they conspired to murder her husband?'

'No, that they are sweethearts.'

'Quaintly put, Arthur,' I told him, with a reassuring slap on the back. Choosing not to prolong further conjecture, I shrugged and made my way to the disrobing room.

'Just heard England's won the first test match against Australia at Trent Bridge by two hundred and thirteen runs,' announced Levi.

'So, your day hasn't turned out too badly.'

'No, as you said you can't win them all.'

'That's right.'

'How do you fancy climbing the town hall clock tower to celebrate your victory, James?'

'You're not serious?'

'I can get the key. Only two hundred and nine steps in all.'

Reaching the one hundred and ninth step – I was counting – Levi panted that he wouldn't work with George Blackburn again.

'That arrogant young upstart proved to be more a hindrance than a help, cost me the case,' he wheezed.

'But you're glad Catherine Tiplady got off?'

'You really think she was innocent?'

'The forensic evidence was fairly conclusive.'

'Ah, the forensic evidence,' sighed Levi. 'You are a great one for doctors, James.'

'Were you not convinced then?'

'I was convinced that the jury would find Catherine Tiplady innocent on Eurich's evidence.'

'But how else could you interpret the post-mortem findings?'

'Just suppose James Wright had tampered with that lethal strychnine bag in some way, or thrown it at Tiplady's feet in a fit of resentment and jealousy. Puff! It had exploded on the barn's stone floor, and his rival in love is soon to be no more.'

'But how would a simple chap like Wright have known the fatal consequences of strychnine inhalation?'

'Although during his testimony he had claimed ignorance, he too had been working in close proximity to the powder alongside Tiplady for years. Surely Tiplady would have warned his apprentice, as it were, of strychnine's deadly potential if breathed in.'

'According to your hypothesis even if Wright had played a part in Brian Tiplady's death there is no proof that Catherine was an accessory.'

Levi's response to this was an ironical shrug.

Two hundred and nine steps, and we stepped out onto a walkway that circled the outside of the clock tower. What dizzy heights. What an eclectic view. Below us was wonderful eastern architecture – minarets and the like – contrasting with ugly belching northern chimneys.

'Things are not always what they seem,' said Levi obtusely.

'Let's go down,' I said, suddenly feeling lightheaded and nauseous. Not from the view but from the thought that with my help the guilty had possibly walked free. On top of this another memory kept buzzing around in my head: Wright's story about the poisoned dogs at Ashberry Hall.

Chapter Fourteen

'I have this recurring nightmare of a girl's body floating somewhere in the abyss,' I told Trotter in chambers the next morning.

'You can't let it go, can you, sir?'

'Let what go?'

'Why, Lydia Bowden's disappearance of course.'

'You think it is she?'

'I think you feel that she is dead and floating around in the ether, floating on the outer reaches of your imagination waiting to be drawn back into the light.'

'Do you really?' I asked, impressed.

'Is there a lake in the grounds of Ashberry Hall?'

'No, the Hall is one of the few great houses not to have a lake.'

'But you suspect that Miss Bowden never left the estate alive and that her body might still be "floating" close at hand.'

'You might be right there, Trotter, but where?'

'That would require a remarkable piece of detective work.'

'Indeed, Trotter. Do you know I've heard the most amazing story that the Marquess' youngest son poisoned two of the gamekeeper's dogs with strychnine.'

Trotter, a lover of all animals, flushed up with anger.

'Surely this is a further reason for you to visit Miss Bowden's mother in the County Lunatic Asylum, sir,' he suggested. 'If she isn't too far gone perhaps you will learn something.'

'Arrange it,' I told him.

* * * * *

The old York Lunatic Asylum, without Bootham Bar, had not always enjoyed the best reputation as I think I've mentioned before. Although housed in a fine Georgian building designed by John Carr in 1777, back at the beginning of the 19th century it was the subject of a national investigation which led to questions being asked in Parliament. During inquiries into alleged abuses at the asylum some records were conveniently burned in a fire which cost four patients their lives. However two different sets of assuasive accounts fortuitously emerged from the flames.

I eventually got to read the inquiry's comprehensive report into the deplorable state of the place written up by Jonathan Gray, a lawyer and alderman of the city of York, with a dedication to William Wilberforce, dated 3rd February, 1815.

A character with the dark surname of Blackader was the nominal head keeper. He admitted that the asylum servants refused to obey his orders. One Backhouse was named as the principal keeper but a man called Henry Dawson was regarded as the power keeper. In short, no one seemed to be in overall authority lest it be the erstwhile physician, Dr Best, who was a master of concealment; or the Steward, Mr Surr, renowned for his questionable bookkeeping; then what about the Governors? – who were certainly neglectful regarding their moral responsibility to those placed in their care. The number of deaths in the asylum was certainly massaged to make better reading. The yearly death rate was in reality horrific. Patients who went missing were recorded as "removed", the bodies of patients who were killed were hurried away to prevent an inquest.

Admittedly before Dr Best's time, two female patients were delivered of male children. One of the fathers was a patient, the other a keeper. The keeper continued to enjoy the confidence of the Governors and was not dismissed but was given a testimonial following his resignation after twenty-six years service.

Mr Higgins, a Magistrate of the West Riding, who had earlier sent a parish pauper into the care of this house, was informed by the pauper's relatives that on his return to society the man showed signs of gross neglect. Mr Higgins, a gentleman with a highly developed Christian conscience, decided to investigate matters for himself. He found the asylum to be in a shocking state and discovered cells previously unseen by those appointed to examine reports of abuse. One of the cells contained a chain and handcuffs affixed to a new board on the floor. Excrement and urine soaked straw was scattered on the ground of all these secret cells, which had been occupied by female patients only the night before.

Accompanied by an architect, a Mr Samuel Tuke – part of a well-known York Quaker family – visited the asylum between ten and eleven o'clock one morning in April, 1814. He reported finding a naked male patient standing in the wash house on a wet stone floor. The man was a mere skeleton, his thighs covered in dried excrement. Mr Tuke described him as being in "the last stage of decay".

But perhaps one of the most poignant stories from this place of horrors is that told by Mary Schorey, wife of the Reverend Butterfield Schorey, formerly of Queen's College, Oxford. The Reverend Schorey became mentally ill and was admitted and readmitted to the asylum over a period of four to five years. During visits to see her husband, Mrs Schorey was shown into the keeper's lodge and her husband was brought to her there. The keepers would push and kick him into the room. Once after the farcically named Benjamin Batty had pushed the Reverend into the room with his foot, Mrs Schorey complained "you should recollect my husband is a clergyman"– Batty replied "he's no more than a dog".

Batty – bats in the belfry – who really were the madmen here? For her husband's tender loving care, Mrs Schorey paid fifteen shillings a week, reduced in his final year to ten shillings due to her straitened circumstances. Reverend Schorey died on 10th December, 1812, aged forty-one.

So here I was, almost a hundred years later, about to pass into one of the worlds we fear most – insanity – the possibility of our own insanity. This asylum, with its previous terrible reputation, strangely shared its parkland site with the Yorkshire Quarterly Meeting Boys' School. This homely arrangement did nothing to calm me as I crossed the green.

On entering the red brick building the first thing to hit me was the smell – the institutional smell of age, ammonia and carbolic disinfectant. I was met with the vacant stares of those for whom the light has gone out of their lives. The patients walking the corridor all looked old, though some were perhaps no older than me. I imagined they had been wizened, lessened by their own tormenting demons. Some men sat on the floor, their backs to the wall, legs sprawling. I was forced to tread with care as I negotiated this obstacle course of limbs before finally arriving outside the superintendent's office. My knock was answered with an immediate 'who's there?'

'James Cairn to visit Mary Bowden.'

'James who?' The chained door opened a fraction.

'James Cairn to see Mary Bowden.' I was aware of a pair of eyes looking me up and down through the slit.

The chain jingled. The door was flung open. A man in morning dress filled the space.

'You need to go across to the women's wards. I'll take you there myself but I must warn you poor Mrs Bowden is not at all well,' he said.

My heart and hopes fell.

'A breakdown due to her daughter's disappearance, I understand,' I responded, as if it wasn't a question at all but it was.

'That's what we thought at first. Who did you say you were again?'

'James Cairn, barrister-at-law.'

'And your relationship, interest in Mrs Bowden?'

I hesitated. 'My interest is actually in her daughter's disappearance,' I explained.

'Tell me, when did you last see Mrs Bowden?'

'A few years ago. I believe I glimpsed her at Ashberry Hall, at a ball,' I added.

'I'm afraid it proved to be much more serious than the mental breakdown you alluded to. You will find Mrs Bowden greatly changed. Her appearance,' he added, as if expecting me to know.

'But how? How can she have changed so soon?' I asked with growing alarm.

'The disease Mrs Bowden suffers from can accelerate cruelly in its latter stages.'

'What disease?'

'I am sure I can trust you with a confidence as one professional man to another,' said the physician superintendent in lowered tones. He took a key from his breast pocket and we entered a long ward. 'The imbecilic ward,' he explained.

True enough there were creatures – the like of which I had never seen – languishing in barred cots on either side of the aisle we walked.

'Mrs Bowden?' he asked a nurse. The woman was dressed in a long white pinafore dress which swished on the floor as she swung round. A matching white cap perched jauntily on her not unimpressive head. The bunch of keys jangling from the belt round her narrow waist symbolic of her power.

She pointed into the distance as a figure stamped towards us with a ridiculous wide gait. She was obviously female but walked with the posture of a seafarer who has just come ashore after a long voyage. The nearer she came, the more appalled I was. I had never seen such distortion of limbs, her poor swollen knees and elbows, joints which appeared unable to fully support her or perform the most menial task. Her face was full of lumps and sores – there was nothing left of the fine attractive woman who had accompanied Lydia to the ball – there was simply nothing left.

'Her face ...'

'Gummata,' said the superintendent.

'"Gummata"?'

'Yes, granulomatous lesions which can ulcerate especially at sites of previous injury.'

'I don't understand.'

'Small rubbery tumours, to you, that can break down,' explained the superintendent all matter-of-fact. 'Associated with tertiary syphilis.'

'"Syphilis"?'

'When am I going home?' asked Mrs Bowden, tottering to a stop an inch or two from us. 'I want to go home,' she insisted, eyeballing the superintendent.

'There's someone here to see you, Mary,' he told her, ignoring what must have been her habitual plea.

'I want to go home,' she insisted.

'Later, later.' The superintendent's voice was reassuring.

'These striking pains deep in my bones trouble me something awful. Can you do anything for striking pains, young man?' she asked me.

'Mr Cairn, here, has come to ask you a few questions about your daughter, about Lydia,' said the superintendent, placing a hand gently on her shoulder.

'Lydia? Have you found her?' Mary Bowden stared at me with expectation.

'I'll leave you two to talk,' said the superintendent.

'I'm not mad you know,' whispered Mary, once the superintendent was out of earshot. 'They think I'm mad in here but I'm not.'

'Tell me about Lydia.'

'Lydia was beautiful, my baby.'

'Tell me about her engagement to Andrew Ashberry.'

'Andrew, poor Andrew, he wasn't up to it,' she cackled.

'T' other one was more a man than he and he was really taken with our Lydia.'

'Which one do you mean?'

'Gerard, of course. He didn't like it, you know. He wasn't happy.'

'Who wasn't happy, Gerard? Andrew?'

'No, no, their father of course.'

'Why wasn't he happy?'

Mary's shrunken shoulders lifted and fell.

'He gave this to me you know,' she said.

'Who did? Gave you what?'

'Freddy.'

'What did Freddy give you?'

'The great pox of course. Though he'll deny it until the day he dies. He gave it to her as well in the end.'

'Who?'

'Her, Geraldine, his wife, the Marchioness of Hambleton, or whatever other fancy name she chose to call herself by.'

'Are you saying you had an affair with the Marquess of Hambleton?'

'An affair,' she scoffed. 'I was his mistress for years.'

'I can hardly ...' I began, thinking this must be the ravings of a mad woman.

'Until ...' she hesitated. 'Until, I heard she was in the family way again. Freddy had told me that side of his marriage was over long ago. He was lying of course as he lied about everything. The fact that she was expecting was the final nail in the coffin for me.'

'Not that he had given you a disease?'

'No, no, it wasn't until a year or two later that I realised he had blighted me with this into the bargain.'

'But your own children, Lydia, Malcolm?'

'Thank God they were spared.'

'Was that why the Marquess objected to the marriage between his son and your daughter? Did he fear that Lydia might not be clean?'

'No, no, there was more to it than that. He must have known which and when one of his poxy whores had contaminated him down in London, that was a few years after our Lydia was born.'

'Did you ever confront him with the accusation?'

'Yes, I did. He denied it of course, said I must have got it from someone else, said I was the source. He told me that I had caused Geraldine's death when Stephen was born early.'

'What, Stephen Ashberry was premature?'

'He was well ahead of time,' cackled Mary. 'A puny little creature if ever I did see one.'

'So was your long affair with Lord Hambleton ...'

'Almost a lifetime's affair,' reaffirmed Mary.

'The real reason for His Lordship objecting to Lydia marrying his son?'

She shook her head.

'Why, then?'

'You will have to ask my son, our Malcolm, the reasons for this and that,' she said, clamping her lips tightly together.

'Then I will,' I told her.

'And your husband, madam, was he not aware of your adultery?'

'Aye, my poor Reggie turned a blind eye for the benefits it brought to the farm and, I can't deny, benefits there were.' She suddenly grabbed the cloth of my coat, balling it up in her claw-like fingers. Her manner abruptly changed. 'Take me out of here, sir. Take me from this terrible place. Take me home with you. They are trying to poison me in here.'

At that point the superintendent arrived as if by magic, alerted no doubt by a staff member.

'Let go of Mr Cairn's coat,' he told her.

'I just want to go home,' she told him again. This time her look was a mix of pathos and desperation.

The superintendent beckoned the nurse with the keys to look after her. I have a fear of keys, of being locked in myself, so I could fully empathise with Mary's predicament.

'Sometimes Mary acts and talks sensibly, at other times, well ...' he told me, drawing a deep breath as he escorted me from the ward.

'So, how much am I to believe? How compos mentis is she?'

'Did she jibber-jabber on about poisoned blood?'

'No, she never mentioned "blood" but she did fear she was being poisoned.'

'And that poisoned blood killed her daughter?'

'No. "Killed her daughter", what on earth could she mean by that?'

'Your guess is as good as mine,' shrugged the superintendent.

'But nobody knows Lydia is dead for certain.'

'Has she told you that the Marquess of Hambleton infected her with syphilis?'

'Yes. Do you believe her?' I asked him. 'Or do you feel the accusation is due to the insane ramblings of a sick woman?'

Again the superintendent shrugged.

'Does it really matter what I believe? Who would take poor Mary's word against that of the Marquess'? And I fear she will not be with us much longer anyway. She has developed heart and breathing problems, the lesions have spread to nearly every bone in her body.'

'Pity,' I said. A pity, I thought too, because there were a lot more questions I would have liked to ask Mary Bowden.

I thought a dash for air and freedom was unbecoming, so I made my way slowly back through the hospital with as much decorum as I could muster.

'Help! Help! Come! Someone come and get me out of here. My God! Help!' The terrible screams of a soiled male inmate tethered to a bed followed me out of the building. It seemed to act as a catalyst for the rest. Others started up. As I quickened my pace across the park, every window in Bootham Park Hospital seemed to echo with the deranged cries of the insane.

Chapter Fifteen

Friday, 16th June – amid great speculation and publicity after our first Test victory, England was due to take the field against Australia's batting order at Lord's on the second day of the second Test match. England hated to lose to Australia almost as much as Australia hated to lose to England – but perhaps not quite so much. The courts were quiet, the criminals were on holiday, and I had a spring in my step as I travelled down narrow Davygate.

Davygate – derived from Davy Hall, the residence of a family whose Norman ancestor, David, passed his name down through succeeding generations. The family held the office of steward of the larder, or Royal Lardiner, and were tasked with keeping the king's larders stocked with provisions such as pork and venison. They also collected certain dues from tradesmen, and were in charge of the king's gaol for poachers which was situated in the Hall. This was a time of forest courts and green sleeves when the majority of England was shaded under a canopy of trees; this was a time when the Forest of Galtres reached the northern walls of York.

It is impossible to move away from the past in York: Roman, Viking, Norman, Medieval residue meets the eye round every corner. Each age can be visually unpicked from the city's fabric like stitches from a garment. And I was very aware on that June morning that a legionary's studded sandals will have tramped the same ground I now trod.

My mouth fell open. I must have looked preposterous to the approaching figure striding purposefully towards me. That is if she had seen me, I couldn't be sure. It certainly wasn't the Roman soldier of my imagination but Winifred Holbrook. I could not believe it. After years of not setting eyes on her, here she was again in just over a month, and this time she was alone.

Our paths crossed outside St Helen's Church, which stands in the angle of Davygate and Stonegate, a short distance from our first ever meeting outside the Mansion House where she had chained herself to the railings in an act of suffrage.

I walked past, dazed, until I heard a well-modulated voice call after me, 'James, James, is that you?'

'Yes, it is I.' I turned shamefaced to face the woman I had loved so much. She visibly stiffened, and in a heart stopping moment I realised that if anything she had become more beautiful with maturity. Her face had become leaner, her mouth firmer.

'Were you going to ignore me?' she asked.

'I didn't think you wanted to know me after ...' I hesitated. 'After your father's ...'

'My father's death and disgrace,' she helped out with apparent indifference.

'Your father's suicide to be precise.'

'Precision is usually your strongest virtue, James, but not in this case. As I reminded you many moons ago, Cedric Holbrook was not my real father but my step-father.'

'Of course, how could he have been anything else,' I reassured her.

'He was not of my blood.'

'Your views and morals were directly opposed.'

'And to those of my mother.'

'Indeed,' I agreed.

'He fooled us all by pretending to be a socialist reformer while all the time he was a member of that abhorrent right-wing organisation.'

'The Brotherhood,' I sighed. 'But Winifred let's not talk about this out here on the street, why don't we step in there for a while,' I pointed to the doorway of St Helen's Church, checking my pocket watch. 'There won't be a service at this time. It will be quiet. Peaceful,' I added.

The church smelt of beeswax. Undecided whether to stand or sit, we completed a half circle of the limestone, cup-shaped font. It was exquisitely decorated with an arcade of semi-circular arches and a band of palmette ornamentation around the rim. I ran my hand over the carving in wonder.

'It's hard to believe that the mason who created this served under Richard the Lionheart,' I enthused to Winifred.

'Hardly served. Richard I only spent about ten months in this country, the rest of the time he was fighting the Crusades. He spoke in a French dialect, *langue d'oïl*, and knew little English.'

'Do you have to annihilate all my romantic notions with pragmatism, Winifred?'

'Well, someone has to keep you grounded.'

'And so knowledgeable. This must be the result of attending that "Infidel Place",' I laughed.

'I did have access to a good library at Girton. However the college taught me less about the past and more about the future of women in politics.'

'Ah, politics. Still a woman of suffrage?'

'Still,' she replied, as we risked the intimacy of a back pew.

'Do you forgive me for exposing your stepfather's criminality?' I asked straight out; sensing it was the time for some candidness.

'What else could you have done?'

'I never felt you were tainted with the affair.'

'It killed her you know.'

'Sorry?'

'The affair, as you call it, the deceit, killed my mother. She died a year later in Scarborough. She retired there to get away from the scandal, but she never really got over it. It corroded her zest for living.'

'I can imagine.' I reached out to touch her hand.

'Don't!' she said, snatching her hand back as if struck by an electric shock.

'I would have liked us to remain friends.'

'We were always that, James. But things have changed, we have changed.'

'You mean your engagement.'

'So, you have heard.'

'And does your fiancé, The Right Honourable John Beardsley, MP, share your suffrage aspirations?'

'Not entirely.'

'As an engaged woman would you risk having tea with me tomorrow afternoon?' I asked; thinking I hadn't a hope in hell of her accepting. 'It would be fun,' I persisted. 'There is this newly built art nouveau restaurant that everyone is talking about just a few yards from here.'

'I would like that very much,' she replied to my amazement. I obviously hadn't taken into account this additional independent strain reinforced by Girton College membership.

Now that something had been decided, we got up to leave.

'See the west window up there which is made up of Renaissance glass, the third figure along is believed to be of Helen, mother of Constantine who was proclaimed Emperor by the troops following his father's death here in York in 306 AD. Born a slave, Helen was pronounced Empress by her son in 324. An intrepid traveller still at the age of seventy-eight, and perhaps wisely choosing to leave the dangerous machinations of Rome, she is said to have visited the holy places associated with Christ's life, founding churches in Bethlehem and on the Mount of Olives. She was a woman with an indomitable spirit like you, Winifred.'

'But I haven't got to seventy-eight yet,' blushed Winifred.

'No, that must have been something of a feat in ancient Rome.'

* * * * *

'My neighbour's daughter tells me Mrs Bowden's condition has worsened,' Trotter informed me that afternoon. 'She says she no longer gets any visitors, not even her son, Malcolm, comes any more. In fact my neighbour's daughter says you were the last person to visit her.'

'What? She remembers me, knew who I was?'

'She was on the ward that day, and they don't get many gentlemen in long Oxford grey box coats visiting the insane.'

'Do you have a problem with madness, Trotter? It strikes me you are afraid of it.'

'Perhaps, a little,' muttered Trotter down towards his feet.

'You hold more prejudices than any other man I know.'

'My father died in there,' he blurted out.

'Died in where?'

'The madhouse, York madhouse.'

'Died of what exactly?' I asked. Incredulous that Trotter had only decided to tell me about his father now.

'Old age, senility, all the things any of us fear we might have to face.'

Trotter had done it again – turned the tables on me – now there was nothing else for me to do but feel sorry for him.

'You'll never believe who I just bumped into,' I told him, deeply ashamed of myself and desperately trying to lift the mood.

'No, and who would that be?' asked Trotter, apparently disinterested or sulking.

'Winifred Holbrook.'

'Indeed, sir.' A knowing look flashed briefly across that otherwise inscrutable and, yes, sad face.

* * * * *

'No play today at Lord's. Match drawn,' shouted huddled newsboys, as the afternoon rain began to pitter-patter on the pavements of York.

'And are you happy with your new man?' I asked Winifred in the room of mirrors and swirling art nouveau.

'It hasn't taken you long to broach that question.'

'I'm interested.'

'What is happiness?'

'Do you love him?'

'Love, love, what is love?'

'I see,' I said, and I did.

'James you do realise there can never be anything between us. This cannot go any further.'

'Of course I do,' I assured her.

Winifred slumped back, visibly relaxed there in her chair in the Davy Hall Restaurant. Indeed we both relaxed, just happy and comfortable to be in each other's company.

I ordered grilled ham, she, smoked salmon. Our order was taken by a waitress who must have been employed for her ability to blend into the background or at least not to distract from the art nouveau.

'Well, well, look who's here, Miss Winifred Holbrook and Mr James Cairn.' Andrew Ashberry raised his hat to Winifred as he passed through to his table. For once no Chatterton, for once he appeared to be alone.

'Oh dear, he's a friend of John's,' she whispered.

'"John"?' I had mentally blocked out the existence of Winifred's fiancé, The Right Honourable John Beardsley, MP.

'Yes, they both were at Stonyhurst College together,' she said, ignoring my lapse.

'But that's a Jesuit college, isn't it?'

'Yes, both John and Andrew come from two of the oldest Catholic families in the land, didn't you know?'

'But you're a Quaker, I seem to remember.'

'I know. I will have to convert,' sighed Winifred. 'Whatever else the Church of Rome has focus.'

'How will Rome sit with Quaker simplicity?'

'I'm not sure,' she shrugged. 'Anyway how do you know Andrew Ashberry?'

'I don't really. We share a mutual friend. I attended a party at Ashberry Hall a few years ago.'

'Did you know Andrew's fiancée?' asked Winifred; clearing her throat and changing the subject, obviously presuming the "mutual friend" was a woman.

'Yes, Lydia, I met her just the once.'

'She simply vanished into thin air, following their engagement party, never to be seen again.'

'Yes, I know. That was the party I attended.'

Winifred's jaw dropped in amazement.

'Was Lydia as beautiful as they say?' she asked.

'Yes, and perhaps more so.'

'As beautiful as your mutual friend?'

'A lot more,' I smiled, thinking of Robert Brown.

'Terrible, it must have been terrible for Andrew.'

Just at that moment Louis Chatterton passed by without seeing us, he was so intent on joining Ashberry's table.

'John always thought those two were, you know ...' muttered Winifred.

'You know what?' I teased.

'Like Oscar Wilde. According to John, Andrew has always had a tendency that way even at school. That's why we were so surprised to hear of his engagement.'

'Not like his father then?' I tested.

'No, no, quite the opposite, the Marquess has a reputation as an awful old philanderer.'

'And where is The Right Honourable John Beardsley, MP, today?' I asked; my turn to change the subject.

'Oh London, Parliament, the usual,' she said.

* * * * *

'Things are getting worse in Russia, sir. It's in all the papers,' announced Trotter, one morning several days later. 'I think you might be right after all about them being on the brink of a revolution. The sailors aboard a battleship called *Potemkin* have mutinied, killing some of their officers, and the ship is sailing the oceans freely under the red flag and their command.'

'Let me see that.' I snatched up the open newspaper from the pile on his desk.

The *Potemkin* had appeared off Feodosia, I read. It had restocked its food supply and sailed for an unknown destination having seized a Russian merchant ship with a cargo of cattle. It was reported that it had also obtained some coal from a British merchant ship. There was no suggestion at all of surrender. The *Potemkin* had set itself the task of sparking off an uprising in all the coastal cities. The newspaper printed a text purporting to be from the manifesto which the *Potemkin* was circulating.

To all civilised citizens and to the working people! The crimes of the autocratic government have exhausted all patience. The whole of Russia, burning with indignation, exclaims: Down with the chains of bondage! The government wants to drown the country in blood, forgetting that the troops consist of sons of the oppressed people. The crew of the Potemkin has taken the first decisive step. We refuse to go on acting as the people's hangman. Our slogan is: freedom for the whole Russian people or death! We demand an end to the war and the immediate convocation of a constituent assembly on the basis of universal suffrage. That is the aim for which we shall fight to the end: victory or death! All free men, all workers will be on our side in the struggle for liberty and peace. Down with the autocracy! Long live the constituent assembly!

I wondered how Winifred would react to this. I was even more curious what The Right Honourable John Beardsley, MP for York, would make of it. But above all I was staggered that Winifred had become intimately involved with a Tory. There was nothing conservative – lowercase or capital C – about Winifred Holbrook. God dammit! – her real father had been an Irish revolutionary.

There was a knock on the door, Trotter walked across the room to open it. Inspector Timon White stood there framed in all his magnificent arrogant glory.

'Mr Cairn.' White entered, Trotter exited. 'A pleasure as always, Mr Cairn.'

Why, whenever White mentioned my name did it always seem more like a reproach than "a pleasure".

'Inspector, what can I do for you?' I tried my best to sound helpful.

'I just called in on the off chance that you would be free and keep you up to date regarding my inquiries into the disappearance of Miss Lydia Bowden.'

'Indeed.'

'I can tell you that she left Ashberry Hall on Saturday morning the twenty-eighth of September, 1901, and that there have been no more sightings of her since.'

'We know that. Is that all you've got?'

'To be absolutely honest with you the Ashberry family has been less than forthcoming.'

Why wasn't I surprised.

'Perhaps this mystery should be approached from another angle,' I suggested.

'What angle?'

'Well, have you interviewed the Bowden family in any depth?'

'Of course.'

'Have you seen Mrs Bowden?'

'She is away in the mental hospital.'

'As you are well aware, she is in Bootham Park Asylum just round the corner from here to be precise.' At that point I decided to admit to White that I had visited Mary Bowden without making any reference to her syphilitic condition.

'You've seen her? Was she as insane as her husband and son make out?' asked White agog.

'That is hard for me to say. She did tell me that the Marquess of Hambleton was very much against the match between his son and Lydia. She said I would have to ask her son, Malcolm, the reasons for this and that.'

'Did she? Well, I haven't exactly found him to be a helpful and grieving relative either to date. He seems to have a profound dislike of the police.'

'I wonder how he feels about barristers.'

'Indeed.' From a thoughtful frown the rugged face smoothed into something approaching a smile. 'What if you were to follow Mary Bowden's advice and ask her son "the reasons for this and that"?'

'And report directly back to you?'

'Quite so, Mr Cairn,' said White with his most ingratiating smile.

Chapter Sixteen

Far from the going concern that Mary Bowden had portrayed, Broadshaw Farm appeared to be a rundown sort of place. A wooden ladder bridged the space where outside steps had once led to the upper storey door of a barn. The farmhouse itself had a depression in its roof, more a basin for catching rainwater than a roof. If a building could be said to have lost the will to live – this had. A broom handle kept the door closed on a small closet shape of a building, the privy perhaps. An old hay cart stood rotting in the yard. A grizzled dog ambled towards me. I stood stock still, uncertain of its intentions. After sniffing around my boots for a while, assessment completed it began to bark loudly before retreating back to its kennel. Nobody came out, only a latchless bedroom window above my head knocked eerily in the wind.

I could hardly believe that elegant Lydia had been spawned by such a place, perhaps it had not always been like this, perhaps tragedy had rendered it thus. I appealed back towards my fellow barrister and friend, Digby West, who had given me a spin out here into the Wolds in his new automobile. He remained fixed like a dummy, dominating the small open topped Wolseley 1904 in his leather helmet, gauntlets and goggles.

'There's an axe over there by that pile of wood,' he shouted, pointing and pulling a face.

I retraced a few steps towards him; his head still sticking ridiculously above the steering wheel, above the parapet.

'I said Lydia Bowden lived here not Lizzie Borden.'

'Don't care,' he told me. 'I'll stay put.'

Digby had swapped his two-horse phaeton a few years ago to become the fully modern motorized man. Digby always had an eye to fashion, he could afford to have, his father was a successful Northampton boot manufacturer and Digby had been brought up to be what could best be described as an outrageous snob. Perhaps that was why he was now firmly fixed in his powder-blue – his favourite colour – black leather upholstered vehicle, shaking his head vehemently and refusing to budge an inch to enter the portals of Broadshaw Farm.

On our way over from York, Digby had little conversation other than the specifics of the six horsepower Wolseley.

'It is conventional in most respects,' he told me.

Not from the glances of passers-by, I thought.

'It features a forward mounted, horizontal, single-cylinder engine with bore and stroke of four point one by five inches. Final drive is provided by a central chain and its most popular guise is its two-seater configuration. Cooling is provided by the Wolseley feature of distinctive gilled tubes wrapped around the bonnet.'

'Really,' I said. This information wafted over me like so much hot air. All I could think of was my possible interviews with Reginald and Malcolm Bowden.

I knocked on the peeling door – no answer. I turned the knob slowly and walked in. Summer flies circled and fed on the remnants of a meal left out on the bench table in the centre of the parlour. There was a fetid smell to the place. I did not see him at first. He was seated by the fireless hearth. He didn't turn or move. I thought he was dead.

'That you, Malcolm?' he asked, still refusing to turn from his fireplace contemplation.

'Mr Bowden?' I asked, beginning to think if not dead he might be blind. 'Mr Bowden, my name is James Cairn.'

'She's dead, you know,' he snuffled. A woollen sleeve, more holes than sleeve, lifted to one eye and then the other to wipe away gathering tears.

'Who's dead?' I asked, placing a comforting hand on his shoulder. He did not react to my touch.

'*She* is dead,' he enunciated slowly making his meaning clearer.

Shocked, I took a deep breath. Exhibiting such distress, he could only mean that his wife, Mary Bowden, had died or that they had found Lydia dead.

'I'm so ...' I began my commiserations.

'Yes, I've had her for twelve years,' interrupted Mr Bowden.

'"Twelve years"?' Mr Bowden wasn't making any sense.

'Rain was the best collie hereabouts.'

'Rain? A dog?'

'No, a bitch. A pure bred bitch, cost me a fortune. She was always Lydia's pet really. She's never been the same since Lydia vanished.'

'Perhaps it is Lydia you are really missing,' I suggested.

Reginald Bowden's eyes narrowed at this. The look he gave me was cunning, wary, unfathomable.

'Maybe,' he said. 'Who did you say you are again?'

'My name is Cairn, James Cairn from York,' I repeated. 'I met your daughter at the Ashberry ball the night before she disappeared.'

'Oh, aye.' He seemed disinterested. 'Never to be forgotten, eh?'

'Indeed, Lydia was very striking.'

'Lots of men thought that of her, too many men for her own good.'

'I had occasion to meet your wife at ...'

'Don't want to hear nowt about her.' Again he interrupted me, this time the ragged sleeves lifted over his ears.

'But surely ...'

'Don't want to hear,' he snarled.

'Haven't you visited your wife in the ... the hospital?' I asked in astonishment.

'Not once. I leave that sort of thing to our Malcolm.'

'Don't you care, don't you care how your wife fares?'

Again he pierced me with a look that I realised was now bordering on hostility.

'What's it to you? What's poor country folk's business to a posh gentleman from York?'

A difficult question. I was deciding what reason to give for my presence when the door was flung open. I turned half-hoping Digby had had a change of heart. But it wasn't Digby standing there but Malcolm Bowden, he was holding a shotgun across his chest.

'You come in that fancy carriage outside?' he asked. I nodded. Though I recognised him straightaway, he didn't seem to know who I was. But then why should he, he had only seen me the once at Ashberry Hall with Gerard's body.

'What fancy carriage?' croaked the older man.

'One of them new automobiles, Pa. The colour of the sky on a good day,' explained Malcolm. 'And a fellow all trussed up in it like a turkey cock.' I could not help smiling at this colourful description of Digby. 'He gobbled too like a turkey when I came up behind him.' Malcolm began making strange noises, strange movements with his mouth. I wondered if he was mentally sound. 'Friend of yours?' he asked.

'Yes, he brought me here,' I reluctantly admitted.

'So who are you and what can we do for you?'

'I am a barrister and I met your sister on the night before she disappeared. I am interested in finding out what happened to her.'

Reginald flashed his son a look that again I couldn't quite fathom – was it fear or warning? Malcolm paled.

'Really,' he swallowed. 'Well, I can tell you what I think happened to her.'

'Please go ahead,' I told him. 'I'm all ears.'

'They killed her.'

'Who killed her?'

'The Ashberrys of course.'

'Which Ashberry in particular?'

'Andrew, no doubt with the help of his father. They waylaid her, killed her and buried her somewhere in the grounds of the Hall.'

'But why would they do such a thing? What motive could they have?'

'The Marquess didn't want his son married to a tenant farmer's daughter, and when it came to it Andrew couldn't go through with it either.'

'Why not? Lydia was a beautiful girl.'

'But she hadn't as much to offer as Louis Chatterton had for a man like Andrew Ashberry.'

'I've heard rumours but I can't believe ...'

'It's true. I warned Lydia but she wouldn't listen.'

'But what proof do you have?'

'Proof? Proof? It's all in here,' replied Malcolm, jabbing at his temple. He had large strong hands innate in farm labourers. I noticed that his father's hands were the same. But there was a young haughtiness about Malcolm. There was something physically familiar about him too which I hadn't noticed before: a likeness to Lydia perhaps?

'Enough,' moaned the old man. 'I've had enough grief recently without raking all that up again.'

'Your father is very upset about losing his dog,' I explained with ill-disguised irony.

'Is he?' said Malcolm. 'She been dead for years and still he goes on about her.'

'A typical bitch,' spat the old man. 'Alus running wild like t' rest of 'em.'

'Rain was bloody useless as a farm dog,' confirmed Malcolm.

'Just keeled over in t' yard one day,' explained the old man, suddenly watery-eyed.

'Your father seems more upset about his dog than your sister's disappearance,' I dared to suggest.

'That could very well be,' retorted Malcolm. 'They weren't that close.'

'But he must miss his wife.'

'You'd better ask him about that,' shrugged Malcolm, breaking the gun over his knee.

I declined, thanking them both for their time as I made for the door.

'About time,' greeted Digby, shifting his buttocks in irritation on the car's leather upholstery. 'When that muscular young fellow followed in after you, I thought I'd never see you again.'

'You didn't feel obliged to come in and check on my welfare then?'

'How about a drink? I remember passing a nice little hostelry not far from here.' Digby was a master of compromise.

* * * * *

The hills up to Scawton were steep and the Wolseley engine struggled, but the Hare Inn at Scawton was picturesque and worth it. A sow, with numerous piglets at her teats, wallowed in a yard to one side of the building.

'Dinner,' grinned Digby, nodding towards the pigs. 'Yum-yum, I could just do with a dish of suckling pig and boiled new potatoes.'

Instead we were offered braised ham hock with sage mash by the country-cheeked (or was it beer suffused) landlord, telling us it was a specialty of the house.

'There's been an inn here since the twelfth century, as long as there's been a church,' he boasted, presenting us with two tankards of the local brew.

'How did the inn get its name?' Digby asked him.

'Now there's a story for later when you two gentlemen are well in your cups.'

'No, tell us now,' insisted Digby. 'I'll not take any of it in if I'm well in my cups.'

'They say the witches around here would turn themselves into hares in order to get around the locality quicker.'

'So Scawton must have been a witches coven,' I put in dryly, grinning over my ale.

'A notorious fifteenth century witch called Black Agnes lived in the last house down the lane,' continued the landlord, undeterred by my skepticism. 'One day the Bilsdale hounds were chasing a hare and it bolted under the door ...'

'Don't tell us, it bolted under the door of the last house down the lane,' laughed Digby, eyeing up a young maid who was carefully placing our cutlery and plates with generous helpings of hock and mash on the table.

'The huntmaster and huntsmen arrived after the hounds,' continued the landlord. 'And despite a warning from the village blacksmith not to enter the witches lair, they flung open the door to find a bloodied and dying Black Agnes on the floor. That is why the building you are seated in at present is known as the Hare.'

'Fascinating,' said Digby, looking round apprehensively. For all his intelligence, Digby was a man easily swayed by superstition. 'And I suppose you have a ghost.'

'Of course,' replied the landlord; not a man to disappoint.

'This hock is both sweet and delicious,' I proclaimed, tucking in with relish.

'Do you think that serving girl is his daughter or wife?' Digby whispered into my ear a little later.

'Either way, if you pursue that line of enquiry you risk a broken nose or a black eye at best,' I warned him.

The landlord appeared with another jug of ale for our table, saying we must be thirsty with all the dust flying up from the road.

'Might I enquire how you have found yourselves in these out of the way parts, gentleman?' he asked.

'Broadshaw Farm,' I said.

'Ah, Broadshaw Farm,' he replied thoughtfully.

'Yes, the Bowdens.'

'An ill-starred family if there ever was one.'

'Do you know them well?' I asked.

'Should do, until recently the father, Reginald, drank in here many a night. He might be nearing sixty but that old fella's as mean and strong as an ox. Nobody dare cross him, he'd knock your block off as soon as look at you.'

'And Malcolm, did he ever accompany his father?'

'Never. I've seen him around but never in here.'

'Mr Bowden senior seemed very upset by the loss of his dog,' I announced testingly.

'Aye, more than the loss of his daughter or wife, I'll warrant,' replied the landlord.

'They didn't get on?'

'You could say that. Reginald had no time for his daughter and little time for his wife.'

'And Malcolm?'

'Reginald tolerates Malcolm but then he needs him to work the farm. Now Malcolm and Lydia that was a different kettle of fish all together, brother and sister were as thick as thieves.'

'Really?'

'Yes, on a fine day they would walk down the village arm in arm more like lovers than brother and sister. Their collie was always following on. Strange, one of the customers, Jess Onion, reported hearing that dog howling near the Windypits on numerous occasions.'

'Eerie, like a wailing banshee,' put in Digby.

'Windypits? What are Windypits?' I asked, ignoring Digby's supernatural reference.

'Don't say you haven't heard of them. They are vertical clefts in the earth which discharge warm or cold air to meet that on the surface. Above ground they sometimes cause small whirlwinds. In cold weather, mist-like steam can be seen rising from the fissures miles away. Skeletons of the ancients have been found in them too.'

'Come to think of it, I do remember hearing about them now. Didn't the Reverend William Buckland explore one of them in the first half of the previous century?'

'Aye, he might have been the first but not the last, I'll warrant.'

'Going back to the dog, perhaps it just liked hearing its own echoes,' I suggested.

'But to die like that, sprawled out at the top of an Ashberry Pit,' said the landlord.

'I understood it died in the Bowden's backyard.'

'No, no, some local Rievaulx fella found the dog as stiff as a board early one morning. It lay on its belly with its head dangling down over the edge of the pit as if about to fall in.'

Chug, chug, the car bounced along the rutted road over Scawton Moor on our drive back towards York.

'Stop!' I shouted across to Digby.

'What? What's wrong?' He slewed the narrow spoked wheels to a stop in a cloud of dust.

'I need a moment to collect my thoughts,' I told him.

Chapter Seventeen

Why had Reginald Bowden lied? The landlord of the Hare said his dog was found dead by an Ashberry Windypit – not in the yard of Broadshaw Farm – just one casually dropped comment and I had stayed awake most of the night fretting over it.

'Trotter, contact Inspector Timon White either by telephone if possible or if not by telegraph,' I told my clerk of chambers the next morning.

'Straight away, sir?'

'Yes, straight away.' Surely the urgency in my voice wouldn't escape even Trotter.

'By the way, sir, there was a letter for you in the first post this morning.' Trotter handed me an envelope. It was addressed in a poor hand and stamped with a Kirk Hammerton postmark.

> Dear Sir,
> We owe you a favour.

My eyes flicked to the signature: James Wright, I racked my brains for a second or two. Then I remembered, James Wright, the farmworker involved in the Catherine Tiplady case. "We owe you a favour" – I took this to mean he and Catherine owed me a favour. My attention moved back up the page.

> You seemed very interested in the goings on at Ashberry Hall. Well there has been further happenings on that front. Folk round about there are saying that someone at the great house did away with a young lass and that they've got away with it, when us ordinary folk would have hanged for the same.

If not the envelope, the note was surprisingly well-penned and I wondered if Wright had got someone else to write it for him. I could not help cringing at the moral outrage it contained, when perhaps "we" ourselves had got away with the murder of a husband and boss mole catcher, Brian Tiplady.

* * * * *

Inspector White stood before me at the appointed hour a day later. He pulled a chair up to my desk and sat down as I laid out my circumstantial evidence before him. I told him about my interview with the Bowdens at Broadshaw Farm; about the dog that supposedly keeled over in the yard, and then about the conflicting evidence that a local man had actually found it dead above a Windypit.

'Which Windypit?' asked White. 'There are a few of them over Ryedale, aren't there?'

'Ashberry,' I told him.

'Ah, the one nearest to the Hall.'

'You know the area then?'

'Mr Cairn, do you really think we haven't already explored that locality with a fine toothed-comb for the missing young woman?'

'Well, it looks as if you will have to search in even greater detail, deeper in fact.'

'Indeed,' sighed White. 'I've heard you are a fossil collector, Mr Cairn. What are your climbing skills like?'

'As a matter of fact ...'

'We'll see you in Ashberry Wood this Saturday at eleven a.m. then,' he told me, before I had time to relate any of my most recent climbing exploits. 'I am desperate to be accompanied by a man with mountaineering experience.'

'I wouldn't say ...'

'I'll not take no for an answer. You are that man.'

'Before you go, you'd better take a look at this then,' I passed him the note from James Wright.

'What folks think and say is often far from what is,' said White. 'And I like to conduct my investigations without any preconceptions.'

* * * * *

I travelled on the 8-30 a.m. train from York to Helmsley and there hired a carter who knew, if not the Windypits, then Ashberry Wood. Luckily, the day was fine for an open ride.

The topography on either side of the River Rye is amazing. It is made up of wooded hillsides and steep ravines. The Windypits themselves are a series of fissures on the west bank of the river, believed to be caused by earth movement and fracturing in the Hambleton Hills.

Ashberry Windypits are the most northerly of the group and are set apart from the rest. From Helmsley, White had told me to take the Old Byland Road rather than the road to Rievaulx Abbey, turn right at Ashberry farm, and keep going alongside the hill. It wasn't hard for me or my driver to locate our destination as a policeman stood guard on a rough forest track leading off the road, and I could hear male voices and the baying of the assembled bloodhounds high above us. The forest was full of the rasping calls of pheasants. I thought what a beautiful wild place this would seem if the task ahead wasn't so onerous. As I approached the top of the hill another officer directed me off the track towards an open field with an adjoining ridge running along the morning horizon. A hare ran out in front of me, its usual isolation interrupted by the unwelcomed assembly.

'Good of you to come, Mr Cairn.' White offered me his hand as I reached the crest of the hill dotted with sparse vegetation and the occasional slender saplings.

'What a climb,' I spluttered, stamping my boots to free them of the clogging clayey soil.

'Glad to see you are dressed appropriately in your mountaineering tweeds,' said White.

He was surrounded by several uniformed officers, and one or two other yawning officials whose profession it was difficult to ascertain. He was obviously expecting to find something.

Four long rope ladders were strewn on the ground together with various coils of climbing ropes. Officers beat metal pegs into the ground, tying ladders and ropes both to them and the odd more robust tree bowing over the chasms. I ventured cautiously forward to one of the two pits. This smaller one seemed to descend vertically. The second pit was wider – a gaping mouth of a hole coated with ferns and mosses – it was awesome.

'Shall we take this one first?' I asked White, pointing down the bigger one. He nodded.

'Good God!' said a police sergeant, flinging the ladders and ropes, now hopefully safely secured on the surface, down into the darkness where they disappeared.

'How do you know they are long enough?' I asked White.

'Prayer and local knowledge,' he replied.

'I have read some of these fissures go down a hundred feet.'

'Not this one,' he smiled.

I flung a testing stone into the void but heard nothing.

'Are you coming down too?' I asked White.

'Of course, but after you.'

'Thank you,' I said with undisguised sarcasm.

'Why Mr Robert Brown was full of stories of how you clamber up and down crumbling cliffs in search of ancient molluscs and suchlike. No better man for the job, he assured me.'

If I survive this, I thought, I must remember to kill Brown following my return to York.

True enough I was experienced at descending cliff faces but usually in healthy sea air, never down into the fetid depths. And true enough at first the pit smelt of damp earth, plaster, stone – and then of something else.

'I don't like this at all,' I shouted up to White, clinging to the swaying rope ladder for dear life.

'It was you who directed us all here,' he replied unsympathetically.

I reached out to touch the rock from my ladder perch. It was smooth, substantial and comforting. It was the only reassurance I had in this dark world.

'You'd better come down now,' I called up to him as my feet made ground.

I took a flashlight out of my jacket pocket as White landed heavily next to me. He wore a more efficient miner's oil-wick cap lamp that nodded and dazzled as he moved his head about examining our surroundings. Without a word we started to inch along a short narrow corridor. We weren't exactly trailing the sickly sweet decomposition of fresh death but it was something akin. It wasn't long before we found it. It was resting in a supine position just to one side of the drop. I was amazed to see in that reduced window above, the sky and scudding clouds were behaving as they always did because nothing felt the same to me now.

The partially mummified skeleton was macabre in the extreme. It was still draped in red velvet.

'Lydia,' I whispered.

'How can you tell? How do you know?' asked White.

Stooping down I lifted up the cross pendant draped on her chest.

'Lydia,' I repeated. 'And the hair, it's her hair, Saxon hair.'

'Sorry?'

'Blonde, Lydia had blonde hair like this.'

'Must have fallen straight in,' said White.

'Or been pushed.'

'Why would she have been up here in the first place? Dressed like that in a red velvet coat. Hardly the clothing for scrambling up hillsides.'

'Nor the shoes.' I lifted up a black Oxford lace-up shoe a yard from Lydia's remains.

'Hmm,' pondered White. 'Must have come off during the fall. Suitable for a walk from Ashberry Hall back to home at Broadshaw Farm but not for coming up here.'

'But in God's name how did she get here? It would have been impossible for say two men, let alone one man, to have transported and deposited her body down this pit.'

'That is supposing she was killed elsewhere.'

'What reason could possibly have brought her up here the morning after the ball?'

'To meet someone perhaps.'

'Again, dressed like that when she was on her way home?' I gestured in the direction of the bundle on the floor of the pit.

'A mystery to be solved,' said White. 'Didn't I read that you once used an eminent medical man in one of your previous cases?'

'Two men in fact in the Robertshaw case. One, a Mr Thomas Scattergood, was an expert in forensic medicine. Unfortunately he is dead now.'

'And the other?'

'Dick, Dick Tate. Oh, Dick is still around and kicking right enough.'

'Umm! Dick Tate as in dictate,' laughed White.

'No, Dick Tate as in senior pathologist at the General Infirmary, Leeds.'

'You all right?' The sergeant shouted down to us.

'Yes, we're all right,' sighed White. 'But we'll need the stretcher.'

An eerie silence developed above as the canvas stretcher was lowered down on creaking ropes.

Before ascending to the surface we decided to investigate a little further down the rock corridor looking for clues of possible foul play. I glimpsed out of my eye corner what I took to be two more skeletons deeper in a lower chamber with what appeared to be the skeletal remains of some animal – perhaps a large dog or a wolf even. From the brown fragile appearance of the human skeletons I took them to be ancients, displayed victims of some ritualistic killing.

'Perhaps these two are best left for someone else to find at a later date,' said White, with a pragmatism that surprised me but which I whole heartedly agreed with.

Lydia's remains weighed nothing lifting them onto the stretcher, but the realisation that this was all that was left of such a vital young creature was to weigh heavily on my soul for a long time.

* * * * *

'What time is your train back to York, Mr Cairn?'

'Five fifty-eight from Helmsley station.'

'May I give you a lift?' offered White. 'My sergeant here has a pony and trap waiting at the bottom of the hill.'

Once White and I were settled in the trap with the sergeant driving, White suggested we had plenty of time before my train departed and why didn't we take a detour to view Rievaulx Abbey.

'Might not get this way again in a long time,' he said.

He was right, Rievaulx Abbey was well worth a visit. The sergeant remained with the trap as White and I began to explore the ruins. Unlike much of Henry VIII's handiwork a good deal of the building's fabric remained. Set into the hillside the nave and north transept were slightly elevated, its pillars and arches appeared to be tiered like a wedding cake. It looked very French to me. Cistercian, I would have said.

'This is one of the first Cistercian abbeys to be built in this country,' confirmed White. 'Because it was surrounded by such good agricultural land, worked by an army of lay brothers, it was meant to be the focus of many substantial daughter houses throughout northern Britain.'

'I didn't know you are a medievalist,' I told White.

'There is a lot you don't know about me, Mr Cairn.'

'What a beautiful spot on which to build your abbey,' I said.

'And what a beautiful abbey,' he agreed.

We scaled a wall and began exploring, marvelling at the sculptured arched pillars and remaining cloister where men from another age once walked in safe contemplation. A blessing that those monks were unable to foresee their Tudor future.

'This place has inspired artists and romantic poets for centuries,' said White.

'I am not surprised.'

'At the beginning of the previous century, Turner himself made some preliminary sketches here to work on later.' Just as White was explaining this the sun disappeared behind a leaden cloud and the whole atmosphere at Rievaulx changed.

'Broadshaw Farm is just down the road from here. Lydia must have once played in these grounds, flirted here, loved here.' I felt as if I could see her, and I wasn't sure if it was this painful image or the missing sun that made me shiver.

'But whom did she play with?' asked White.

'If we knew that it might unlock this whole unpleasant business.'

Chapter Eighteen

'Hand delivered this morning.' Trotter handed me a note with a twinkle in his eye – a twinkle is something rarely seen in Trotter's eye. I didn't recognise the writing on the addressed envelope but it was certainly a more educated hand than James Wright's.

> *Dear James,*
> *Could you possibly meet me tomorrow lunchtime at the church as before? I have some news that might be of interest to you.*
> *Winifred*

That was all it said – that simple. My heart began to thump. Had she called off her engagement? There was certainly something clandestine about the reference to "the church as before". How would I be able to contain myself in the hours from now till then?

'Everything all right, sir?' asked Trotter.

'Perfectly.' I bit my lip, unable to contain the quaver of excitement in my voice.

* * * * *

Winifred was already seated in the same back pew of St Helen's Church. I almost missed seeing her at first.

'How are you?' My banal opening.

'I'm well enough,' she replied.

'Did it take you long to get here?'

'I live here, here in York.'

'Don't you still have the family house in Heslington?' I asked, a little dismayed. Why do we never accept that other people's lives change? Our own circumstances change but we expect those we have known and loved to remain in their same appointed boxes, continuing life's same little routines. I realised on our previous meetings I had been so taken with Winifred I had failed to ask her about the mundane.

'No, no, we sold the property in Belle Vue Terrace when mother moved to Scarborough. Cedric is away at school and I have taken rooms here in town.'

'Where in town?' I asked.

She did not answer, saying instead, 'James, we have to be cautious, Parliament is now on summer recession and John is in York holding talks with some of his constituents. We don't want to risk our innocent meetings being misunderstood.'

'No, of course not.'

'I knew you would see it that way.'

'Certainly I do. I have no wish to compromise you.'

'John has some very powerful friends.'

'I expect he does,' I said; thinking *but so have I.*

'And I am not sure he would approve of me tittle-tattling to you.'

'I am sure he wouldn't,' I agreed; thinking *God, Winifred you are such a beautiful woman.*

'But it's important.'

'Look, Winifred, what is this all about?' I asked, tiring of the prevarication.

'Well,' she gulped. 'The corridors of power at Westminster are buzzing with talk and innuendo regarding a scandal involving an important Tory party member and peer of the realm.'

'Oh, and what are they saying?'

'That either the peer or one of his sons is involved in the murder of a young girl. They say both men reside at the family seat in the North Riding of Yorkshire.'

'Ashberry Hall,' I sighed.

'Must be,' she agreed. 'I read that Lydia Bowden had been found down some awful pit and foul play was suspected. And I remembered you telling me that you'd met her once, James.'

Both alive and more recently dead, I acknowledged silently to myself.

'I know one of the senior policemen investigating this case,' I admitted instead. 'Though what you have told me is only rumour do you mind if I share it with him?'

'Well, I don't know. If it should come back on John for telling me.' She looked irresolute, frightened, not her usual self at all.

'Winifred, a young woman the same age as you, or at least she would have been had she lived, has been murdered in the most horrific circumstances. Surely it is up to us all ...'

'"Murdered", you say. So are they sure it is murder now?'

'Yes.'

'Tell him,' she said, her voice clipped. 'Tell this friend of yours what I have told you but you must emphasise that it is only Westminster gossip.'

'Look, where can I find you should any more information come to light?'

She hesitated awhile before opening her purse and tearing a page from her diary.

'You can leave word at this shop, only if you have to,' she insisted; her slim fountain pen thoughtfully balanced.

I risked a kiss on the cheek before we ploughed back onto the street, into the populace, to go our separate ways once more.

* * * * *

'Well, I must admit, that pathologist friend of yours over in Leeds is a clever chap,' said White.

'Who, Dick?'

'Yes, he's found the victim's hyoid bone was fractured consistent with the act of strangulation rather than any injury sustained from a fall. However, because of the degraded state of the body, he was unable to find any signs of petechial haemorrhaging. Doctor Tate felt she was most probably dead before she was thrown into the pit.'

A week after my meeting with Winifred, White had arrived at my chambers to personally inform me that my suspicions, and his, had been confirmed. Lydia was no longer young and vivacious Lydia but a dried up corpse at the bottom of a pit, a victim. How easily and quickly death dehumanizes us.

'This is now officially a murder investigation, Mr Cairn,' announced White with some ceremony.

It was then that I decided to tell White about the whispers travelling the corridors of power.

'Where did this information come from exactly, did you say?' he asked.

'I didn't.'

'Didn't what?'

'Say, exactly where it came from.'

'So, are you going to tell me?'

'I'd rather not say at the moment.'

'Well, perhaps you are better keeping the identity of this person to yourself if what they have told you is only Westminster tittle-tattle. But I must warn you in the near future I might have to insist you reveal where this information came from.'

'Although you don't like to work under any preconceptions, that note from the farm worker, James Wright of Kirk Hammerton, expressed the same sentiments as my Westminster source.' I took Wright's note out of my top drawer and passed it across to White.

'Hmm, Kirk Hammerton isn't far from here.' White gave a satisfactory sniff. 'I think a visit to Mr Wright might be called for. A starting point to put an end to all these rumours and innuendoes, don't you think, Mr Cairn?'

'Indeed,' I replied, feeling a sudden mixture of suspicion and apprehension regarding the man seated opposite me. Did this mean White was a man who would be easily intimidated, fobbed off by his powerful masters? Why was I getting the feeling that White was holding something back from me?

The words of dying Mr Brown senior suddenly came to me regarding Andrew Ashberry's forthcoming marriage, "I feared for that young girl's safety then". I remembered my own sworn promise, all those months ago, in All Saints Church to Lydia Bowden. It was time to do a little more private investigating on her behalf.

* * * * *

'Letter for you, sir, by special delivery,' announced Trotter the next afternoon.

It was from Algernon Tucker, the physician superintendent of Bootham Park Asylum, regrettably informing me that Mary Bowden had died peacefully in the night.

Why do people always say peacefully? – when death isn't always peaceful, I thought.

To those watching on, Mr Brown senior's death had been difficult not peaceful.

Tucker explained that Mrs Bowden had insisted that he send me a note after her death. I would find this note, written by her, enclosed herewith.

Like father, like son.

Those four words were the only words written on the note. Of course I knew the phrase well but what did Mary Bowden exactly mean by it?

I spent the rest of my evening at home pondering that question. I researched it, found that the saying itself was first recorded in 1787, coming from the *London World Fashionable Advertiser*, where it read: "For between ourselves, it was like father, like son." But I could not escape the feeling that in Mary Bowden's shaky hand it expressed a portent of biblical significance.

Without appearing heartless and calculating, I saw an opportunity here. I would attend Mary Bowden's funeral.

'Trotter! Trotter!' I shouted out to my clerk the next morning. 'Find out where and when Mary Bowden is to be buried from the physician superintendent of Bootham Park.'

* * * * *

As fortune would have it, I had a few days off before my next case. My client, William Sanderson, had been found drunk in charge of a horse drawn carriage. In 1872 it had become an offence to be drunk while in charge of carriages, horses, cattle and steam engines. The penalty for which was at that time a fine not exceeding 40 shillings or, at the discretion of the court, imprisonment with or without hard labour for a term not exceeding one month. With the intervening years, the seriousness of the offence had not lessened. Mr Sanderson had been seen driving his carriage down Blake Street in York, in a wild and erratic manner, by a policeman and several witnesses before depositing his terrified passengers outside the Assembly Rooms. The passengers agreed with the policeman that Sanderson was well in his cups. Sanderson did not deny that he was drunk on the night in question but maintained that he had had just cause as his wife had left him for a coalman. A straightforward case, I advised him to plead mitigating circumstances and hope for a reduced sentence or fine.

Chapter Nineteen

On Friday 21st July – the same day Jewish girl, Dorothy Levitt, set her first Ladies' World Speed Record, while competing at the inaugural Brighton Speed Trials where she drove an 80 horsepower Napier at a speed of 79.75 miles per hour – I was trundling in a horse and cart back up the hill to Scawton from Helmsley railway station. The carter dropped me and my bags off at the Hare Inn. It was the day before Mary Bowden's funeral. I decided to take a look at St Mary's Church myself as I was interested in old churches and had already read up on this one.

Since sitting with Winifred in St Helen's Church, I seemingly had become obsessed with fonts. The workmanship on the font in this minor village church looked to be very old. At a guess the mason happily worked on this particular piece of church furniture rather than taking up arms for this or that medieval skirmish.

'Beautiful, isn't it?' said a voice behind me. 'It is said to have come from Old Byland Church in eleven forty-six when this church was built.'

So my loose estimate was pretty spot on, I noted, turning with smug satisfaction.

'Arthur Lionel Whitaker, Rector of St Mary's.' The rector stuck out his hand.

'The wooden bell cover is very unusual too,' I said, reluctant to introduce myself.

'Seventeenth century.'

'That old?'

'Are you holidaying in these parts?' asked Whitaker.

'No, no, I've come to attend Mary Bowden's funeral tomorrow.'

'Ah,' he said. 'Ah,' he repeated somewhat guardedly.

'Did you know Mary well?' I asked.

'Quite well, more so towards the end. Mary was only a Bowden through marriage. The Bowdens are from very old farming stock in these parts.'

'And Lydia?' I asked.

'Ah, Lydia,' he pondered. 'Before I talk about Lydia let me tell you something about the church where her mother is to be buried. It is unique.

It was founded by an order of Savigniac monks, later to become Cistercians, who lived at Tylas, a mile or two up the river from Rievaulx. Originally harried from their house at Calder in Cumberland by marauding Scots, they wandered the countryside homeless for a year with all their worldly goods piled high onto a single wagon pulled by eight oxen. Gundreda de Gournay, wife of Nigel d'Aubigny, finally took pity on them and ceded them land at Tylas. Thirty-one years later these same destitute monks built Byland Abbey.

'Tell me more about those three arches dividing the chancel and the sanctuary. I've never seen anything quite like them.' I decided to indulge the antiquity passionate Arthur Whitaker before returning to the thorny issues of the Bowdens and Lydia.

'I suspect the two smaller side arches might have been used by priests as squints so that they could observe the abbot at the main central altar and act in unison during religious services. Let me show you something amazing,' Whitaker beckoned me forward. 'See here, behind this relatively modern altar, something of great rarity.'

'A stone altar.' I ran my fingers over each of the small inscribed corner crosses. 'Not many of these left in Britain.'

'No, they were outlawed at the Reformation. See the trouble they went to with these chamfered edges.'

'You are right to call this altar amazing. Its survival alone through so much turbulent history is a miracle in itself.'

'Ah, a miracle,' smiled Whitaker. 'The church doesn't acknowledge too many of them.'

'Indeed.' I paused, feeling the chamfered edges of this ancient symbol of sacrifice and the tombs of the martyrs. 'I went to visit Mary Bowden in Bootham Park Asylum,' I told him more abruptly than I had intended to.

'So did I, poor creature,' he replied.

'Do you know what she was suffering from?'

'Of course, tertiary syphilis, I have see it many times while administering to the needy.'

'Do you know how she came by it?'

'No, she would not tell me.'

'She told me that she had been infected with the disease by the Marquess of Hambleton.'

Whitaker hesitated and paled before admitting, 'That wouldn't surprise me.'

'Why, wouldn't it surprise you?'

'Let us say, the Marquess has something of a reputation in Ryedale.'

'And Lydia, what do you make of Lydia's murder?'

'"Murder", you say?'

'Yes, almost certainly murder.'

'Her father and brother were distressed enough over her disappearance, her death, and now this ...'

'Were they as distressed at losing Mrs Bowden?' I interrupted. Whitaker did not answer. 'What do you really know about the tenants of Broadshaw Farm?' I asked him.

'I know Malcolm was devoted to his sister. She and he were always together along with that collie of theirs.'

'Rain,' I acknowledged.

'Yes, that's right. Many a summer's evening I've seen the three of them running through the grounds of Rievaulx Abbey as free as the air.'

'But not now ... you'll never see them doing that again.'

* * * * *

That Saturday started fine enough. By the time I had walked through the village to St Mary's Church, every bench seat was taken and I was forced to stand with my back to the famous stone font which came from Old Byland Church.

I could see all the Ashberrys were seated on the front bench. Chatterton was not there. Unlike the last time I saw him at the shooting dinner, the Marquess was no longer his apoplectic self. His shoulders were bent forward and heaving, his head was in his hands, he was crying inconsolably. Andrew sat upright next to him. He made no movement towards comforting his father. Next to Andrew, Stephen Ashberry lolled at the end of the bench, one foot stretched out into the aisle.

Whitaker, the rector, was resplendent in ceremonial robes. He and his clerks sang out the words, 'I am the resurrection and the life, saith the

Lord; he that believeth in me, though he were dead, yet shall he live; and whosoever liveth and believeth in me shall never die.'

Slowly they progressed ahead of Mary Bowden's sturdy but simple coffin. A forlorn looking Malcolm and his father followed on.

As soon as White releases Lydia's body they will have to follow her coffin in here too, I quietly acknowledged to myself, at least her mother has been spared that.

'I know that my Redeemer liveth, and that he shall stand at the latter day upon the earth. And though after my skin worms destroy this body, yet in my flesh shall I see God: whom I shall see for myself, and mine eyes shall behold, and not another.'

How macabre, I thought, the worms have already destroyed Lydia's flushed young skin, turned it into lacerated parchment. In the name of the woman we were burying today, I was more determined than ever that someone would pay for that abomination.

'We brought nothing into this world, and it is certain we can carry nothing out. The Lord gave and the Lord hath taken way; blessed be the Name of the Lord.'

I really wished I could fall in with this, share in this belief, but my cynical soul could not embrace it.

'I said, I will take heed to my ways: that I offend not in my tongue. I will keep my mouth as it were with a bridle: while the ungodly is in my sight.'

My eyes fell to the ground like a naughty schoolboy caught out as Whitaker spoke the psalm – did he mean me?

So the lessons went on and I endured, all the while trying to gauge the reactions of the mourners from my disadvantageous position. I got an occasional glimpse of a profile but I was mainly confronted by backs.

'Now is Christ risen from the dead, and become the first fruits of them that slept.'

My luck had to change, was about to change, as we all trooped out of the church to the graveside.

'Man that is born of a woman hath but a short time to live ...'

Some shorter than others – I recognised ironically.

As the coffin was lowered down into its final resting place, my gaze fell onto the grave that soon would be Lydia's grave too. Indeed looking around there were several Bowden headstones scattered about, no doubt branches of this same Wolds' farming family.

But hadn't Lydia been destined for greater things than her ancestors. Surely it was intended at the end of her life she would be entombed with her husband – the rest of the Ashberrys – in some grand family mausoleum, not sharing this humble trench atop her mother.

Her intended husband acknowledged me with a dismissive nod – Andrew's attitude had been contemptuous throughout the service. But it was Stephen who really caught my eye. He was not as I remembered him at all a few years ago at the ball. Indeed, he could have been a different person. Yes, he had the same beard and, of course, the same miniature stature, but his face had changed completely. I was almost as shocked seeing him as I was when I had first set eyes on Mary Bowden's in the asylum. Rhagades ran from his mouth like dried up riverbeds, the bridge of his nose appeared to have collapsed as if he had been smashed in the face. Less of the gentleman now, more the pugilist, the bare knuckle fighter. When Stephen smiled – and he did smile at me (or perhaps leered at me is a more accurate description) – he smiled uneven notched teeth.

Malcolm and old Mr Bowden stood stiffly at attention by the grave. This public attention and ceremony was way beyond their usual experience in the fields. It did not ride comfortably on what looked to be Reginald's borrowed black coat. The rector nodded to them to cast the earth upon Mary Bowden.

'Forasmuch as it hath pleased Almighty God of his great mercy to take unto himself the soul of our dear sister here departed, we therefore commit her body to the ground, earth to earth, ashes to ashes ...'

The Marquess shook his head over the offered handful of soil. I had seen no gesture of recognition pass between him and Reginald Bowden.

'Funny lot them,' muttered a villager next to me.

'Who?' I asked. 'The Bowdens?'

'No, no, them over on t' other side.' With his eyes still cast on the hole in the ground, the man's head gave an almost imperceptible movement towards the Ashberrys.

'The grace of our Lord Jesus Christ, and the love of God, and the fellowship of the Holy Ghost, be with us all evermore. Amen.'

'Fancy you coming all this way to attend Ma's funeral,' said a voice behind me as I made for the gate accompanied by my new friend. Malcolm Bowden smiled, rubbing the soil from his hands. My friend continued on his way leaving me alone with Bowden.

'I had occasion to visit your poor mother during her confinement at Bootham Park Hospital,' I told him.

'Did you?' He looked both interested and surprised.

'She seemed to think you knew the real reason why Lord Hambleton was so set against your sister's engagement to his son.'

'That was a terrible place to visit, don't you think?' he asked, ignoring my slanted question. 'Fancy Ma finishing up like that, a physical and mental wreck locked up in a madhouse. Makes you think, Cairn, live for the day and bugger the rest of 'em.'

'The rest?'

'All of 'em. Does anything matter if you're going to lose your mind in the end?'

Chapter Twenty

'Trotter, will you send a telegram to my friend Dick Tate at the General Infirmary, Leeds, asking if he's free to dine with me next week here in York?' I leaned back in my chair, hands folded behind my head, I was safely back in the fold.

'Of course,' replied Trotter. 'It will be lovely to see Doctor Tate again. But how did your trip to Scawton go for Mary Bowden's funeral?'

'I'm not sure. I need a walk, air, time to think things through. Achoo!' I sneezed.

'You're getting a cold, sir.' Trotter looked alarmed, whether from fear of contagion or genuine concern for my wellbeing I wasn't sure.

'Nonsense, just paper dust. Achoo!' I sneezed again, giving greater credence to Trotter's hypothesis.

'What you need is whisky, hot water and lemon, sir.'

'I can hardly drink in chambers,' I pointed out.

'It looks like rain out there.' Trotter nodded discouragingly towards the "out there". 'You'll catch your death.'

'It always looks like rain in Yorkshire.' All the same, peering out at the leaden sky though the window, I reached for a Newmarket style waterproof overcoat off the Bentwood stand which seemed to grow coats and hats weekly in the corner of our office. To whom the coats and hats belonged – I was never quite sure – some remained unclaimed.

Trotter pulled a disapproving expression as I rejected my topper for a bowler.

'Are you going to the races, sir?' he smirked.

'You can't really expect me to expose my best silk hat to a storm?'

'A gentleman always dresses like a gentleman whatever the weather.'

'Then I am not a gentleman and stop mollycoddling me, Trotter. One minute you tell me to stay indoors and the next you insist I dress unsuitably,' I said, slamming the door behind me.

Once outside on Bootham, I felt I could breathe more freely. I made for the river Ouse down towards Marygate Landing. To my amazement I chanced upon Winifred Holbrook yet again. She was walking up Marygate on the opposite side of the street past the Bay Horse. It was as if we were moths drawn to each other. Then I suppose it wasn't really surprising with her lodging in York now. But every time I saw her, I couldn't rid myself of the shock following years of neglect. Indeed I never really believed I would see her again after being instrumental in exposing her stepfather's corruption and extreme political beliefs.

'Winifred!' I shouted. She appeared not to hear me. 'Winifred!' I crossed the street and ran after her back towards Bootham. It began to rain in earnest. I finally caught her up and grabbed her arm. She turned. Her cheeks were wet under the fedora hat. At first I wasn't sure if it was from rain or tears until I saw her anguished expression.

'What's wrong?' I asked.

'I can't speak to you, James.'

'What's wrong?' I persisted; my heart thumping heavily. I gently stroked her face to rub away the tears.

'Don't!' She jerked her head out of reach.

My left hand held onto her right arm as if she was about to evaporate.

'Let go! You're hurting me.' She shook her arm dislodging my grasp.

'Winifred?'

'Leave me alone, James.' She looked about her like a frightened chicken.

'What's the matter, Winifred?'

'Just leave me alone,' she repeated.

I could only stand and watch the fedora hat disappearing round the corner at something between a walk and a run. The same fedora hat made famous by Sarah Bernhardt, the most polished actress I had ever seen on stage, that is until I met Winifred Holbrook and was subjected to all her dramas. There and then I decided that Winifred and her suffrage principals had always meant trouble for me. I would cast her from my life and thoughts forever. The woman was impossible.

I turned on my heels and made for the river once more, this time with an even greater incentive to clear my mind. A wind had blown up and the Ouse had changed its usual bland character – out in mid-stream it no longer oozed along but was driven by rolling waves – rain made broken patterns on the calmer shallows near the landing.

What was it Trotter had said? – "It looks like rain."

Rain, Lydia's dog, they were inseparable and the faithful dog had died sprawled above one of the Ashberry Windypits. Rain must have known that his mistress was down there in the pit. But how? And why would Lydia have been up in that isolated location in the first place in unsuitable footwear, when she had only intended walking home to the farm from Ashberry Hall? But if she had been killed before being thrown down into the pit, how could anybody have transported her body to such a difficult location? And, again, I asked myself why had Reginald Bowden lied, saying that the dog had died in Broadshaw farmyard?

* * * * *

'What's wrong with you, James? Aren't you glad to see me?' asked Dick, as we shared a roast of seasoned lamb at the Black Swan. 'Such a long face. But this place isn't bad at all. I like this place, full of character,' he pronounced before I'd got a word in edgeways.

'It's my local,' I explained.

'Your "local"?' he repeated as if I had just told him something amazing.

The Black Swan was the sort of dark archaic building that always had a fire even in July. Although it was built for a William de Bowes, merchant and Sheriff of York, in the early 15th century, everything about its exterior was Tudor from its timber-framed frontage to its twin gables. It was set on Peasholme Green, so called because it was once a water meadow used for the production of peas.

'So come on, why the long face?' persisted Dick.

'I've had a cold. Started with a sore throat and left me with a cough for a week.'

'"A cough"?' More incredulity.

'Yes, a bad cough.' I gave one brief hack of confirmation. 'It keeps me awake at night.'

'You didn't get me over to York to tell me that. I am a pathologist, for God's sake.'

'I've bumped into Winifred Holbrook again,' I finally admitted. 'She's taken lodging here in York.'

'Really?' Dick's eyes glowed as brightly as the embers in the fire grate. 'I always felt she might be the girl for you.'

'If only ...'

'If only what?'

'Everything was perfect at first, just as it had been before. Now suddenly she won't speak to me again. And there's a fiancé.'

'Ah! There's always a fiancé for every eligible woman.'

'But what can I do, Dick, if she continues to ignore me even on the street.'

'Ask yourself this one question, James, why is she giving you the cold shoulder.'

'She doesn't like me.'

'No, no,' said Dick, shaking his index finger. 'You simply do not understand the workings of the female mind, do you, James? It is because she is afraid.'

'"Afraid?" Afraid of what?'

'Of her true feelings for you.'

'You're teasing me.'

'No, I am not.'

'So how do I get her to acknowledge her true feelings then?'

'Fight. Fight for her, of course. You've always been besotted by her, James, you know you have, admit it.'

I shook my head, not daring to admit such a thing even to myself and certainly not as things currently stood between Winifred and me.

'Tell me,' I asked, changing the subject. 'What would your diagnosis be of an adult patient who suddenly presents themselves to you with a saddle nose and uneven notched teeth?'

'Not Winifred?' asked Dick with undisguised alarm.

'No, not Winifred,' I assured him. 'It is someone I am distantly acquainted with.'

'Notched teeth can be otherwise known as Hutchinson's teeth.' Dick now smiled his own flawless set of fangs. 'From your description your distant acquaintance could be suffering from congenital syphilis. Have you ever seen Rembrandt's portrait of Gerard de Lairesse? – Lairesse was a painter himself and art theorist.'

'And when do these changes occur in someone suffering from the disease?' I asked, ignoring Dick's examination of my familiarity with the Dutch School.

'At anytime between the ages of five and thirty. Although a late manifestation in an adult is rare.'

'And would either the female or male, mother or father donor of syphilis exhibit symptoms?'

'Not necessarily. Some carriers possess a high degree of immunity others do not. It is possible for a person to remain ignorant that they have contracted the disease at all. That is why it is so dangerous. There are instances where syphilis remains dormant and asymptomatic in some individuals, and they unknowingly pass it on to others through genital contact.'

'Or uncaringly,' I added.

'That happens too.'

'So some people don't exhibit any symptoms?'

'No, nothing too visible. They might have an ulcer where you wouldn't wish to have one.'

'"An ulcer"?'

'Yes, a red oval ulcer known as a chancre. Look, James, is this something to do with that lass from over Helmsley way whom I performed a post-mortem on the other week?' he asked. I nodded. 'Your friend, Inspector White, said he had sent the body across to Leeds on your recommendation.'

'That's right.'

'Are you involved in that case?'

'A little,' I admitted. 'I helped White find the body.'

'You know I can't really discuss any post-mortem results with you without authorisation.'

'White has already told me something of your findings.'

'Has he?' Dick lifted an eyebrow in surprise.

'Can I get you another pint, Dick?'

On my return from the bar with two brimming glasses, Dick leaned forward and whispered in my ear, 'There was no sign of syphilis in that lass's body if that's what you're wondering.'

'I wasn't. But that's interesting because her mother died of tertiary syphilis recently.'

'Well,' sighed Dick. 'The most obvious conclusion is that her mother contracted the disease after she was born, unless she was one of those unusual asymptomatic types.'

'Do you know it has always been believed that a passageway, dating back to when the house was first constructed, ran from here under the road to St Cuthbert's Church?' Again I rapidly changed the subject.

'Really,' replied Dick with little interest.

'Yes, it must have been a hundred yards or so long.'

'Really,' replied Dick still preoccupied.

'Built by the same man, William de Bowes, who built the house in which we are now sitting.'

'Umm, William Bowes,' grunted Dick.

'Are you actually listening?'

'I'm thinking, James.'

'About what?'

'Do you know what you are getting involved in? From what I learnt from White, the person or persons unknown who murdered that young girl went to a lot of trouble to conceal her body.'

'A brilliant piece of deduction to find her though, don't you think?'

'I do. I also fear it won't be long before all and sundry know it was you who worked out where to find her body.'

'Including the murderer or murderers unknown?' I feigned bravado.

'Including her, him or them. Look at the difficulties you got into over that Mortimer Blakely affair a few years ago. It nearly cost you your life.'

'But this is a parochial victim, a rural crime. I bet the perpetrator is a spurned jealous lover, something obvious like that.'

'A *crime passionnel*, you could be right there but that doesn't mean you're not in grave danger with a madman about.'

'So, you think he must be a madman?'

'Anyone who commits murder and risks the gallows is a madman by my reckoning.'

'I'll be all right,' I bluffed.

'Hello, James, fancy seeing you here tonight.' Speaking of bluff and bluster, Digby West sloshed his pint down on our table and pulled out the vacant chair smothering it beneath his fulsome backside.

Knowing this was the end of my interesting tête-à-tête with Dick, I reluctantly introduced Digby to him.

'Heard they found that young lass out Helmsley way,' continued Digby, impervious beneath gathering clouds of resentment. 'Bet it was her father, that old farmer, who did away with her.'

'Keep your voice down, Digby. You mean Reginald Bowden?' I was incredulous.

'Yes, I got a strong feeling of foreboding, dread, when we visited that farm,' he whispered. 'Now what was it called?'

'Broadshaw,' I help out.

'Yes, that was it, but there was nothing broad about that place. Insular, claustrophobic, was the way I would best describe it. A chill runs down my spine at the thought of that place. And when his son, what was he called?'

'Malcolm,' I filled in.

'Yes, Malcolm. When Malcolm followed you into the farmhouse holding that shotgun ...' Digby paused, turning to Dick, 'I really feared that was the end of James.'

'Can I get you two gentlemen another pint?' I asked. Digby nodded enthusiastically. Dick shook his head and said he must be making a move back to the station to catch the Leeds train.

'Car's outside. I'll give you a lift,' offered Digby. 'You, James, will have to walk home.'

Digby kept his promise but not before consuming several more pints in quick succession. From the worried look on Dick's face as he clambered into the passenger seat of the open sporty Wolseley, I smiled and counted my blessings.

As Digby cranked up the engine, Dick leaned across to me conspiratorially, 'Who did you say had congenital syphilis?'

'I didn't.'

'What's that? What's that you two are muttering about together?' asked red-faced Digby.

'Nothing,' I told him.

'It can bring about mood and personality changes in the sufferer,' Dick whispered to me.

Enough to lead to murder, I wondered as the powder-blue vehicle chugged off up the street.

Chapter Twenty-One

'We've won!' shouted Gerald Fawcett, flinging the pink *Sporting Times* across my desk. 'We've beaten the shackle draggers.'

Shackle draggers – Trotter looked at me askance.

'A highly pejorative term for Australians,' I sighed my explanation.

'We've beaten 'em anyway,' said Fawcett; his glee undiminished.

Not wishing to cross words with my colleague so early in the day, I picked up *The Pink 'Un* and read on as Fawcett quit my room. The third Test at Leeds was drawn; the fourth Test at Manchester was won by England and was long gone; the fifth Test at Kennington Oval was drawn again. England's captain, Stanley Jackson, had not only won the series 2–0, but also won the toss in all five matches and headed both the batting and the bowling averages. Just as I was absorbing this wonderful news with Trotter, a boy brought in the morning post. There was one letter addressed to me and this time I immediately recognised the generous hand.

16, Church Street –15th August, 1905

Dear James,
Please forgive my attitude towards you the other day. You must think me dreadful.
Just before I bumped into you along Marygate, John Beardsley had broken off our engagement. He accused me of being unfaithful. Someone must have told him that we were together in the Davy Hall Restaurant.
Yours,
Winifred

But was she really mine? Was there now a possibility that she might be mine? This time she had given her private address.

Again the rain was teeming down as I walked down the narrow street of Georgian red brick shops and houses off St Sampson's Square. I hoped the rain wasn't a bad omen. I knocked on the door of 16 Church Street – known a long time ago as the feminine Girdle Maker Street – a white face peered out of the flat bay window above my head. I hardly recognised Winifred as she opened the door. Her sorrel hair hung in limp tresses about her face. She had raccoon rings round her eyes. She did not smile on seeing me.

'James, you've come,' she said. 'I've not slept for a week, I've been feeling so wretched.'

'Why didn't you tell me on Marygate that your engagement was over?'

'I thought you might feel compromised.'

'I wish you had compromised me a long time ago,' I told her as she ushered me up the stairs into a comfortable if modest living room.

'Did you really?' She seemed genuinely surprised. 'You never showed it.'

'You never gave me any encouragement.'

'There was so much going on back then.'

'And you wanted to fulfil yourself in your own right.'

'Of course I did. I took every opportunity to educate and better myself. I never wanted to be the sycophantic little housewife waiting at home.'

'You could never be that,' I laughed.

'I *would* never be that.'

'I would never want you to be.'

'I think that's just what John wanted me to be.'

'Is the engagement really over between the two of you?' I asked.

'When I look at you, it is.'

I took her in my arms then – embraced our torrid history – more out of a wish to comfort than romance, saying, 'I am showing I care enough now.'

'You know when Andrew Ashberry saw us together in that Davy Hall Restaurant, half of me wished he would believe we were a couple,' she whispered. 'It must have been he who told John that he had seen me with you, don't you think?'

'I am not too sure Ashberry and I are on the best of terms following suspicions regarding his own fiancée's disappearance.'

'And I thought it was me he was intent on making trouble for. Perhaps it was you.'

'Perhaps,' I said, blowing into her hair. 'But what intrigues me more is why you never told Beardsley you were dining with me in the first place.'

Winifred's pale cheeks turned red. She pushed me away a little and looked intensely into my eyes.

'Because I acknowledged, on my part, any meeting between the two of us could never be regarded as innocent,' she said; her wonderful modulated voice even deeper now. 'I knew that from the moment I sat next to you in St Helen's Church. However because of my late stepfather's right-wing sympathies, I thought you would never consider a relationship with me.'

'That was him, this is you. Where we go from here is what matters now.'

'We must be patient.'

'Patience isn't my strongest virtue.' That is when I kissed her – kissed Winifred Holbrook properly on the mouth for the first time – other than in my dreams.

'Careful, James,' she warned me, drawing back. 'John could be having me watched. He has a ruthless streak. I don't know what he's capable of.'

Her high colour had run to white again. I noticed a small bluish black mark on her cheek bone. I ran my fingers across it.

'Did Beardsley do this to you?' I asked.

'Just the one slap.'

'Is The Right Honourable John Beardsley still in town?'

'He could be. He's not due back in Westminster until the second of September. We must wait, James,' she reiterated.

'I will have my day with that gentleman,' I told her.

* * * * *

I was just enjoying reading my morning newspaper in chambers – enjoying the photographic spectacle of the Ancient Order of Druids initiating hundreds of its white robed followers at Stonehenge – when Robert Brown burst through the door unannounced.

'There's been a terrible kerfuffle at the Hall,' he huffed and puffed.

'What hall, where?' I asked, irritated by the intrusion.

'Ashberry Hall of course.'

'What sort of kerfuffle?' I felt a sinking feeling in the pit of my stomach.

'The Marquess rang me.'

'Rang you?'

'Will you stop repeating everything I've just said, James, and just listen.'

'I am all ears. Being a rich man the Marquess obviously has a telephone.'

'He is a modern man.'

'As you yourself are, Bob,' I scoffed.

'Never mind all that. The police have arrested his son.'

'Which son?'

'The Earl of Fadmoor.'

'Who?'

'Remember, that's Andrew's official title.'

'Why has he been arrested?'

'For the murder of Lydia Bowden of course.'

'On what evidence?'

'They are suspicious about him selling her engagement ring so soon after her disappearance, and it seems your pathologist friend, Dick Tate, turned up some further incriminating evidence against him.'

'Really,' I said, really interested now.

'Yes, and the Marquess wants me to act for him.'

'Well, there are no surprises there. You are the Ashberrys' family solicitor.'

'Yes, but he also wants you to represent his son and heir in court.'

'Now that is a surprise.' I carefully pondered the implications. 'And do you know what additional evidence Doctor Tate has found against Lord Fadmoor?'

'Tate found something in the skeletal grasp at post-mortem and it looks very bad for my client, I must concede.' Brown's customary anxious expression turned to one of furrowed concern.

'What did he find?' The suspense was killing me. White had told me nothing about this but then he wouldn't have done would he?

'A gold cufflink engraved with two interlocking A's.'

'Andrew Ashberry,' I moaned.

'Yes, and it gets worse. Recall that jeweller in Coney Street, James Inglis, the same jeweller who created Lydia's engagement ring?' asked Brown. I nodded. 'Well he has identified the link, found by Tate, as one of a pair Lydia had engraved for Andrew Ashberry prior to their engagement.'

'Has Andrew offered any explanation as to how one of his cufflinks could be in the grasp of the dead woman?'

'He said he never owned such a pair, knew nothing about them, Lydia never gave him any like that.'

'Perhaps she intended giving him them on their wedding night,' I suggested.

Brown's frown deepened if anything, he didn't seem convinced.

'You tell that to a jury,' he said.

* * * * *

As I worked on other more minor briefs, I questioned whether I was suited to represent such a prominent family as the Ashberrys. I had made my name as a counsel for the outsiders, society's outcasts – Catherine Tiplady, Edwin Holroyd, Philip Cubitt and the like – now I had been called on to defend the Establishment. My previous interview with Andrew Ashberry regarding his sale of Lydia's engagement ring had been terse if cordial. Then there was Winifred's suspicion that it had been Andrew who had maliciously informed John Beardsley about seeing us dining together at the Davy Hall Restaurant. I was taking all these considerations into account, when there was a knock on my office door and Louis Chatterton minced in. He was obviously in such a highly agitated state that he made no attempt to disguise his effeminacy as he had done on previous occasions.

'Please, please, Mr Cairn, you have to do something for poor Andrew. He's having a terrible time in that awful place,' he squeaked, flapping his wrist.

'What place?'

'Northallerton Gaol of course.'

'Yes, I have heard it is less than salubrious.' I said, remembering the complaints of Edwin Holroyd let alone the Earl of Fadmoor.

'It's just awful, Mr Cairn. The food is awful, awful.' Another flap of the limp wrist and I thought that only happened on the musical halls.

'I can imagine daily cocoa and gruel must be extremely unpalatable to a man used to champagne and *pheasant au vin*,' I commiserated halfheartedly.

'His cell is damp,' added Chatterton, in an attempt to give weight to his argument.

'And rat invested, no doubt.'

'Can't you get him bail, Mr Cairn? He has done nothing wrong.'

'One, I have not decided yet whether or not I am taking on his defence. Two, I am not sure that even a nobleman would be granted bail indicted for a capital offence.'

'John Beardsley, the MP, visited Andrew in prison the other afternoon.'

'Really?' My interest was again piqued.

'They went to school together.'

'So I have heard.'

'Mr Beardsley has offered to stand bail for Andrew, but Andrew will have none of it, he hates him.'

'Does he?' Andrew had immediately gone up in my estimation.

'Said Beardsley was an awful bully at school.'

'Is that so?'

'Although it was Beardsley who recommended you to the Marquess as the best defence counsel around.'

'Did he?' My mouth gaped open stupidly.

'However, apart from Andrew's distaste of Beardsley, the Marquess wouldn't allow him to stand bail. Whatever the cost the Marquess will foot the bill.'

'As I've already said, I'm not sure bail is an option.'

'But Andrew has done nothing wrong,' reiterated Chatterton. 'He's an innocent man.'

'So who do you think killed Lydia Bowden?' I asked him. Chatterton fell silent for awhile. 'Mr Chatterton?' I prompted.

'Stephen,' he whispered.

'Stephen, his brother?' I gauped. Chatterton nodded. 'Stephen who doesn't like killing things?' I persisted. Chatterton nodded silently and seriously again.

'Stephen doesn't like killing things during field sports,' he explained. 'Too clean a kill for him. He'd rather capture and torture birds and rabbits slowly to death than dispatch them quickly. Andrew told me his younger brother has had this worrying disposition to hurt things since childhood. The family always put it down to his motherless state.'

A memory glinted in the back of my brain. That was it, I remember now: James Wright, the mole catcher, had told me after the Tiplady case that he'd heard gossip that the Marquess' youngest son had poisoned two of the Ashberry gamekeeper's dogs with strychnine.

'Have you heard anything about a cufflink being found with the deceased Lydia Bowden?' I asked. Chatterton nodded and looked to the floor. 'Do you know that the pathologist found that inscribed cufflink actually in Lydia's grasp?'

'Yes, I have heard something of the sort,' Chatterton reluctantly admitted.

'Bearing the initials of two interlocking A's?' I persisted. Chatterton nodded again. 'Have you any explanation for that?'

Chatterton shook his head saying, 'I know it looks bad for Andrew but I don't believe he is capable of murder.'

'If I told you how many times I have heard that same affirmation, Mr Chatterton, given on behalf of the vilest criminals.'

'There's something you don't know, Mr Cairn, something Andrew got me to swear I wouldn't tell anybody.'

'Then perhaps you shouldn't.'

'But if it will save Andrew's life.'

'Anything said in here is in the strictest confidence,' I reassured him.

Chatterton sucked in air. 'Andrew didn't find Lydia's engagement ring in Gerard's pocket at all. He found it days later in a drawer in Stephen's room. He lied to protect Stephen. The whole family is habitually engaged in protecting Stephen.'

'Conditioned to preserve his distorted sense of reality,' I suggested.

'Exactly so,' Chatterton readily agreed. 'That's the main reason Andrew wanted to get rid of the ring quickly. He felt guilty and torn about suppressing the truth and verbally placing the ring in Gerard's pocket.'

Chapter Twenty-Two

'Highly risky! Highly risky!' bellowed Gerald Fawcett over afternoon tea.

'Oh, I don't know,' said the studious looking Thomas Leacock. 'If James is successful and gets the Earl of Fadmoor off.'

'I'm not so sure I like the "if",' I told Leacock.

'A big if,' sneered Fawcett.

'Talk about chalk and cheese, you and Leacock disagree on just about everything. We haven't had a really big murder case in chambers for years. I, personally, think James should take the Ashberry brief,' advised Andrew Carlton-Bingham. 'What do you think, Trotter?'

Trotter mumbled something inaudible and shrugged.

'Trotter?' insisted Carlton-Bingham.

'Mr Cairn never listens to the likes of me, sir. He always goes his own way.'

'There you are, Trotter agrees,' laughed Carlton-Bingham, ignoring the Trotter cynicism.

'And I agree,' enthused Leacock.

'I don't,' announced Fawcett sulkily. Fawcett who had been trying for years to get rid of Leacock.

'That's just too bad, you're outvoted, Gerald,' said Leacock.

'Gentlemen please,' appealed Carlton-Bingham.

After plenty of soul searching, I decided to follow my boss's advice and take on the Ashberry case. Although nobody in chambers was ultimately responsible for my decision, I have to confess that my real and overriding motivation was Beardsley. It was Beardsley who had recommended me as the best advocate to defend the Earl of Fadmoor – his only reason for doing that must have been that he felt sure I would fail – the challenge was on.

* * * * *

The red-bricked square slab that was Northallerton Gaol was grim beyond Dickens. It was built in 1783 on a the site of a swamp and the town's rubbish dump. This House of Correction, corrected with stints of solitary confinement and cat o' nine tail whippings. It was famed in the previous century for having the largest corn grinding treadmill in the world – once ground the corn was thrown away because of fears that it would damage the local economy. What a waste when malnutrition was rife among prisoners. Another reason for this starving Northallerton prison population was the meagerness of the human spirit: it was said that one regular priestly prison visitor kept his dogs alive for ten years on food purloined from the gaol's kitchen. "Better is the poor that walketh in his uprightness, than he that is perverse in his ways, though he be rich" – I hope this man of the cloth's Sunday sermons to his uninitiated parishioners sounded convincing.

Various structural changes were made to accommodate more and more prisoners until, like Leeds, this northern lock-up had become the embodiment of Pentonville.

Hadn't that infamous prisoner of our age, Oscar Fingal O'Flahertie Wills Wilde, first enjoyed the pleasure of the treadmill at Pentonville before being transferred to Reading? Speaking of Wilde, seeing my prospective client brought into the visiting cell by a beast of a warder, I was immediately put in mind of him. Although he had already lost some weight, Andrew Ashberry still had the soft, rounded good looks of a young Wilde. Then again, I guessed Ashberry was actually little short of forty-six – the age the playwright died looking like an old man.

'Unfortunately your solicitor, Mr Brown, is unable to attend today due to illness but he has assured me you are happy to be interviewed by me alone.'

'You've got to get me out of here, Cairn,' were His Lordship's first words to me. 'The grub in here is terrible.'

'"Grub"?' I asked surprised.

'My pathetic attempt, old chap, to fit in with the lingo in here.'

'I see,' I said.

'The other inmates think I'm a poof because of the way I speak. Talk about working class snobbery.'

'Do they really?' I dared to ask.

'Do they what?'

'Think you are a homosexual?'

'I ...'

'Louis Chatterton came to see me. He is very concerned. Said John Beardsley had visited you and offered to stand bail.'

'Ya,' sniffed Andrew unconvinced. 'Can't stand that Beardsley chap, he's all talk and top show. Anyway, Pa will stand bail.'

'I don't think bail is an option for a capital offence,' I pointed out as gently as I could.

'Oh, God! God!' exclaimed Andrew. 'You mean I have to remain in this sodding dungeon until a date is set for my trial?'

I nodded, acknowledging that perhaps the biblical reference was an unfortunate one for Fadmoor to use, while realising that the lack of *pheasant au vin* would soon take its toll on this man as it had on Wilde.

'Don't sleep a wink at night because of other fellas shouting. And the rats, this place is invested with rats,' he moaned.

'Cockroaches too,' I suggested.

'Them too,' he confirmed, suddenly looking preoccupied with something much bigger than cockroaches. 'Pa says they are burying Lydia next Friday.'

'I know. I heard the coroner has just released her body.'

'So, you're not going to her funeral either then, Cairn?'

'No, I decided not to.'

'And might I ask why is that?'

'That is obvious, Lord Fadmoor, I have become too involved in this case.'

'I understand that it was you who helped find Lydia's body down Ashberry Pit?'

'To my deep regret.'

'"Deep", being the operative word.'

'My Lord, this isn't a matter for flippancy.'

'Do you see me laughing, Cairn?'

'Lord Fadmoor,' I decided to get on a more official footing with my prospective client. 'Did you murder or conspire to murder Lydia Bowden on the twenty-eighth of September, 1901?'

'No, I did not.'

'But you did tell me that you found Lydia Bowden's engagement ring, bought by you, in your dead brother Gerard's pocket, did you not?'

'Yes,' agreed Andrew cautiously.

'When you actually found that ring in your youngest brother Stephen's bedroom drawer?'

Andrew turned a ghostly white.

'Who told you that?' he growled.

'It doesn't matter. You told a falsehood to a man whom you now want to act as your defence counsel in a court of law.'

'I did,' he admitted. 'And I'm sorry but there was a good reason for it.'

'There is never a good reason to lie.'

'Perhaps not.'

'How do I know you won't fabricate further information?'

'It won't happen again, you have my word on it.'

'Tell me more about your brother, Stephen.'

'There's not much to tell.'

'Perhaps we could start with the disease he is afflicted with.'

'I am not sure I know what you mean.'

'Stephen suffers from congenital syphilis, does he not?'

'I'm not ...'

'The same disease that Mary Bowden died of.'

'How do you know that?'

'Is that why the family is so protective towards him?'

'Our mother died giving birth to Stephen. He only knew a wet-nurse's love.'

'Which isn't much,' I commiserated.

'No, it's not much at all,' acknowledged Andrew.

'Nevertheless, if we are to work together to clear you of this serious charge, Lord Fadmoor, we must have full transparency from now on in all things.'

'Cairn, could I ask you to do a favour for me?'

'That depends on the request, My Lord.'

'Would you be kind enough to send a wreath of late summer roses to ride on Lydia's coffin? Add it to all your other expenses.'

It seems that was it – as simple as that – I was hired with roses.

* * * * *

During the month of July, York had enjoyed long periods of sunshine. August had been wet and unsettled, now into September the days began to cool though the nights remained mild. However, one day was never the same. There was change in the air and a sense of instability. Then one afternoon ...

'Crash!' Bootham Chambers shook as daggers of light slashed across a darkening sky.

'What on earth was that?' asked Trotter, his head jerking up from his work as if physically struck.

'Thor is angry,' I laughed. 'Perhaps he will finally clear this muggy air.'

We both made as one for the office window to observe the thunderstorm. Below, a carriage was drawing up outside.

'It looks like someone else is intent on clearing the air,' said Trotter, indicating a rotund figure alighting from the stationary vehicle with great difficulty, despite a helping hand from a footman, before making its way up our steps at a snail's pace.

'Lord Hambleton, what a pleasant surprise,' I lied.

'It's been a long time, Cairn, since I've had the pleasure. Again we meet under unfortunate circumstances.'

'Indeed, My Lord. Tea,' I offered.

'No time for tea. I've one son dead, another a dullard, and now my heir, the Earl of Fadmoor, is under arrest for murder. What do you say to that, Cairn?'

'A truly sad state of affairs.'

'But what can be done about it? – that's what I want to know. Brown says you are the best man to sort things out, eh?'

'He is, My Lord, he is.' Trotter would have to get his embarrassing pennyworth in.

'Trotter, perhaps you would be kind enough to leave us for a few minutes, so I might have a private word with Lord Hambleton.'

Trotter flounced out like an indignant courtesan.

'What's wrong with him?' asked the Marquess.

'He's a sensitive soul,' I explained.

'Speaking of sensitive souls and sensitive issues, Andrew tells me you think Stephen might be involved in Lydia's death, Cairn.'

'He was missing from the shoot all day, and he had Lydia's engagement ring in his bedroom drawer. He had the time and he had the ring.'

'Nonsense, the boy's not got the wherewithal to kill anyone.'

'But he has got a disease that can affect one's mental processes.'

'What on earth are you talking about, Cairn?'

'Congenital syphilis, My Lord.'

'Please!' exclaimed the Marquess, raising his hand to silence me. 'I refuse to discuss such unspeakable things.'

'I fear you might have to, you might have to in open court should you wish to save Lord Fadmoor. So better we get this matter out of the way now than later.'

'If we must,' sighed the Marquess wearily.

'Is it true that you had a liaison with Mrs Bowden?'

'Always had an eye for a pretty girl and Mary was extremely pretty, believe it or not, once upon a time.'

'Until she contracted syphilis?'

'I know nothing about that.'

'But you do admit having a long term adulterous affair with the wife of one of your tenant farmers?'

'Listen, Cairn, not so long ago the Lord of the Manor had the right to break in any virgin of his choosing on his estate.'

'Ah, we are talking *droit du seigneur*. Alas, I hate to disillusion you, Lord Hambleton.' I was now loath to give this odious old man the courtesy of his title. 'Those rights were purely a fiction – the feudal lord's entitlement to sleep on the first night with the vassal's bride etcetera, etcetera.'

'You forget, Cairn, power is a great aphrodisiac.'

'That maybe so. But do you deny that it was you who infected both Mary Bowden and your wife, the Marchioness, with syphilis, and in turn through your wife your youngest son? You, who have "always had an eye for a pretty girl".'

'And you are impertinent, sir,' spat apoplectic Ashberry. 'Look at me, do I look like a man with syphilis?'

'No, you do not. But I have it on good authority that your failure to exhibit any symptoms does not discount you from carrying the disease.'

'I'll not listen to this anymore.'

'I advise you to remain where you are, Lord Hambleton, unless you want to see your eldest son swinging from the gallows rope because of your own sordid misconduct.'

That settled His Lordship's hash, that steadied him.

'What in God's name am I to do, Cairn?' The Marquess was on the point of tears now.

'Tell me why were you so set against the engagement between your son and Lydia?'

'I cannot say.' The Marquess shook his head from side to side observing his silk stockings.

'Did you consider she wasn't good enough for him?'

'She was a tenant farmer's lass,' sneered the Marquess.

'But that wasn't the real reason, was it? That wasn't the main reason that you were against the match?'

'Both Mary Bowden and I were determined it wouldn't happen, could never happen. We did our level best to discourage the pairing. Until ...' The Marquess hesitated.

'Until, you learnt that Lydia was already expecting Andrew's child,' I helped out. 'A fait accompli.'

'Exactly that,' agreed the Marquess.

'I have already guessed the real reason for your objection.'

'Yes,' sighed Ashberry, 'I expect a clever chap like you has.'

'Lydia was your illegitimate daughter.' I stated rather than asked. Ashberry nodded. 'And Malcolm?'

'My bastard son and the finest of the lot,' roared Ashberry. 'Gerard had his weaknesses but he was at least a soldier. The remaining two are nothing but a couple of milksops. If only I could recognise Malcolm as my own, my one true heir.'

'And did Reginald Bowden know the truth of this?'

'He must have done. He's as impotent as a newly castrated lamb, always has been according to his late wife,' said with a sneer.

'But he was happy to bring up Lydia and Malcolm as his own.'

'Must have been.'

'And neither Lydia or Malcolm knew that Andrew, Gerard and Stephen were their half-siblings?'

'Not to my knowledge.'

'And vice versa?'

'Not to my knowledge,' repeated Ashberry. 'Otherwise Andrew would surely never have wanted to go through with the marriage, would he?'

'You do realise, My Lord, this gives you a strong motive for murder. How could you allow the eventual heir to the Ashberry Estate to have been conceived through an incestuous relationship?'

'It won't be the first time,' mumbled the Marquess.

'Lord Hambleton.' I decided to put the same question to the father that I had asked of the son only days before. 'Did you murder or conspire to murder Lydia Bowden on the twenty-eighth of September, 1901?'

'No, I did not.'

'This case is going to take some entangling, sir,' I pointed out.

'Indeed,' he agreed.

'If you and your son are happy for me to represent you in court, then I am happy to do so.'

'Just get on with it, Cairn,' snapped the Marquess.

'As I have already pointed out to Lord Fadmoor, I do not feel bail will be an option here. One, because of the seriousness of the indictment drafted against your son. Two, the prosecution will argue that Andrew has every means available to him to jump bail.'

'Do what you have to do,' sighed the Marquess wearily. 'No expense spared, Cairn.'

Chapter Twenty-Three

Following the departure of the not-so-honourable, Most Honourable Frederick Marquess of Ashberry, over the next few intervening days I began to consider the case. I began to fret that perhaps I had made a mistake taking it on. When all was said and done the Ashberrys were not the most salubrious outfit to be representing.

Winifred had begged for caution and patience. Nonetheless, the absence of her wholesome presence in my life was killing me as I mixed daily with society's poor and rich transgressors. At least hunger and poverty could be argued as mitigating circumstances for crime, whereas the affluent's substantiation was usually indefensible greed.

Winifred suspected that 16 Church Street was being watched, that Beardsley could have employed a private detective to follow her, so much so that she discouraged even the possibility of a furtive night visit on my part. Was Winifred being paranoid? – a condition she had been accused of before – and as before I didn't think so. Nothing Beardsley, the politician, did would surprise me.

So far my love affair with Winifred Holbrook had been conducted through letters. Beautiful letters as they were I was not a man to be easily deterred. I sensed summer was drawing to an end. I began to formulate a plan. In a week's time I saw a small window of opportunity in my mundane portfolio of fraud, petty thefts and pub brawls.

Déjà vu – I clambered onto the same 8-30 a.m. train from York to Helmsley that I had travelled on some weeks earlier. I had little difficulty locating Winifred in one of the prearranged carriage compartments. Thankfully she was alone, and we remained alone until arriving at our destination. Déjà vu again – I hired the same carter in Helmsley town centre but this time I gave him instructions for a very different location to that of the Windypits.

'I have to show you the most perfect Cistercian abbey I have ever seen,' I told Winifred.

'Like that day you took me and Lucy Alexander to Kirkdale to see the most perfect minster you had ever seen,' she laughed. I suspected she laughed freely for the first time in a long time as we bumped intimately along together in the back of the cart.

'Would you say you were deeply involved with John Beardsley?' The green-eyed monster, seeing her relaxed, whispered in her ear.

'What do you mean?' she responded; not that relaxed.

'Were you sleeping together?'

'James,' said with great indignation.

'I would like to know.'

'So that you can torment yourself?'

'If you like.'

'We were engaged, dammit.'

'Oh, yes, and you are a modern woman,' said with jealous anger.

'So, what about your fancy, married London actress friend then?'

'How on earth do you know about that?'

'People talk.'

'Well, those same talking people should have told you that relationship was over years ago.'

'As is my involvement with John Beardsley now over.'

'So we are equal then?'

'Equal,' she said, taking my hand in hers and surprisingly kissing it like an act of penitence.

'Don't do that,' I told her.

'Why?' she asked. 'Why so prickly?'

'Forgive my prying and never devalue yourself on my behalf. You are far too precious to me for that.' I took her hand in mine, the long fingers still and artistic in mine.

The cart trundled on and we fell silent. There was no necessity to speak. Just being together was everything. We were as one.

It was one of those misty autumn days. Only the red pantile roofs of the village cottages surrounding the abbey had any colour to them. The main church, built into the valley side, loomed like a skeleton over the ruined plot. Mysterious, airless, it looked as if it was about to rise above the tall background hills. For some bizarre reason I was reminded of the church of Santa Felicita in Florence and Jacopo Pontormo's painting of the *Deposition from the Cross* – one of the lightest colourful depictions of Christ seemingly lifting towards God.

'I must take you to Florence one day,' I told Winifred. 'You will see things there that you have never seen before.'

'You've already been I take it?'

'Just the once with my sister. An experience I will never forget.'

'And you have been here just the once too?'

'Yes, the last time I visited Rievaulx was in the company of a police inspector.' I helped her down from the cart which we'd arranged to wait for us.

'Was that when you found ... ?'

'I swore I would come back here,' I told her, changing the subject.

'Like Florence?'

'Yes, like Florence but not so far away. I've read everything I could get hold of on this place.'

'I'm glad to hear you've done your research, James, as you did with St Gregory's Minster and the Kirkdale Cave,' said with a wry smile.

'Yes, always be prepared for any academic challenge,' I laughed.

'What, from me?' Her eyes widened in mock surprise.

'Henry the Eighth has a lot to answer for, doesn't he?' I pointed across to the ruins.

'And yet there is beauty here too, beauty in dissolution.'

'Yes, strange isn't it. Maybe we should take a closer look.'

We picked our way through piles of cream sandstone, tomb-grey masses of limestone and marvelled at the remnants of carvings left discarded here and there. I explained to Winifred that in the 1160s the abbey was home to a community of nearly six hundred monks and lay brothers. The site then occupied over ninety acres, now nearer fifteen. The church was not built on a traditional east-west alignment but a south-north axis because of its restricted location. A local man told me during my visit here with White that the course of the river Rye had to be altered three times in the 12th century.

'It's worthy of a picture,' said Winifred.

'I believe Turner actually did paint a wonderful high summer scene from the bridge back down the road.'

'Come to think of it, I'm sure I've seen that picture exhibited in London, or at least an engraved version of the original. This entire place seems familiar to me as if I've been here before. So quiet too.'

'Here's where the fulling mill would have once stood for cleaning wool; over there tanning vats; the infirmary here; the abbot's house there; the chapter house or meeting place there; the sacristy, where the priests attired themselves in vestments, there ... ' I began explaining with wide sweeping gestures like a mad man.

Surreal – there he was sat among the ruins near the south transept of the abbey, long muscular legs straddling a tumbled wall – both Winifred and I saw him at the same time. It was as if Malcolm Bowden was sitting there waiting for us. But he wasn't, he hadn't even looked up at our soft grass approach, a man lost in his own thoughts.

'Bowden,' I cried out in amazement. 'Fancy seeing you here.'

He finally lifted his eyes in surprise. 'Mr Cairn.'

'What are you doing here?' I remained flabbergasted.

'I could ask you the same question,' he replied, looking Winifred up and down with obvious if insolent approval.

'I'm showing Miss Holbrook the abbey.'

'Well, I live near here or have you forgotten.'

'Of course not.'

'You haven't introduced us properly, James,' complained Winifred.

'Miss Holbrook, allow me to introduce you to Mr Bowden of Broadshaw Farm.'

Malcolm gave a mocking little bow. I could smell the drink on him.

'I come here to think,' he explained more temperately, despair suddenly clouding his face. 'I come to think about her.'

'About you mother?' Poor chap, I tried to sound as sympathetic as possible.

'No, no.' His hollow laugh echoed off the abbey walls. 'About Lydia. I come here to remember Lydia.'

'You must miss her terribly,' said Winifred; clever Winifred who had worked out the Bowden family connection straight away.

'I miss her beyond words. We ran about these grounds as giggling children to ripe maturity. She was my soulmate.'

'I'm terribly sorry,' I said.

'Aren't we all,' he said, still waspish. 'Has that policeman friend of yours, White, I think he's called, got any nearer to finding the man who killed my sister?'

'Haven't you heard? The Earl of Fadmoor is remanded in Northallerton Gaol at present on suspicion of murdering Lydia.'

'Nobody bothers to tell us ought out here.'

'We'll leave you to your memories then,' I told him; selfishly not wanting to darken Winifred's Rievaulx experience further.

'Fancy, him not knowing that Lord Fadmoor has been arrested,' exclaimed Winifred, once we were out of hearing range.

'Perhaps the police fear local reprisals against the Ashberrys,' I reasoned.

'I noticed you didn't tell him that there is a good chance you will be representing Fadmoor.'

'It wouldn't have been ethical.'

We stood in the middle of the choir, where rows of monks must have once stood at either side of us chanting the *Te Deum*, now only birdsong could be heard above the roofless structure.

'I can't help feeling terribly sorry for that man,' Winifred whispered. 'He must have loved his sister very much.'

'In the same way you love Cedric?' I asked.

'No, not in the same way at all. Much deeper, I'd say.'

'I love *you* deeply,' I told her.

There in the ruined choir of Rievaulx Abbey, Winifred Holbrook sank her head against my chest. Malcolm Bowden had said he missed Lydia beyond words.

'Without words,' were the words Winifred murmured as I enclosed her in my arms.

It must have been almost a minute later that I became aware that we were not alone: Malcolm stood behind one of the arch pillars observing us, his face was black with rage. Perhaps he felt we had breached the sanctity of the abbey with a kiss, the purity of his memories. Whatever ...

'I think it is time for us to go,' I told Winifred, giving our voyeur a brief salute. Malcolm made no response.

We decided not go back to York that night. I gave the carter instructions to make for the Hare Inn at Scawton.

* * * * *

'Do you have a room for the night?' I asked the landlord.

'One room or two, Mr Cairn?' replied the landlord, scrutinising Winifred's ringless wedding finger.

'Just the one,' I insisted.

Winifred could not stop babbling about "how quaint" everything was once we got into the privacy of the bedroom until I placed my forefinger across her lips.

'"Quaint" with old fashioned values,' I yelled, bouncing back on the hard mattress of the mahogany four-poster, pulling her on top of me.

'James, are you sure about this?' she asked.

'Are you?'

Unprepared for an overnight stay, unaccompanied by even the smallest valises, we stood at the small washstand splashing water across our faces before playfully splashing each other. I wasn't used to such sharing – sharing the strawberry decorated pitcher and bowl – a small thing, a small intimacy, but a strange one for me.

We enjoyed an excellent hogget and potato pie which we washed down with an equally excellent claret. There was anticipation, excitement in the air at the little inn at Scawton that evening. Though at first reserved even the landlord began to jettison some of his moral values moulded in the previous century. He started treating us with the reverence of a bridal couple. A bridal couple! God help me, I had never been particularly good at the wooing game.

'Tell me about this actress friend of yours,' said Winifred, closing the bedroom door. 'Why are you so reticent about her?'

'She was lovely but married.'

'Older than you?'

'Yes,' I sighed. 'Quite a bit older.'

'Your first experience of love?'

'Yes,' I sighed again. Where was all this leading to? I could have admitted that it was my only experience of love. Instead I said, 'Our relationship was ... we never fully consummated the affair if that is what you are after.'

'And why was that?'

'I couldn't.'

'And do you think you can now,' she asked; her eyes calm and fixed on mine as her fingers began to undo my necktie.

'I always thought in terms of wedding nights,' I told her.

'James Cairn, my beautiful blushing bride,' she teased.

'Winifred Holbrook, will you marry me?'

'Not just at the moment,' she said, her voice husky with emotion.

I have never loved as simply and easily as I did that night. I have had my problems in the past with animal passion but all before her was mechanical with no real soul to it. My feeling for Winifred was all soul. It was a meeting of minds as well as bodies. It was even more than that it was purity, childlike purity. Her skin shivered velvet beneath my touch. We rolled into one with such intense tenderness it approached pain. I knew I was pleasing her, pleasing myself. Her sighs were light, abnormally high and light from one with such a well-modulated voice.

I could not move, did not want to move, did not want this night to end as Winifred twitched in exhausted sleep against my chest. I filled my senses, my memory with the scent of her hair, her body. She smelt of lemons. An erotic scent from the past. I remember now she was always mad about Bronnley lemon soap, had it sent up specially from London. This was just right, all right. Had this really happened? Was this really happening to me?

Just as I was marvelling at Winifred's capacity for sleep – a state or torpor personally impossible to achieve after what was for me a momentous happening – she opened her eyes and smiled.

She lay there on my chest, her head turned upward staring at the bed's blue damask canopy. She seemed in a trance as if looking to the heavens for guidance. But there were no planets, no stars up there – the only stars were those in her eyes.

'What are you thinking?' I asked.

'I am thinking that this four-poster tester in silk damask is an amazing fixture to have in such a humble inn.'

'But you like it?'

'I like it. I like everything. I like you.' She kissed me before falling back into her trance like state.

'What are you thinking now?'

'I am thinking about Ursula Howell.'

'Ursula who?'

'Miss Howell. She lives in the rooms below me on Church Street and plays patience all day long. *Snap! Snap!* I can hear the cards slapping onto the table in her frustration.'

'Why on earth are you thinking of her?'

'Because Miss Howell is a sixty-something schoolmarm who will never have known this. She hangs like a malevolent influence over 16 Church Street. She hasn't a good word to say about anyone. She is forever correcting other resident's grammar, often incorrectly. She drip, drips poison in everyone's cup. A deeply unhappy woman she is eaten up by jealousy of those about her. She hates those that she considers more successful or fortunate than herself. Her mouth sags downwards in repose.'

'She sounds an awful woman. So why think of her at a joyous time like this?'

'Because whatever happens to me from now on into the future, you've saved me from that. Whatever happens for once in my life I have known love and fulfillment.'

'But we will go on forever, won't we?' I asked bemused.

'Perhaps,' she replied, snuggling deeper into my skin.

Chapter Twenty-Four

Despite my client's father attempting to bring all the influence he could to bear on the magistrate, Denholm Partridge wouldn't budge, refusing to allow Andrew Ashberry out on bail. In certain respects this served to make my job easier. At least I knew that my client wasn't off on some jaunt somewhere with Chatterton and was easily accessible to be interviewed in Northallerton Gaol.

'How are things, My Lord?' I asked him.

'The food is still terrible.'

'I am sorry to hear that.'

'And look, look, see here, Cairn.' Ashberry rolled back the balloon sleeve of his white cotton poet's shirt.

A strange shirt for an earl to wear, I noted.

'I'm being bitten to death by fleas,' he complained.

I felt incapable of registering much sympathy. I remained unconvinced that I was about to represent an innocent man.

As he readjusted his sleeve to cover the offended flesh, I asked him instead about the diamond cross pendant found round Lydia's neck. Had he bought it for her?

'No, no, the ring cost me enough,' he chuckled.

'Who then? Who bought her such an expensive gift?'

'She told me her brother had given her it.'

'Her brother! And you believed her?'

'Why should I not?'

'Forgive me, My Lord, but how on earth could Malcolm Bowden have afforded to buy, let alone give, his sister such a piece of jewellery?'

'He must have sold a few sheep,' Ashberry shrugged. 'You'd best ask him.'

'You're sure Lydia didn't say her *mother*?'

'Brother, mother, it's all the same to me. By the same token how would Mary Bowden be able to give such a necklace?'

'A family heirloom perhaps,' I offered.

'Such an heirloom would have been sold off years ago to pay off Reginald's debts. We are talking about tenant farmers here.'

'A tenant farming family that you were prepared to marry into, My Lord.'

'Well,' shrugged Ashberry indifferently. 'Lydia was the prettiest gal around.'

There was another way, a more realistic way, I reasoned, that such a fine necklace could have found its way round Lydia's neck.

'Perhaps your father gave it to Mary Bowden first and she passed it onto her daughter,' I tested.

'Why on earth would the old man do that?' laughed Ashberry.

I suddenly remembered the Marquess' words: knowing Lydia was his half-sister "Andrew would surely never have wanted to go through with the marriage, would he?" But then would he? Being wedded to his half-sister gave him both marriage status and a perfect excuse never to consummate the union. Perhaps he hoped Lydia would put up with the situation to protect her status. Hadn't her mother before her done just that married to the celibate Reginald Bowden? Had Andrew really no idea of his relationship to the Bowden siblings?

'I have a feeling that cross pendant might be vital to this whole case,' I told him. 'The person who bought it for Lydia, could be her killer.'

* * * * *

York was a tale of two cities. There were the fine Georgian houses in areas such as Micklegate, then there were the back slums of Walmgate and Hungate identified by Benjamin Seebohm Rowntree in his excellent book *Poverty – A Study of Town Life* published by Macmillan a few years ago. This was where working class homes nudged those of the workless class. Where twenty-one houses shared one water tap, seven houses one water closet. Where fathers, mentally pulled under by waves of poverty and drink, refused to work. Where mothers sold their bodies to feed their children. The great escape into district brothels and alehouses was a world all too familiar through my professional life. But Winifred – Girton College educated Winifred – Winifred from the fresh country fields of Heslington, I regret knew nothing of these things. She certainly knew how to make love but nothing of the uncertainty of having nothing – the back-to-back lovelessness of having nothing. I began to wish it was otherwise.

Once back in York, we renewed our discreet affair with letter-writing and occasional get-togethers in various cafes, never the same one twice. However, it was a small afternoon tearoom off the Shambles that was to be our undoing or in the light of events to come maybe our salvation.

Looking into Winifred's green eyes, I suddenly realised that it was her social naivety that was both attractive and refreshing to me. Intelligent, highly educated, a woman of suffrage, she had a middle class blind spot to the unsavoury happenings down the snickelways of her city.

'Why acknowledge it if you can't change it?' she asked.

'What?'

'Poverty.'

'You can read my mind now.'

'You just gave a half crown to that legless beggar sitting on the pavement outside and looked at me as if I should do the same.'

'And you don't think I should have done that?'

'Half a crown is a lot of money to give, a fortune to him.'

'The poor old sod probably lost his legs fighting for us, for our great British Empire.'

'He will spend your half crown on drink.'

'Is this the cynical Miss Holbrook?'

'No, the realistic Miss Holbrook. You think I don't see, don't care.'

'How do you know what I think?'

'Just one or two things you've said lately.'

'You felt you could change the rights of women.'

'We haven't achieved that yet.'

'So why not attempt to change the rights of the poor?'

'One thing at once, the rest will follow.'

'I hope you are right.'

'Of course she's right,' snapped a voice from behind a newspaper.

Winifred jumped to attention like a dog to the command. The newspaper slowly lowered at the corner table to reveal the scowling face of John Beardsley.

'Beardsley.' I scowled back.

'James Cairn.'

'Have you been following us, John?' Winifred's voice quivered.

'Pure chance, sweetheart. Who would want to follow you?'

'Watch your tongue, Beardsley,' I warned him.

'And you watch your back, Cairn.'

'Is that a threat?' I got up to confront the playground bully, relishing the moment.

'Please, please, James let's just go,' pleaded Winifred, catching my arm.

The tearoom proprietress appeared and appealed for calm.

'James, you don't want any trouble with this big case of yours coming up,' Winifred reminded me.

It was only then that I stopped in my tracks, throwing a few coins down on the table behind me, before Winifred dragged me towards the door.

'There goes James Cairn famous for his defence of poofs,' Beardsley yelled after us.

'There sits John Beardsley famous for assaulting women.' I disentangled myself from Winifred and took a step back towards Beardsley's table. 'Your engagement is over. Winifred doesn't want anything more to do with you. Can't you get that through your thick skull?'

'She'll get tired of you too, Cairn, soon enough. Just you see.'

'And you would be better employed improving your constituents' living conditions than wasting your time following a woman who wants nothing more to do with you.'

'What do you know about my constituents' living conditions?' he spluttered.

'I do know. I have had occasion to visit the people you purport to represent in their vermin infested hovels. I've smelt their stinking ash pits. Seen their shoeless kids going hungry for days. I do know,' I told him. '*Bang!*' I thumped my fist down on his table leaving the tea cup rattling in its saucer.

'I'll call the constables,' squeaked the proprietress.

'You do that,' I told her.

'You'd better go.' Beardsley looked genuinely frightened.

* * * * *

Eoforwic – was the Anglo-Saxon name for York – meaning wild boar town. As far as I was concerned, following my encounter with Beardsley, it was living up to its name. I had never seen usually self-possessed Winifred so unnerved by another human being. What had that man done to her? More than ever I felt she needed my protection. Again I asked her to marry me, again she said not just yet. I suspected that this prevarication was due to the bad experience of her previous engagement. Once bitten twice shy ... Holbrook women were not famed for their choice of men. I felt it wouldn't be long before I locked horns with The Right Honourable John Beardsley once more.

I decided to take the train back up to Northallerton a second time to interview Andrew Ashberry. I had to warn him about Beardsley. Again Robert Brown was unable to make the journey, this time due to the pressure of work, I began to fear for my friend's mental fragility following his father's death.

'Louis is extremely concerned about my situation,' whimpered Ashberry.

'As we all are, My Lord.'

'Louis more than most. He is a very emotional man.' Ashberry flung his arms out helplessly.

'I'm sure ...' I began.

'I'm an innocent man, Cairn,' he proclaimed, his eyes welling with tears. 'I didn't do this terrible thing laid at my door. You do believe me? I might be many things but I am not a murderer.'

'So, what are these many things you are, My Lord, other than a murderer?' I decided to confront my suspicions rather then pussyfooting around the issue. In light of Beardsley's "defence of poofs" taunt, I feared a character assassination was in the offing that could seriously jeopardise our case.

'Well, I ...' gulped Ashberry, obviously taken aback by the question.

'Forgive me, My Lord, but it has been suggested that you might be of a certain persuasion.'

'Nothing to apologise for, Cairn. I trust anything I tell you is in the strictest confidence.'

'Of course, I am a professional man.'

'Louis and I ... Damn it, I love him, Cairn.'

'I see,' I said, immediately anticipating all the legal ramifications.

'And you?'

'And me?' I laughed. It was my turn to be taken aback.

'Louis and I did wonder. Then we saw you with Winifred Holbrook in the Davy Hall Restaurant.'

'I am about to be married,' I told him, pushing the truth.

'So was I.' A cold statement without mirth.

'And now she is dead.'

'I understood you had sympathies … ' Ashberry cleared his throat, changed the subject, he was more comfortable talking about love than death. 'Did I not hear that you had defended a priest who liked to wear dresses? I understood you were a great advocate for those on the social fringes …'

'But the Reverend George Hobb was not homosexual,' I cut in quickly. 'Homosexuality, as you know, is against the law.'

'It shouldn't be,' muttered Ashberry. 'Love should never be a crime.'

'But it is between men in this country. Maybe the law will change eventually.'

'Perhaps,' said Ashberry doubtfully.

'Then again there is misplaced love, the abhorrent physical passion for children.'

'My love is not misplaced, Cairn.'

'I am glad to hear it. Might I ask, My Lord, did you mention to John Beardsley that you had seen me with Miss Holbrook in Davy Hall?'

'Certainly not! What do you take me for, Cairn? I've told you I can't stand the chap, never have done. Winifred Holbrook is best rid of him.'

'So it will not be news to you that I suspect John Beardsley is far from the caring old school friend he is presenting himself as. I fear he might prove to be anything but that. Indeed, it wouldn't surprise me if he stands as a witness for the prosecution.'

* * * * *

Winifred sent for me. She asked me to call at Church Street on a given day at a specific time. I presumed that she had become bolder about our affair as it had already been exposed. But no, there was none of her usual warm welcome for me at the door. Her face was distorted, incandescent with rage.

'What's wrong?' I asked as she led me up to her rooms.

'What's wrong! What's wrong!' she spluttered, turning on me. 'You of all people should know *what's wrong*.'

'Well, I don't,' I told her, trying my best to keep calm.

'Beardsley has written to me telling me he has heard that I am due to be married.' She slammed the door behind me. We were locked in confrontation.

'I don't ...' I began.

'Married to *you*,' she mocked.

'How can he have ...' I began again.

'He asked me if I didn't think it was a little unseemly after being so recently engaged to him. Did I not think it appeared as if I had to have a man at any cost? Any man?'

'I only mentioned it ...' I began a third time. Why had I mentioned it? That was it, I had used the probability of a forthcoming marriage to counter any homosexual misunderstanding on the part of Ashberry. But how could I explain that to Winifred?'

'Did you tell Andrew Ashberry that we were due to be married, yes or no?'

'Well,' I hesitated, knowing my future happiness could depend on my answer. 'Yes,' I finally admitted, because if we did not have truth between us then we had nothing.

'I never agreed to marry you,' she railed.

'I know.'

'We're not even engaged.'

'I see it was more wishful thinking on my part,' I retorted lamely.

'I don't want to see you anymore. I no longer trust you, trust any of you.'

'Any of us?'

'Men,' she roared.

'I haven't much faith left in you either, Winifred. I realise now I was good enough to sleep with but not to marry.'

'You're not old enough to be married, James, you're still a child.'

'And you can't carry corn, Winifred.'

And so the recriminations went on and on until I left. She had been in floods of tears, me angry now. Back in my Gillygate townhouse, I reran the scene in Church Street over and over again in my head.

"She'll get tired of you too, Cairn, soon enough. Just you see." Like Miss Howell, Winifred's fellow lodger, Beardsley had dropped his poisonous words into my cup in the tea room off the Shambles.

But I loved Winifred Holbrook, always had done. I was heartbroken and in that mood I wrote out my withdrawal from the Lydia Bowden murder case and the reasons why to Andrew, Earl of Fadmoor.

Chapter Twenty-Five

Andrew Ashberry was incensed. He denied having any sort of communication with Beardsley since my last visit to the gaol. He reminded me, by return post, that he couldn't stand Beardsley and begged me to reconsider resigning from the case. What was going on? Ashberry was the only person I had been foolish enough to make my idle, inaccurate marriage speculation to. Had this merely been an intuitive guess on Beardsley's part? But then how could Beardsley have known to give Ashberry as the source for his information?

I decided to do nothing for a few days, sit on the problem, until Trotter announced Mr Robert Brown was seeking an audience with me immediately. I realised that both my throne and problem were about to get extremely sticky and difficult.

Enter all of a fluster, hot-under-the-collar Bob Brown.

'Is it true, James? Is it true that you have resigned your brief in the Fadmoor case? I've just received this ...' he said, wafting a letter in my face. 'From Freddy Ashberry, saying you are refusing to represent his son. I don't believe this, James. Tell me it isn't true?'

'It is true,' I admitted flatly.

'All because of this Beardsley business?'

'That's right.'

'Andrew swears he never informed Beardsley of your forthcoming marriage.'

'Forthcoming nothing, not even a friendship exists between Miss Holbrook and myself now.'

'I'm sorry but you only have yourself to blame for this, James. What ever possessed you to fabricate the truth?'

'I wished it to be so. I wished to be betrothed to Winifred so much that I fooled myself into believing she felt the same.'

'She has always been the one for you, hasn't she? Despite fate continually arriving to intervene against the match.'

'You are beginning to sound like Winifred.'

'Maybe at some future date the situation will right itself,' reassured Bob, ever the optimist.

'But if not Andrew Ashberry, who could have told Beardsley that Winifred and I were about to be married?'

Bob gave me a long hard stare.

'I have my suspicions,' he said, 'but no proof.'

'Not Chatterton?'

'I can't be sure. Andrew will not say, only that it wasn't him.'

'Not chattering Chatterton?' I moaned again.

'James, I implore you to reconsider taking on this brief. If I believed for a moment that Andrew was guilty of this horrendous crime then I wouldn't be so concerned.'

'Crime or crimes?'

'What?'

'Don't you see that there is still a strong possibility that whoever murdered Lydia could have murdered Gerard? The probability of two young related deaths in such a limited time span is highly unusual.'

'But the coroner found Gerard's death to be accidental.'

'As you well know, Bob, coroners are not infallible. Do you remember the wording of that anonymous note you received a while back? There was one sentence in it that intrigued me referring to the Marquess: "But more than this, he is culpable in the gross crime of filicide, not just a son but a daughter too".'

'I didn't understand that either. I presumed it was some lunatic but I did as you advised and handed the note over to the police. If it was accusing Freddy of murdering Gerard, his son, that was one thing but Lydia wasn't his daughter.'

'Do you remember I speculated that the writer could have intended "daughter-in-law"?'

'Yes, I remember.'

'Well, I have come to the conclusion that he meant exactly "daughter" – "his daughter".'

Once more Bob gave me the long hard stare – before long hard stare changed to disbelief.

'As the Ashberrys' family solicitor I think you should know that The Most Honourable Frederick, Marquess of Hambleton, was indeed Lydia's father through his liaison with Mary Bowden.'

'So that was why Freddy was so against his son's match with Lydia.'

'Indeed. Further more, I have no doubt that this state of affairs will come out in open court soon enough. It is a crucial element in this case.'

'Does this mean you have reinstated yourself, James?'

'Give me a day or two to consider my position. Whoever your anonymous letter writer was, he was privy to this well-guarded family secret.'

'Could he be the murderer?'

'Anything is possible in this case.'

* * * * *

'I'm sorry it was me, Mr Cairn. I'm truly sorry if I have been the cause of any personal grief. I was the one who told John Beardsley of your impending marriage. Believing it to be true, I wanted to hurt him because men like him despise men like us. I have an inkling that Beardsley intends standing up in court against Andrew. You can't really mean to withdraw your professional services from this case, Mr Cairn. Andrew needs your expertise to get to the truth, to set him free. He is an innocent man, Mr Cairn,' pleaded Chatterton, close to tears.

'That's enough, Louis,' Fadmoor told him, palm raised in Chatterton's face.

'How do you fare, Andrew?' asked Bob Brown; concern furrowing his brow.

Ashberry shook a woeful head. 'Not well, not well at all, Brown.'

The prisoner's cell at Northallerton Gaol was beginning to resemble a crowded steam bath after a rugby match. Brown had finally agreed to accompany me on this visit. Louis Chatterton was already there when we arrived. The Marquess was just leaving, muttering on his way out something to the effect of 'whatever was the world coming to with so many fairies in it?'

'Fairy I might be, Pa. But your son and heir isn't a bloody murderer,' the younger Ashberry screamed after his father.

The Marquess turned in the doorway, rasping in disgust, 'Can't you do something about this ghastly mess, Cairn?'

'I haven't quite decided if I will renew my interest in your son's case, Lord Hambleton.'

'No, but you're here now, aren't you?'

'To discharge my duties to the full, I have to be convinced of my client's innocence.'

'Do as you please,' he growled. Pushing the warder out of the way with such venom, the man was nearly knocked to the ground.

'For God's sake, I can't stand much more of this,' complained Fadmoor. 'Can't you two gentlemen get me out of here, whatever it takes?' he asked, turning to me and Brown.

'We are doing our best, Andrew,' placated Brown.

'Remand,' he grunted. 'Innocent until proved guilty. But no, you still have to get down on your knees and polish the floor, buff up the lustre on your brass basin, scrub the table until your hands are raw, fold up your bedding and arrange any paltry piece of cell furniture in exactly the same position every time. This place is soul destroying.'

'Well, Andrew,' sighed Brown. 'Things were much worse forty years ago.'

'Yes,' I agreed. 'At least the Separate System has been diluted. Prisoners were once forced to wear leather hoods, known as peaks, pulled down over their faces so that they could only look forwards when infrequently allowed out of their single cells. Penned in individual cubicles, I hesitate to call them pews, they weren't even able to associate with fellow inmates during chapel. Their heads were only visible over the woodwork to the duty warders and chaplain.'

'Yes, the intention was that you reflected on your sins, alone and in silence, during your period of incarceration,' added Brown.

'The rule of silence would hardly act as a deterrent for me,' sniffed Ashberry. 'There isn't anybody in this place that I would wish to converse with.'

'Pity Mr Wilde isn't still available,' said Brown; unwisely, I thought.

'Puh! Poor old Oscar. See what grinding prison time did to him. It broke his will, killing him in the end,' retorted Ashberry.

'But Wilde was a convict, you are not,' I pointed out.

'Not yet,' moaned Ashberry.

A sneeze caught in my hurried 'goodbye'. And then another one forcing me to reach down into my coat pocket for my handkerchief.

With so much negativity buzzing around the fetid cell, nothing more was to be gained for the moment. Brown and I finally escaped into the free world.

'What do you make of it all, Bob?' I asked, filling my lungs with satisfying gulps of fresh air as we crossed the prison yard.

Before he could answer we heard a running tap, tap, behind us. Louis Chatterton flounced up.

'You've forgotten this, Mr Cairn,' he said, handing me my fountain pen. 'It must have fallen out of your pocket.'

'Thank you,' I told him. Indeed I was extremely grateful as the pen had been a memento from New York City a while back.

'A Waterman,' he acknowledged. 'It must be very precious to you.' I nodded. 'Mr Cairn, Mr Brown, there is another matter I would like to discuss with you both before you catch your train.'

'Go ahead,' Brown told him impatiently.

'I do wish you would look into my theory regarding who might be responsible for all this,' said Chatterton with a nervous giggle. 'Though Andrew will have none of it.'

'Please, get it off your chest, man. We have a train to catch,' pressed Brown.

'I have already mentioned my suspicions to Mr Cairn. Now more than ever I am becoming convinced that Andrew's brother, Stephen, could have been the one who killed both Lydia and Gerard,' announced Chatterton flatly. 'He came across them in the Doric Temple. Heard them discussing something he did not like. She left and he shot Gerard with his own gun. Who other than a brother would Gerard allow to handle his gun? He then waylaid Lydia sometime afterwards on her way home.'

'But the coroner recorded Gerard's death as an accident,' reaffirmed Brown, as he had done to me after I had queried the finding.

'Puh! Didn't you know the coroner was an old friend of the Marquess'? He had him and his wife round to dinner following the verdict. Frederick was terrified that his heroic second son would be put down as a suicide.'

'However, you, sir, are talking of murder, double murder,' I pointed out.

'That's right, Mr Cairn.'

'And have you proof to support such an accusation?' I asked.

'Stephen is far from normal. There are all those animals he tortures. Horrible, he does horrible spiteful things.'

'Have you any irrefutable proof to support your accusation?' I persisted.

'No, but if you agree to represent Andrew I will get you your proof.'

'A deal,' I said, shaking hands with Chatterton to the astonishment of Mr Brown.

'You're not really taking on this case because you believe Chatterton can deliver on his promise of evidence against Stephen Ashberry, are you?' Brown asked me on the train back to York.

'Of course not,' I replied. 'I have finally decided to take on this case because it is intriguing. There are so many suspects, so many scenarios, so many motives.'

'Is there ever a sound motive to take the life of another human being?' asked Brown dryly.

'It happens all the time in war but then war changes the rules.'

'Not in peacetime society though.'

'No, Bob, not for the likes of you or me either. We would way up the pros and cons of our actions, the risk of capture and punishment, then there's conscience. However, I think civilised behaviour is just a thin veneer covering the primitive. The murderer must feel the necessity of committing his brutal act outweighs the risk of discovery and the hangman's noose. If we can understand the perpetrator's reasoning then perhaps we will find him.'

'But just suppose he is a killer without reasoning, someone who is insane.'

'Then we have a problem,' I agreed.

'So you don't believe Andrew Ashberry killed Lydia, despite one of his cufflinks being found in her clench fist?'

'A little staged, don't you think, Bob?'

Chapter Twenty-Six

Planted evidence, planted innuendoes, planted seeds of doubt in Winifred's mind. I wasn't doing too well recently.

'Trotter, dig out that paper work on the Ashberry case, if you would be so kind,' I asked my clerk the next morning.

'*Rat-a-tat-tat*' – five minutes later Trotter's familiar knock on my door. He reappeared arms laden with documents and files.

I began to form my defence, carefully sifting through witness statements and affidavits. I had previously made my own statement to the Crown, revealing that I, along with Inspector White, had discovered Lydia Bowden's body at the bottom of one of the Ashberry Pits. It was unprecedented for a defending barrister to have found the victim, but the discovery had been made well before my original appointment to act for Andrew Ashberry. I heard nothing for months so I presumed I was free to go ahead with the Ashberry defence. I had had no personal contact for months either with Inspector White or my old friend Dick Tate who I believed would be appearing for the prosecution. However, I already had asked for disclosure of Dick's post-mortem results as was my right. It made interesting technical reading, although merely confirming what White had already told me: Lydia died from strangulation presumably prior to the fall.

I knew from previous experience that strangulation was an intimate crime – a crime which nearly always resulted from passion or extreme emotional hatred or both – however, the taking of a life face to face is an unusual occurrence.

Another piece of information to catch my eye was that Dick had confirmed that Lydia was pregnant.

Trotter's familiar knock again. His expression was fixed, impassive.

'Miss Winifred Holbrook wishes to see you, sir,' he announced.

'You are joking?'

'No, sir, I am not.'

'Here, now?' I asked. He nodded. 'Well, show her in, man,' I told him; my face reddening as I struggled to my feet.

I offered Winifred my hand but she looked at it as if it was a dead thing. I went round my desk and gave her a brief kiss on the cheek which she treated with equal indifference. I retreated back to my chair like one of Massarti's circus lions whipped onto its stool.

'James, I have something to tell you.' There was no warmth in her voice.

'Something else,' I groaned.

'Yes, something important.'

'Please,' I offered her a seat. This she did not decline.

'It has to do with John Beardsley.'

'I thought it might. Are you seeing him again?' My spirits fell to rock bottom.

'No, no, of course not.' Her laugh was brittle, humourless.

'Thank goodness for that.'

'I bumped into Charnley Lodge the other day.'

'Charnley who?'

'Charnley Lodge.'

'Who on earth is he? He sounds like a gatehouse.'

'He was John's secretary.'

'So you "bumped" into him?' I was growing uneasy – where was this leading to now?

'Yes, I bumped into him in the same way I bumped into you.'

'Are you walking out with this Lodge fellow now?'

'No!' Winifred's eyes widened, blazing with anger. 'John sacked Charnley a few months ago.'

'Why did he sack him?'

'Some ethical disagreement or other. Something like that. I don't exactly know the details. The point is Charnley told me about a connection that you might find interesting.'

'Between whom?'

'Between John and Frederick, Marquess of Hambleton.'

'And what does this connection involve?'

'Business, it is a business partnership. They intend opening a quarry on the Marquess' estate.'

'"A quarry",' I repeated, some memory rattling in the back of my mind. 'Where exactly on the estate?'

'Near Broadshaw Farm, on fields worked by the Bowdens.'

'This is news indeed,' I told her, sensing a tightness in my throat.

'Yes, I believe John is using his political influence to push the plans through.'

'Thank you for taking the trouble to come and tell me about this, Winifred.'

'Surely though the Bowdens have some rights?'

'The law is complex in regard to manorial estates but basically it remains feudal.'

'You mean Frederick Ashberry could simply push the Bowden family off fields they have worked for generations?'

'I am not privy to any agreement that might exist between them, although I know someone who might be.'

'Who?'

'Unfortunately, I am not at liberty to say. But in my experience should there be a tenancy agreement it nearly always favours the landowner.'

'How shocking. I believe in fairness and justice just as much as you do, James.'

'That being the case, it was Louis Chatterton not Andrew Ashberry who told Beardsley of our engagement.'

'There was no engagement, no proposal, no acceptance and you admitted that rumour originated from you.'

'Can't you accept, Winifred, it was just wishful thinking on my part?'

'No, James, I can't forgive you. You live in a world of talk and theatricals. I have to survive in the real world. My brother and I have had to overcome a terrible legacy left to us by Doctor Holbrook.'

'None of which was your fault.'

'That is not how most people perceive it.'

'Those sorts of people aren't worth bothering about. Let me take you out to lunch, Winifred, and make amends. At least let us remain friends.'

'No, no.' She flapped her hand across welling tears and rushed out leaving the door ajar.

Almost immediately, Trotter arrived to close it.

'Oh, dear,' he said.

Left to myself, I began to mull over Winifred and that morning's events.

I really had made a mess of things. But it wasn't until I was comfortably ensconced back at home in Gillygate – cuddling a large glass of brandy – that I remembered the anonymous letter to Bob Brown. The letter White said hadn't been written by Malcolm Bowden. The letter that said that the Marquess planned to rob many of his tenant farmers of their livings by selling off land to quarry for stone. If not Malcolm then why couldn't the composer have been Reginald Bowden? The only thing that troubled me about that hypothesis was that the writing was incongruous with the cheap paper it was written on – the hand was assured and professional.

* * * * *

I instructed Trotter to send for Mr Robert Brown first thing the next morning. Fortunately, the solicitor had his office just round the corner in St. Leonard's Place. However, he didn't arrive at Bootham Chambers until late afternoon. He was flustered and his appearance somewhat dishevelled.

'Sorry, James, I couldn't get here earlier. I've had a hell of a day. So much paperwork to get through, so many appointments to meet.'

'I expect Frederick Ashberry's quarry project alone keeps you busy.'

'What quarry project?'

'The quarry he is intending to open on rented Bowden land.'

'What?'

'Don't tell me you don't know about it, Bob, you're the Ashberrys' family solicitor.'

'I am telling you, I know nothing about a proposed quarry. Freddy must be taking advice from elsewhere for some reason.'

'Hmm, perhaps he felt you wouldn't approve, being a man of principle.'

'It's happened before. I recently learnt that Freddy had settled a small annuity on Mary Bowden through a London solicitor.'

'And now she is dead.'

'Yes, and following her death it was to be passed on to Lydia.'

'And now she too is dead.'

'Quite.'

'Tell me, Bob, have you still got that anonymous note vilifying the Ashberrys? Do you remember it mentioned something about quarrying for stone?'

'No, Inspector White kept it. I must confess all that got pushed to the back of my mind following my father's death. But yes, come to think of it, I do remember a reference to a quarry. You don't think Lydia's murder and the accession of land could be linked?'

'Is that something you've just thought of, Bob?' I smiled.

* * * * *

Two days later, Brown was back with larger than life Charnley Lodge in tow. Lodge looked like a walking buddleia bush. He sported a deep blue satin waistcoat covered in embroidered butterflies.

Not the usual quiet sartorial fashion of an MP's secretary, I noted. No, this man was obviously a dandy.

'Encountered a friend of yours the other day, Mr Cairn. The lovely Miss Holbrook. What a stunner,' he enthused, before a wincing Brown could make any formal introduction.

'Really,' I said.

'Yes, really,' he replied. 'Glad that gal ended her engagement to John Beardsley Esquire.'

'Miss Holbrook is a very independent young woman,' I pointed out.

'So I understand. But what a waste it would have been, a fine young filly like her married to a fella like him.'

'But he was your employer.'

'Only for six months. Didn't really like Mr Beardsley from the start but it took me that length of time to work out how much of a cad he really is.'

'Why cad?'

'Tell him, tell Mr Cairn what you've just told me,' interrupted Brown.

Lodge sighed deeply at the tedium of having to recount the tale. 'The Marquess of Hambleton had devised a plan to turn part of his estate into a stone quarry, so depriving a few of his tenant farmers of their valuable grazing rights on common land.'

'Common land, not fields, you say?'

'Yes, common land initially,' confirmed Lodge.

'The law regarding such land is complex,' explained Brown.

'Does the landowner have the right to open a quarry?' I asked.

'Well,' hesitated Brown, 'this is the difficulty. The landowner's rights are restricted regarding common land, the commoners have rights of usage, although the landowner retains other rights to the land, such as rights to minerals and large timber, and to any common rights left unexercised by the commoners.'

'The commoners being the Bowdens.' My turn to sigh.

'Yes, them mainly.' Brown examined the floor. 'Them almost exclusively.'

'Listen, Mr Cairn, if you already know about this please don't allow us to bore you by covering familiar ground,' put in Lodge.

'No, pray continue, in your own words,' I told him, unscrewing the top of my pen.

Lodge turned to Brown in some alarm.

'It is better this way, Mr Lodge,' Brown reassured him. 'It is better to give your testimony here today, voluntarily, rather than suffer the humiliation of *subpoena ad testificandum*.'

'The trouble was the Marquess did not envisage merely a small quarry on the common,' continued Lodge, still looking uncomfortable. 'But a huge industrial process that over time would spread out by stealth and eat up the majority of Reginald Bowden's historically cultivated pasture.'

'Did the Marquess consult Bowden senior?' I asked.

'Yes, but only regarding the common land. Of course the old man, who is shrewder than he looks, refused. That is when the Marquess brought in John Beardsley, and through him a sinister lawyer who, I swear, was the living image of Mr Dickens' Vholes in *Bleak House*.'

'So, the Marquess chose not to consult his usual solicitor, Mr Brown here, for this transaction?'

'I believe they knew Mr Brown wouldn't sanction what was going on. For a share in the quarry profits, Mr Beardsley had agreed to use his political influence to push things through.'

'Did the Earl of Fadmoor know about his father's business proposition?'

'As far as I know Lord Fadmoor knew nothing. Again, like Mr Brown here, they knew he would be opposed to the manner in which they were attempting to push it through.'

'And they weren't agreeable to offer any compensation to the Bowdens, I suppose?'

'Not a penny. Indeed, they were bent on driving them out completely. The thinking being that they could convert Broadshaw Farm and its outbuilding into offices for the business.'

'Was it because of your disapproval regarding this scheme that Beardsley sacked you?'

'I believe so.'

'And is the quarry to go ahead?'

'When I left John Beardsley's employment the decision had been deferred.'

'Why was that?'

'Because of the discovery of Lydia Bowden's body and Andrew Ashberry's arrest of course,' said Lodge, swatting his sweating brow with his silk millefiori pattern handkerchief.

I slid pen and paper across the table for Lodge to sign his statement, praying he wouldn't ruin my precious gold nib.

'Well, gentlemen, thank you both for furnishing me with this information.' I got up to show them out.

'Do you think this quarry business might have some relevance, James?' asked Brown with a backward glance.

'"Relevance", I should say so,' I replied.

We were into the first week of October. The Wright Brothers' aeroplane, Wright Flyer III, had stayed in the air for thirty-nine minutes. Wilbur had been airborne longer than any other man living – apart from me, that was, with this new information about Beardsley's and Frederick Ashberry's business association, I was floating on air too.

The whole complexion of this case was changing daily. It was like riding a roller coaster.

Chapter Twenty-Seven

The sensation of floating on air was not destined to last long. A day or two later I came down to earth with a bump. The Hilary term ran from January to April. I heard from Trotter that the trial date for the Ashberry case had been set for Monday, 15th January – the beginning of the new year – I had only three months in which to prepare the Earl of Fadmoor's defence. Standing against me for the Crown was a Mr Jonathan Black. Mr Black was unknown to me. According to Trotter's research he had been carefully picked. Black was a KC who had previously travelled the Western Circuit. He was lean, keen, up-and-coming. More importantly, he had no connection with the Ashberrys.

On top of this not so "uplifting" news, I had a chance meeting with Charnley Lodge in High Petergate. One I would rather not have had.

'Happened to run into the lovely Miss Holbrook again,' he leered.

'Really,' I said, wondering what had happened to his butterflies. They appeared to have flown off to more salubrious fields. Today he wore a more sober striped waistcoat vest in light grey wool.

'Yes, she's going to work in Paris.'

'Work? What sort of work?'

'Political work, she told me.'

'Women's suffrage,' I moaned. 'She's going to rally the troops over in France.'

'She didn't say exactly,' replied Lodge; obviously a little worried by my reaction.

'She didn't have to,' I moaned again.

'I'm sorry, Mr Cairn, I didn't realise ...'

'There is nothing to realise, Mr Lodge,' I told him, before walking on.

Oh, but there was. I was facing this difficult case and all I had as fact was one dead girl, and that Frederick Ashberry had previously approached her family about throwing them off their tenanted land. Did Lydia know about this? If so would she not have told Andrew about it? Apart from the complex relationships between his children was this an additional reason Frederick Ashberry didn't want the marriage to go ahead?

Winifred was going. Any chance of a reconciliation was going. My heart was heavy. How I could have done with her support.

When I got back to chambers, Trotter handed me a note from Bob Brown. In it he told me he intended to visit Andrew Ashberry in Northallerton the next day. There were some outstanding financial affairs to be sorted out that had arisen during His Lordship's incarceration. Was there any message that I would like to convey to our client?

One message, I wrote back, the trial date was set for Monday, 15th January, next year. And one question: did the Earl of Fadmoor know anything about his father's intention to quarry common land used by the Bowdens?

* * * * *

The following week – autumn was on the turn, winter was on its way – and I was seated at my desk fantasying about following Winifred Holbrook to Paris. I heard Trotter's knock on my door.

'Come in,' I shouted.

Trotter had barely set one foot into my office before a little rodent bustled round him and, without so much as a by-your-leave, took a seat.

'Mr Vincent Smail of *Wincup and Smail Solicitors*,' announced Trotter with obvious disapproval.

'Mr Cairn.' Smail reached his small paw over my desk.

I took it. It was bony and cold.

'I don't think I have had the pleasure,' I told him, struggling to release my hand from his grasp.

'No, I don't expect you have because I've just come up from London,' replied Smail cleverly.

'"London"?'

'Yes, I am the Marquess of Hambleton's London solicitor.'

'"London solicitor", I see,' I said, and I did. So this was the Mr Vholes that Charnley Lodge talked about.

'Now look here, Cairn, the Marquess is very upset to hear that you've been rooting around in his business affairs.'

'Have I?' Damn that big mouth Charnley Lodge was my first thought.

'Yes, asking his son, the Earl of Fadmoor, about a project that has been temporarily suspended.'

'Has it?' Sorry, Lodge, was my second thought. Bob's visit to Andrew Ashberry in Northallerton Gaol must have stirred all this up – this immediate response.

'Yes, obviously.'

'"Temporarily", you say?'

'The Marquess has more to worry about at present with his heir in gaol accused of murder, don't you think?'

'No, I think the young Earl has more to worry about,' I replied dryly. 'And anything that might help his cause is worth investigating.'

'How can a business proposition help his cause?' sneered Smail.

'A proposition that greatly upsets other people,' I suggested.

'I'm sorry, I don't see the connection.'

'Don't you really? Such financial propositions can be the motive for murder. Lydia was about to marry into a family that was seizing common land. She finished up being pushed down a pit and if her fiancé is hanged for her murder all the better. Gerard, the next Ashberry heir, has been shot dead. That only leaves Stephen and he is …'

'I know, I know, an imbecile.'

'Is he actually that?' I asked surprised.

'Well, he's not far short of one.'

'Why, is that?' I faked ignorance.

'Because as you have already unkindly informed the Marquess, his youngest son is suffering from congenital syphilis.'

'Did I really?'

'Yes, you did.'

'You seem to know a lot about Ashberry affairs, sir.'

'I must admit I do enjoy a good working relationship with the Marquess.'

'And a lucrative one, no doubt.'

'Should the quarry go ahead it would be of terrific benefit to the nation,' replied Smail unfazed.

'And to the Ashberry family in particular?'

'Yes, to them too.'

'And it would provide much needed employment in the local community,' I offered, having heard this argument time and time again regarding various greedy landowner projects.

'Of course.'

'So would the Marquess go ahead with his quarry scheme if he had no competent heir to leave it to?'

'I don't think so. That is why it is important to get Andrew safely acquitted.'

'Merely so this business venture that you are representing can go ahead?'

'No, no, of course not. But I feel it is in your best interests, Cairn, to concentrate on the important matter in hand.'

'Are you threatening me, *Mr Vholes*.' A terrible slip of the tongue.

'Pardon?' (Irritated.)

'Sorry, silly of me, Mr Smail of course.'

'Are you feeling quite well, Cairn?'

'Do you mean am I of sound mind, Mr Smail?'

'Yes, if you like,' he snapped.

'I think I am, Mr Smail, but perhaps you could assuage some of my nervousness regarding one point?'

'I'll try,' said with a bored groan.

'If the Marquess was so sure of the legitimacy of his scheme to turn common land into an industrial enterprise, why had he failed to mention it to his heir, Lord Fadmoor?'

'Well, that's obvious.'

'It is?' I asked. The lawyer made no reply: he saw the jaws of the trap too late. 'You mean it is "obvious" because the Marquess chose not to tell his son he was after land farmed by his fiancée's family for generations?' Again no reply from Smail. 'And it wasn't merely the common land he wanted, was it? Eventually, he intended his quarry to spread out into valuable farming land. Indeed, the Marquess was bent on driving the Bowdens from their farm entirely, was he not?'

'Who's told you all this?' Smail found his voice at last.

'That doesn't matter for now. What matters is that for any of the parties involved this appropriation of tenanted land could be yet another motive for murder.'

'Well, well, I doubt ...' floundered the lawyer.

'Good day, Mr Smail.'

Smail had only just scuttled off when Trotter arrived with the lunchtime post.

'A small rude man, with a small mentality, our Mr Smail,' commented my clerk.

'Alas, I disagree, Trotter. Rats are highly intelligent and highly dangerous,' I retorted, frowning as I recognised Winifred's handwriting on the envelope. I couldn't stop my hand shaking as I tore it open.

16, Church Street -13th October, 1905

Friday, the 13th October, was this an omen.

> *Dear James,*
> *I am going away to Paris for a while. I have*
> *to think things through. Please don't attempt*
> *to follow me.*
> *Winifred*

That brief, that cold. I had to think things through too on that cold golden October day. Winifred had read my thoughts about pursuing her to Paris – how well she knew me, how little she knew me.

I paid my shilling and took a lunchtime stroll through the Museum Gardens, created by the famous landscape architect, Sir John Murray Naysmith, on the former grounds of St Mary's Abbey in the 1830s. The gardens had been given by the Royal Family to the Yorkshire Philosophical Society in 1828. Making my way down towards the river Ouse, my pace quickened, my sole intention was to walk Winifred Holbrook off. But my body physically ached for her – a sharp physical ache – I could no longer conceal the truth, any spiritual harmony that had existed between myself and Winifred Holbrook had, for me, become overwhelmed by sexual desire. Just the once – just the one taste of that delicious fruit – only to have it snatched from me. How cruel was that? Under that blue northern sky, above the slow moving water, I decided then and there that I would be better rewarded placing all that terrific energy into my career than pursuing an indifferent woman.

The wind was now set fair for me to give *Rex v Andrew Ashberry* my full attention. However, I realised this was no easy task with so many players in the cast, so many suspects who might have wanted Lydia Bowden dead.

* * * * *

Mid-October I learnt that Justin Black was not standing against me in the Ashberry trial after all. The poor fellow had recently suffered a seizure and died. He was to be replaced by someone from Middlesex. Obviously the Crown was maintaining its determination not to risk any accusation that its man might be tainted by familiarity to one of England's powerful aristocratic families. Dry crinkled leaves began to fall to the ground along Bootham and October moved into November, November into the mild December of 1905. Nothing very much happened apart from my participation in cases that amounted to little more than misdemeanours. York was enveloped in low cloud for many days and fog clung to the surface of the Ouse as if fatally attracted.

Other than the forthcoming Ashberry trial, the main talk in chambers was the approaching General Election. On the 4th December, the Conservative Party split over tariff reform. This led to the resignation of the Tory Prime Minister, Arthur Balfour. Henry Campbell-Bannerman took over for the Liberal Party, pending a general election in the new year.

'I believe the Liberals have an up-and-coming young man in their ranks,' Carlton-Bingham told us over tea and cake. 'A Mr Winston Churchill.'

I kept my own counsel but I too particularly liked the sound of this Member of Parliament for Oldham. Last year Randolph Churchill's son had crossed the floor from the Conservatives to join the ranks of the Liberal Party.

'Puh! The fellow is little more that a traitor,' said Gerald Fawcett, blowing out a cloud of cigar smoke which threatened to choke us all to death.

'I agree,' said Trotter, another dyed-in-the-wool Conservative.

'I don't,' I finally announced. 'Churchill firmly believes in free trade without tariffs, in stark contrast to the Liberal Unionists and their

Conservative allies. And as a newspaper correspondent who covered the Boer War, he also believes in magnanimity to our enemies. But what really attracts me to him is his opposition to that obnoxious Alien's Bill against Jewish immigration in all its forms. From what I have read about Mr Churchill, despite his aristocratic birth, he is a true Liberal in every sense and I would like to buy him dinner.'

'Really?' responded Fawcett.

'Yes, *really*,' I replied.

'But would he come, Cairn, do you think?' scoffed Fawcett.

'Come where?'

'To dinner with you of course.'

'That's not the point. He would be invited whereas you would not be, Fawcett.'

'Gentlemen, please,' appealed Carlton-Bingham.

'*Clap! Clap!*' Thomas Leacock stood applauding me in the doorway with a wry smile on his face.

When I got home that evening, I found Kate had left a letter in the silver tray in the hall for me. It was a letter from my mother, complaining that she had not heard from me in quite a while and inviting me down to London for Christmas. Torn by both duty and guilt, I nevertheless penned my regrets for the next morning's post. I could not face her and my sister's efforts to be jolly when I felt so wretched myself. I could not deal with the softening process of their love when my sanity and survival depended on me remaining tough. I would only have spoilt the party.

* * * * *

Christmas came dry and clear. About to embark on a miserable Christmas, I personally would have welcomed back the fog to conceal my loneliness. York was always dead over the festive season. However my maid, Kate, who is without close family, began to prepare our Christmas feast – and a feast it would turn out be – for the first time ever I invited Kate to take a place at my table.

Pheasant soup to start with followed by fish mayonnaise accompanied by some fine Rhineland hock.

"'A Merry Christmas to us all; God bless us, every one",' I quoted Tiny Tim over Kate's exquisitely basted stuffed goose.

'There are only two of us, sir,' she pointed out. Was she being flirtatious here? Yes, I thought I saw a sparkle in her eye that I had not seen there before although it could have been a trick of the candlelight.

I raised my glass of claret in a toast to the cook.

'Cook and friend, I hope, sir.' She smiled.

I was reminded of a scene in Henry Fielding's novel, *Tom Jones*, where Fielding draws parallels between lust and gorging.

How prettily and neatly she ate. How pretty she was. Why had I never noticed before?

The plum pudding she presented me with was full of flavour, full of currants and candied fruits and served with brandy butter. I watched her opening her mouth, spooning the dessert delicately onto her tongue compared to my own hungry devouring. However, when she opened her empty mouth to enjoy the next morsel and I made her laugh, I could see right back to her pink tonsils.

My arousal would have been obvious if it wasn't for the saving grace of the tablecloth.

Mince pies and Yule pastries followed. By the time I opened the port there was no longer just two of us but an intoxicated blurred half of each of us left – we were extremely inebriated and a distinct possibility crossed my mind – would she be agreeable to our two drunken halves staggering into one? She yawned, her eyes looked dull and lazy now. I was tired and ready for bed, was she?

Chapter Twenty-Eight

I woke up bleary-eyed to a year of change. I woke up on the morning of the Ashberry trial – a trial that had many transgressors, too many possible suspects other than the Earl himself.

Walking towards York Crown Court I had no clear idea of how this case would be resolved, let alone how my personal life would pan out. I had plenty to mull over as I beat out my path to heaven knows what waiting fate.

The love of my life had gone to Paris. My ridiculous compensatory overtures to my maid, Kate, over Christmas dinner had been rejected and it was "touch and go" – forgive the pun – whether she would remain under my roof much longer. The sobering cold breeze funnelling down Blake Street was the only reassurance, certainty, in my life at that moment.

I had represented a Down's syndrome man, a priest who liked wearing dresses, now I was about to embark on the defence of a member of the English aristocracy in yet another cause célèbre. Although Andrew Ashberry was at the higher end of the social scale from my other two clients, he was confronting the same horrific possibility of the hangman's noose as the Down's syndrome man, Daniel Robertshaw, who had been indicted for the murder of a young girl.

Change was certainly in the air. The Friday before the trial, Sir Henry Campbell-Bannerman's cabinet, which included among its members H. H. Asquith, David Lloyd George and Winston Churchill, embarked on sweeping social reforms after a Liberal landslide in the general election. Perhaps the Liberals weren't dead and buried after all.

Numerous Atlantic disturbances heralded the new year too. They skirted our coasts and moved inland like a marauding army. January matched my mood – exceedingly unsettled and boisterous. I struggled to gain some equilibrium as gowned and bewigged I entered the crowded courtroom.

Catherine wheels of whispers hissed and cracked around the body of the court as my client came up from the depths into the dock. I could see his eyes blinking and searching me out. He looked a little disorientated at first in this unfamiliar setting of boxes, benches and hurdles. Finally seeing me, he gave a quick nervous jerk of his head in recognition.

'All rise,' shouted the clerk of assize.

Mr Justice Bloom mounted his dais. Thelonious Bloom was such a rounded name but the judge was anything but rounded; he was wizened and thin like the pared blade of a fillet knife and just as sharp by reputation. His scarlet pleats and black sash of office hung loosely from his frame – curtains from a rail – as he folded into his lofty perch.

'Andrew Ashberry, Earl of Fadmoor, you are indicted and the charge against you is murder in that on the twenty-eighth of September, 1901, at Helmsley, in the County of Yorkshire, you murdered Lydia Bowden. How say you, Andrew Ashberry, are you guilty or not guilty?' asked the clerk.

The court held its breath, gentlemen from the press held their pencils at the ready.

'I plead not guilty,' replied Andrew softly. He had lost all his field sport colour, all his dinner party robustness. He *was* a shadow of his former self.

Detached from all subtle human considerations, the mechanics of justice began to crank into action and the jury was empanelled and sworn.

'Members of the jury, the prisoner at the bar, Andrew Ashberry, Earl of Fadmoor, is indicted and the charge against him is murder in that on the twenty-eighth of September, 1901, at Helmsley, in the County of Yorkshire, he murdered Lydia Bowden. Upon this indictment he has been arraigned, upon his arraignment he has pleaded that he is not guilty and has put himself upon his country, which country you are. It is for you to inquire whether he be guilty or not and to hearken to the evidence.' The clerk gave a little bow in the direction of Bloom and retreated back into the bowels of the court.

'May it please your lordship, members of the jury,' began opposing counsel as he clambered heavily to his feet. If the court was full of lean men, this wasn't one of them. George Wombwell KC had all the elegance of an elephant seal attempting to flop out of deep water onto sharp rocks.

The sharper the rocks the better, I hoped. I expected him to fall back at any moment barking onto the bench seat. But looks can be deceptive and I hadn't forgotten my previous bruising encounter with a then QC of similar proportions, Cuthbert Henge, in the Robertshaw trial. Henge had been a brilliant adversary.

'Miss Lydia Bowden disappeared on the morning of the twenty-eighth of September, 1901, the day after her engagement to the Earl of Fadmoor at his family seat, Ashberry Hall,' continued Wombwell in a smart London drawl. 'To say a relationship between a tenant farmer's daughter and a peer of the realm wasn't one made in heaven would be an understatement. Although hosting the Earl's lavish engagement party, privately the Ashberry family were very much set against the match. Indeed the Earl himself seemed to regard both his future bride and their forthcoming nuptials with, to say the least, a cavalier attitude. It is the Crown's intention to explain the reasons for the prisoner's unusual attitude and bring forth evidence showing how his hand had been forced into this unfortunate union. Miss Bowden's body was found on ...' Wombwell's fat fingers shuffled around in his notes. 'Here it is. Her body was found by an officer in the North Riding Constabulary at the bottom of one of two pits on the Ashberry Estate, otherwise known as a Ryedale Windypit, on the first day of July, 1905. She had been missing for over three years ...'

'Almost three years and nine months exactly, my lord,' I piped up.

'Please, Mr Cairn, do not interrupt counsel when he is in the middle of his opening speech,' rasped Bloom.

'Sorry, my lord, I was only trying to be helpful.' My bottom lip jutted out in mannered sulkiness to the amusement of my team.

'I stand corrected by my esteemed learned friend,' assuaged Wombwell with a smile. 'My learned friend who, I believe, had first hand knowledge of the condition of the body as he was present at its discovery having been seconded by the police to explore the cave. It would seem that counsel for the defence is known locally as an excellent mountaineer.'

'He'll need to be to conquer this case,' tittered Wombwell's junior.

'So if it pleases the court and Mr Cairn, allow me to continue. This unfortunate young woman's body was found in a partially mummified state due to the peculiar climatic condition during her three years and *nine months* entombment,' emphasised Wombwell, simpering across at me. 'The body's excellent state of preservation allowed the pathologist to give a detailed analysis of her condition prior to death. He concluded that Miss Bowden had died from strangulation at the hands of another, most probably before being disposed of down into that dark miserable hell.'

'He's laying it on a bit thick, isn't he?' Trotter's breath wafted down the back of my neck. Trotter was seated on the bench behind, next to Robert

Brown. Thomas Leacock, who had agreed to help out in Fadmoor's defence, was seated next to me.

'Don't underestimate this man,' I whispered back to Trotter.

'I don't,' he replied. 'He's not lost a single case since taking silk.'

'How long has he been a KC?'

'QC, KC, too many years,' sighed Trotter.

'The Crown intends to show that Andrew Ashberry waylaid Miss Bowden on her way home sometime during the twenty-eighth of September. Perhaps under the guise of a lovers' tryst, he enticed her up the forested lane to that isolated spot known as Ashberry Pits. Here he cynically and callously strangled her before throwing her down one of the pits to conceal his foul deed. We will show he had a sound motive for seeing his fiancée dead, and we will lay before you evidence linking him to the scene. I will be ably assisted by my learned friend, Mr Justin Reed. We have spared you a great deal of detail which it will be necessary to call to your attention later, but there you have a brief outline of the prosecution's case. Permit us to call the evidence before you,' concluded Wombwell, crashing back onto the bench we shared. The bench juddered its entire length as if experiencing an earthquake.

Puppet-like, Justin Reed was on his feet as Dick Tate was sworn in. If Wombwell was bumbling and fat, Reed appeared youthful, energetic and was unquestionably reed-like.

'Doctor Tate, you are the senior pathologist at the General Infirmary, Leeds, are you not and an expert in the forensic sciences?' he asked without further ado.

'I am.'

'Did you examine the body of a young woman in July of last year?'

'I did.'

'Did you feel this young woman had died of natural causes?'

'No, I did not.'

'How so?'

'She had a small depressed fracture in the right temporal bone.'

'Caused by a blow?'

'Possibly a blow or a fall. But in addition the hyoid bone in her neck was fractured, consistent with strangulation.'

'"Strangulation"?'

'Yes. I would suggest the deceased died of asphyxiation caused by manual strangulation.'

'Throttling at the hands of another, do you mean?'

'Yes.'

'Would you be kind enough to tell the court more about this hyoid bone, Doctor Tate?'

'Otherwise known as the lingual bone it is a horseshoe shaped bone located just about here.' Dick pointed to a spot above his own Adam's apple. 'It is situated in the anterior midline of the neck above the thyroid cartilage.'

'Was Miss Bowden wearing anything that might have caused this fatal injury during her fall? Such as a scarf catching on a piece of rock say?'

'She had a diamond cross pendant about her neck but that would have broken if caught on anything or tightened with any force.'

'"Force", you say?' Reed obviously put great weight on emotional emphasis.

'Yes, to break the hyoid bone of a young person would have taken considerable strength.'

'Such as a rugby player might possess?'

'My lord, I must protest ...' Assisting Thomas Leacock sprang to his feet.

'Mr Reed,' warned Bloom.

'So, the fact that a valuable pendant was left in place discounts theft, wouldn't you say, Doctor Tate?' Young Reed was apparently a master of deflection too.

'I am not qualified to make such judgments,' replied Dick resolutely.

'No, but you are well qualified in the science of pathology, are you not?' Reed's question came out more as a statement. A self-evident truth that Dick didn't trouble himself to answer. 'Tell the court and gentlemen of the jury, did you find anything else of interest, Doctor Tate?'

'The deceased showed signs of an early pregnancy.'

'How early?' asked Reed.

'The foetus appeared to be approximately three months in development.'

The court fizzed and buzzed over this. Journalists' pencils scratched on notepads. Thelonious Bloom frowned.

'Am I to understand that you found a dead child within the body of the deceased?' he asked.

'Yes, my lord, I'm afraid I did.'

'Two lives destroyed by one brutal act of murder, isn't that so?' continued Reed.

'Yes.'

'My lord, I would like to draw your attention, and the gentlemen of the jury's attention, to Exhibit Five.' Reed instructed the usher to initially present Dick with Exhibit Five. 'Do you recognise the piece of jewellery before you?'

'Yes, I do.'

'And when did you last see this cufflink.'

'During my post-mortem examination. I found it clasped in the deceased's fist.'

'A gold cufflink found in the prisoner's dead fiancée's hand bearing two interlocking A's, isn't that so?'

'Yes,' confirmed Dick.

Reed nodded to the usher to pass the cufflink next to his lordship and then to the jury.

'A's, which I suggest stand for the initials Andrew Ashberry,' commented Reed. He gave the hushed court time to suck this in before announcing, 'I have no more questions for Doctor Tate.'

'Doctor Tate, allow me to clarify that you actually performed the post-mortem yourself in Leeds, is that not so?' Leacock struggled to his feet gamely.

'Yes, sir, I did,' replied Dick. Following his previous damning testimony, did I detect a slight hint of relief that it wasn't me cross-examining him?

'Not *in situ* then?' reaffirmed Leacock.

'No, I believe only the most experienced climbers were able to reach the victim's body *in situ*,' smiled Dick.

'Although as soon as possible after recovery from the Windypit, Miss Bowden's body was transported by train to you at the General Infirmary in Leeds, is that correct?'

'That's right.'

'Some sixty miles or so?'

'Approximately, I should imagine.'

'Was there much deterioration in the corpse's condition by the time it reached your post-mortem room?'

'No, not really, because of the mummification.'

'And this did not hinder your findings?'

'No. If anything it helped to preserve her.'

'But this unusual state of preservation would preclude any possible signs of petechiae, would it not?'

'"Petechiae"?' queried Bloom.

'Petechial haemorrhaging, my lord, small red spots found in the eyes or on the face usually associated with strangulation,' explained Leacock.

'Cases are becoming so technical these days,' sighed Bloom, to the court's amusement.

'I can attest, my lord, that these spots can be extremely difficult to find even in the best of circumstances and usually require strong lighting,' explained Dick.

'So, apart from a blow to the head and damage to the hyoid bone there was no other apparent trauma to Miss Bowden's body,' asked Leacock rather desperately.

'I think the force applied to fracture that bone would be enough to kill anyone,' said Dick.

'Have I got this right, death wasn't actually caused by damage to the hyoid but pressure on the windpipe?' enquired Bloom.

'Exactly so, my lord, the fracture merely indicates the power involved,' elucidated Dick.

'Face to face, would you say?' asked Leacock.

'Sorry, I don't understand,' said Dick.

'Would Miss Bowden's assailant have been looking at her as he pressed his hands round her neck?'

'Yes, he could well have been,' said Dick.

'A very intimate crime then, would you say?'

'I would,' agreed Dick.

'Finally, Doctor Tate, would you be good enough to reaffirm that you are ninety-nine per cent certain that Miss Bowden's fatal injury couldn't have been caused by an accidental fall down into the pit?'

'Almost impossible.'

'Tell me, did you find any other broken bones during your examination of the deceased?'

'Yes, she had a spiral fracture to her left femur.'

'So, even if she had been alive, she wouldn't have been able to climb out of the Windypit?'

Not without ropes, I sighed to myself.

'No, not with a broken femur,' Dick told Leacock. Adding cynically, 'nor after being strangled to death.'

'No more questions,' Leacock quietly bowed out.

'Find the father of the child, find the murderer,' murmured Brown from his row behind.

'I think we will take this opportunity to adjourn for lunch,' said Bloom, rising in his swathe of scarlet.

* * * * *

Lunch was a rather gloomy affair for our defence team at the Golden Fleece Inn, known only as the Fleece to those regular legal frequenters, black shoes tapping across the stone tiles to recharge their glasses, desperate to take the opportunity of just one more before the afternoon sittings.

Apart from the contemporary imbibing judiciary, this three storey building of Flemish-bonded brickwork had an even more colourful past. The beheading of Thomas Percy, a Tudor Catholic recusant, took place on 17th August, 1572, on the Pavement just opposite my present window seat. It was carried out by Edward Blackwell, who travelled to York to do his queen's bidding. No doubt for a fat purse and a comfortable night's stay at the inn, a very different timber-framed house then I suspected.

'Things don't look good,' Trotter, ever the pessimist, was saying to Thomas Leacock.

'I did my best,' retorted Leacock. 'The medical witness was implacable.'

'Oh, Dick's that all right,' I put in wearily.

'Bloody clever too,' said Robert Brown. 'Do you remember how he got to the bottom of the forensic evidence in the Robertshaw case?'

I left them to argue the toss as I mulled over my own memories of Dick's disclosures regarding the strangulation of Estelle Parke during my defence of Daniel Robertshaw. Dick had been on my side then. Estelle's murder had been a very different affair to this, she had been garrotted from behind. The words *face to face* kept impinging on my imagination – *face to face* is a familiar concept – *face to face* is a very personal crime. This did nothing to rule out my client, Andrew Ashberry, of course, but there were several other possibilities it didn't exclude either.

'More wine,' offered Brown.

Putting my hand over my glass, I pointed out that I needed a clear head for the afternoon session.

'Mr Cuthbert Henge maintained that a glass or two at midday always helped him to elicit the truth,' said Trotter.

'If my memory serves me well, truth wasn't Mr Henge's main objective – winning was,' I retorted.

Trotter and Brown chuntered on. I meanwhile had a problem. I was reminded of when I was a small boy and my mother had given me a Betts' jigsaw puzzle, *The Parable of the Sower*. I had just stared at the wooden pieces in total confusion. Finally, my small fingers had attempted to fumble the few irregular pieces into one picture. The Ashberry case was like an even more complicated jigsaw puzzle – so many separate pieces – that refused to fall into place. Frederick Ashberry had had a long time affair with Lydia's mother, a tenant farmer's wife. He had privately admitted to me that Lydia was his daughter. What about slighted Reginald Bowden then? How did he really feel about being cuckolded? – being Lydia's father in name only? He was due to stand in the witness box after lunch. If both Lydia and Malcolm were the unacknowledged children of the Marquess, then they shared the same father as Andrew, Stephen and the late Gerard Ashberry. Lydia was Andrew's half-sister. The blood ties were close, too close. Both Mary Bowden and the Marquess had done their best to discourage the match. Ultimately, the marriage between Lydia and Andrew could never have gone ahead. The trouble was Mary and the Marquess were trying to end the match without revealing their guilty secret. Mary suspected that Gerard too had unknowingly fallen in love with Lydia. Perhaps he had, perhaps because of their confused genetics – the likenesses – Gerard had confused homologous chemistry with love.

Chapter Twenty-Nine

'Call Reginald Bowden,' cried the clerk of assize.

Reginald had done little to improve his appearance for the court. Where his cardigan previously had several moth dinners eaten into it, today I saw only one hole at the elbow of his old tweed jacket. Someone must have been busy with needle and thread. His thin face however was still neither bearded nor clean shaven but had a grizzled appearance. Unkempt, for all the world to see, he stood there a man unloved – a man who didn't even love himself.

'I would like to express my and I am sure the rest of the court's condolences for your sad loss,' began Wombwell.

'Eh?' mumbled Reginald gruffly.

'Your loss, sir. Your daughter,' reiterated Wombwell.

'Thank you,' said with a sullen reluctance. 'I thought you meant the missus there for one moment.'

'Of course for your loss of the late Mrs Mary Bowden as well,' commiserated Wombwell: counsel for the prosecution was nothing if not thorough.

'Might I enquire what your wife died of, sir?' asked Bloom.

'The pox,' mumbled Reginald.

'What did he say?' asked Bloom again.

'The witness has just explained that his wife died of syphilis, my lord,' translated Wombwell.

The court fizzed and buzzed again.

'And are you yourself affected by the disease?' pressed Bloom.

'No, nor did she get it from me,' spat out Reginald.

'Oh, I see,' exclaimed Bloom, looking askance across at prosecuting counsel.

'Now can you tell the court and the gentlemen of the jury when you last saw your daughter?' continued Wombwell smoothly, too smoothly, surely he wouldn't let this opportunity pass as to who had infected Mary Bowden.

'The day of the party at the big 'ouse. The day our Lydia pledged herself to 'im,' Reginald nodded across at the prisoner in the dock in disgust.

'Now we are talking about Friday, twenty-seventh of September, 1901, are we not?'

'Aye, summat like that.'

Wombwell and his lordship let this go.

'Was your daughter in good spirits at the prospect of her engagement to the prisoner?' Wombwell asked instead.

'Aye, our Lydia was alus of good heart, made the best of things.'

'Are you expressing some reservation as to her state of mind regarding her engagement, Mr Bowden?'

'Well, as you ask and looking back on it, her mother did say our lass had been a bit quiet of late.'

'So Miss Bowden wasn't completely happy at the prospect of marrying the prisoner?'

'That's right, she did seem as if summat was up from time to time.'

'Could it be that the prisoner, your future son-in-law, had learnt that his intended might have syphilis and the unborn child in her belly likewise?' asked Wombwell. 'A good reason for murdering her, I would have thought.'

'My lord, my learned friend is calling for a conclusion from this witness which he is not qualified to give,' I interrupted.

'The jury will disregard counsel for the prosecution's last comment,' instructed Bloom.

'Thank you, Mr Bowden, I'll not trouble you anymore,' announced Wombwell, glaring gleefully across at me.

'Mr Bowden,' I remained standing. 'I do appreciate what an ordeal this must be for you but in the interests of truth and justice I must ask you a few questions.' Reginald nodded a sort of half-recognition. Whether or not it was acceptance of the questions I was about to ask or actual personal recognition, I was unable to tell. 'Now, sir, would you be kind enough to tell the court how you felt about your daughter's engagement to Lord Fadmoor?'

'Can't say I was bothered one way or t' other.'

'You weren't concerned about her making an unhappy match?'

'It didn't matter what I thought. She alus went her own way, they both did.'

'By both, do you mean Lydia and her brother, Malcolm?'

'That's right.'

'Did you attend the engagement party at the Hall on Friday, twenty-seventh of September, 1901?' I asked, already knowing full well the answer.

'No, I wasn't invited.'

'What, you weren't invited to your daughter's engagement party? Why was that?'

'I wouldn't have wanted to go any rate,' shrugged Reginald.

'Was that because the Ashberrys had plans to quarry land tenanted by you?'

'That's right,' replied Reginald, more warily this time. 'They wanted to take the whole lot.'

'But you had no objection to your daughter marrying into a family with designs on your land?' I made no attempt to conceal my incredulity. 'Land that your ancestors had worked for generations.'

'What could I do? I only rent the land.'

'You could have objected. You have rights the same as any man, particularly grazing rights on common land.'

'Do I really?'

'Yes, sir, you do.'

'Hasn't happened yet though, has it?' cackled Reginald, grinning one or two good teeth.

'No, sir, it hasn't because other events have superseded its importance.'

'That's right, that's right,' cackled Reginald shrewdly again.

'Permit me, my lord, to take this opportunity to read out an anonymous letter that was posted to Mr Robert Brown, the defendant's solicitor, almost a year ago. Exhibit Eight,' I instructed the court usher.

'And has it a bearing on this case?' enquired Bloom.

'Yes, my lord, very much so. Exhibit Eight caused the police to reinvestigate Lydia Bowden's disappearance.'

'Then please proceed, counsel,' instructed Bloom.

'"Dear Sir",' I began, '"I understand that you are the legal man who acts for the Marquess of Hambleton and his brood. Let me tell you, sir, you are representing a hornet's nest. At best the Ashberrys are driven by avarice." Would you say that is an accurate assessment of the Ashberrys, Mr Bowden?'

'How should I know,' shrugged Reginald.

'"The Marquess plans to rob many of his tenant farmers of their livelihoods by selling off land to quarry for stone." That refers to you, does it not, Mr Bowden? You are one of those tenants, are you not? In fact you are the tenant with most to lose, isn't that so?' This time Reginald chose not to answer at all. '"But more than this",' I continued reading. '"He is culpable in the gross crime of filicide, not just a son but a daughter too." *Filicide*? Now what on earth does the author of this vilification mean by that?' Reginald shook his head. '"Take my advice, sir, and withdraw your services before it is too late." This was the writer's recommendation to the Earl of Fadmoor's solicitor. The note is signed, "Yours faithfully, A Well Wisher." Are you that Well Wisher, Mr Bowden? Did you write this?'

'No, I did not,' roared Reginald; the sleeping lion was waking at last.

'I have no more questions for this witness, my lord.' I smiled back across at Wombwell as I took my seat.

Smug Beardsley was next up. How I hated this man.

'You are the Right Honourable John Beardsley, and represent this city in Parliament, do you not?' asked Wombwell. Senior counsel for the prosecution wasn't leaving this peach for his junior to chew at.

'Yes, I do.' Beardsley smoothed back his already slicked back dark hair.

'Did you see that? Did you see that?' muttered Brown. 'The self-satisfied swine.'

'And are you acquainted with the prisoner over there in the dock,' asked Wombwell.

'Yes, I am. I have known him most of my life, since we were lads at school together.'

'Was the prisoner a popular boy at school?' asked Wombwell.

'Well, he …'

'Were you friends?'

'Well, no, not exactly,' hesitated Beardsley.

'Mr Beardsley the court isn't really interested in the minutiae of your personal feelings,' censured Bloom, who from his expression was determined not to be impressed by Beardsley or his position. 'Please do not digress from a simple "yes" or "no" where possible to counsel's questions.'

'Well, no, I wouldn't say I was an intimate friend of Andrew Ashberry's at school.'

'So, you wouldn't regard yourself as being in the Earl's group of chums as a youngster?'

'No, they were extremely esoteric in their philosophy, shall we say.'

'Ah, esoteric, from the Greek *esoterikos*, meaning belonging to an inner circle.'

'Yes.'

'The Ancient Greeks had a certain way of looking at things, did they not?' Wombwell smirked.

'Yes,' replied Beardsley.

'In addition to *esoterikos*, they felt that love between boys and boys and boys and older men was acceptable behaviour, did they not?'

'Yes they did.'

I heard Trotter's groan behind me.

'To say the Earl and his friends shared an esoteric philosophy is a polite way of saying they did not believe in behaving like other boys, is that not so?'

'That is correct,' replied Beardsley. 'They were sexual inverts, the whole lot of 'em. Andrew Ashberry was particularly well-known for his sexual inversion at school and beyond.'

The court protested its collective abhorrence of anything Greek. Immediately I was on my feet.

'My lord, this is outrageous. This is an unsubstantiated slur on my client's character and reputation.'

'Might I remind the witness that the allegation he is making is a serious one,' pointed out Bloom. 'Given royal assent by Her Majesty Queen Victoria in 1886, the Criminal Law Amendment Act 1885 outlawed sexual relations between men in England.'

'But, my lord, it was well known at my school that Ashberry was a sissy,' persisted Beardsley.

'Was he homosexual though?' persisted Bloom.

'He was, my lord. From his first term at school he was regarded as fag meat by the prefects and older boys.'

'"Fag meat"? I have not heard that term before,' quipped the bemused judge. 'Even though, hard as it may seem now, I too enjoyed the infinite pleasures of once being a small vulnerable boy in our public school system.'

'My lord, throughout his whole time at school Ashberry's courtesy title was corrupted to "Fagmoor",' persisted Beardsley.

No one laughed, certainly not the judge.

'*Corrupt, corrupted*, perhaps these words should carry more weight and meaning than "fag meat" or "Fagmoor" in this courtroom today, Mr Beardsley.' Bloom frowned. I looked at his lordship in a new light. I felt like applauding this fellow sufferer of an English education.

'Puh! All this from Beardsley who was useless at rugby,' roared Frederick Ashberry in disgust. 'Beardsley, who couldn't catch the bloody football for the life of 'im. Bawled his eyes out every time he was tumbled.'

I could not help mentally applauding this too, finally seeing a fault line developing between the old business partnership of the Marquess and Beardsley. Perhaps here was something that could be exploited.

'Order! Order!' screamed Bloom, struggling to restore a semblance of command. 'I'll not have dissention from the public gallery from whatever source.'

Meanwhile the Marquess' son's prison pallor turned to green. Andrew slumped in the dock, water was fetched.

Beardsley stood in the dock shaking his head after his dressing down, still insisting, 'It is the truth, my lord. I have only told the truth.'

'Mr Beardsley, unless you can provide factual evidence of an indecent act or acts taking place between the Earl of Fadmoor and X, I must insist that you desist from making these serious, if flimsy, allegations or I will be forced to hold you in contempt,' Bloom told him. 'And I would like to remind you, Mr Wombwell, that the prisoner is not indicted here today for homosexuality but for the capital offence of murder. Please try to keep any future questions relevant to this case.'

'I will, my lord,' replied Wombwell, bowing with fake reverence. 'Mr Beardsley, did you ever observe the prisoner showing any genuine affection towards Miss Lydia Bowden?'

'No, never. He had no interest in her,' grunted Beardsley. 'How could he have?'

'I have no more questions for this witness, my lord.' Wombwell scratched his rather large bottom with satisfaction before taking his seat.

'How vulgar,' muttered Trotter from behind.

'Never mind that,' I whispered back, struggling to my feet to make amends. 'Wombwell knows the seed has been planted in the jury's mind, the damage done.'

Beardsley writhed uneasily in the witness box as I held off until I judged my timing was perfection.

'Did you?' I finally weighed-in.

'Did I what?' retorted Beardsley edgily.

'Have any interest in Lydia Bowden?'

'Of course not,' he snapped.

'Perhaps you would be good enough to tell the court, sir, why you offered to stand bail for the defendant if he was such a disreputable character at school?'

'Well, I ...'

'Please answer the question,' instructed Bloom, on his mettle now.

'I felt sorry for him.'

'Well, well, sorry for a man you've just accused in open court of being a sodomist, is that not so?' I asked. Beardsley made no reply. 'Wonders will never cease,' I muttered. 'Tell me, did you confide your and the Marquess' intention to start a quarry on the Ashberry Estate to this man you felt so sorry for?'

'No, I did not.'

'Why not?'

'We just never got round to it.'

'You didn't ask the future heir of the Ashberry Estate for obvious reasons, did you?'

'What obvious reasons?'

'Why, the Earl was about to marry the daughter of a tenant whom you were intending to kick off his farm and land for your scheme to be realised, isn't that so?'

'It simply never occurred to us.'

'"Us"?'

'The Marquess and me.'

'No, I don't expect it did.'

'It was the Marquess' business if and when he decided to inform his son.'

'Nevertheless, it would have suited your own personal business ambition to have both Lydia Bowden and Andrew Ashberry out of the way, would it not?'

'Now look here.' Beardsley appeared flustered.

Wombwell waddled onto his feet.

'My learned friend isn't just leading this witness, he is trying to lead him into deep water,' he objected.

'I would suggest, Mr Wombwell, we are merely in the shallows at present,' smiled Bloom. 'I feel there is much further to go in this trial. Because of the importance of Mr Cairn's question, I am going to allow it in this instance. Please answer counsel's for the defence's question, Mr Beardsley.'

'No,' snarled Beardsley.

'No? No you will not answer or having Miss Bowden and the Earl out of the way would have been of no benefit to you?' I asked.

'You're talking nonsense.'

'Am I, sir? The same sort of schoolboy nonsense you've delivered here, today, in your crude and vicious attempt to assassinate the good name and character of the Earl of Fadmoor.'

'Please, Mr Beardsley, answer counsel's original question,' intervened Bloom.

'I had no wish for Miss Bowden and the Earl to be out of the way.' Beardsley sounded bored but the razor parting in his slicked back hair looked rumpled, less sharp.

'You finally have your answer, Mr Cairn,' muttered Bloom disparagingly.

'Though it was like drawing blood from a stone,' scoffed Leacock.

'I have no more questions for this witness at the present time but I might wish to recall him at a later date, my lord.' I quickly regained my seat, fearing further Wombwell recriminations.

'Before we adjourn for today,' said Bloom, 'I would like to take this opportunity to ask the jury to disregard all Mr Beardsley's references to the prisoner's sexuality. Mr Wombwell, your anti-character witness provided not a shred of factual evidence to substantiate what amounts to nothing more than a schoolboy slander based on innuendo and tittle-tattle. I will further remind you that you have simply wasted the court's time. Should the accused be acquitted of the capital offence for which he is indicted, then it will be up to his legal representatives to decide whether they wish to pursue this matter further. I would like to see you, Mr Wombwell, in my chamber forthwith.'

Bottom scratching Wombwell didn't look quite so satisfied anymore.

* * * * *

Although I had scored a small victory regarding Beardsley and his testimony, I felt gloomy about the overall prospects of an Ashberry acquittal.

I faced a cold miserable night ahead of me in Gillygate. Kate had taken the night off again. Indeed since my clumsy attempt at romance, she had been taking more and more nights off at short notice. For both our sakes, I would have to consider asking her to leave if things continued as they were. But for the present the Ashberry trial was consuming my thoughts there alone in my sitting room.

Taking a slurp of brandy, I dismissed the bitchy evidence of John Beardsley as the judge had done, as I hoped the jury would do but I wasn't so sure about them. Beardsley had gone too far casting Andrew as a villainous sodomite. Sodomite he might be but a villain I doubted very much. Still, we would have to wait and see what transpired in this case. In short, although I was sure there was a good deal of truth in some of Beardsley's allegations, he had overplayed his hand. What a strange business it all was – the complicated relationships between Andrew and Chatterton, the Ashberrys and the Bowdens – the ambiguity of the cuckolded Reginald Bowden's position, his apparent indifference. "She alus went her own way, they both did," he had said referring to Lydia and her brother. What did he exactly mean by that? What did this man of the earth truly feel bringing up children sired by his landlord?

Surely, Reginald Bowden had as much cause for murder as anyone. He wasn't even invited to his "daughter's" engagement party but then neither was brother Malcolm. Both Bowden men were men never at the party.

Somehow the prosecution had veered round Frederick Ashberry's part in all this. They had skirted round the obvious question: if Bowden hadn't given his wife syphilis then who had? Examining my reflection there in the brandy glass, I wondered how much longer we could keep the Marquess' paternity out of this trial.

Chapter Thirty

'Call Malcolm Bowden.'

'Mr Bowden, you are the younger brother of the late Lydia Bowden, are you not?' Wombwell commenced battle on that bleak January morning.

'I am, sir.'

'Would you be good enough to tell the court what the age difference was between you and your sister?'

'Just two years. Lydia was twenty-two when she disappeared, I would be twenty.'

'Both in your prime of life then?'

'We were.'

'And by all accounts your sister was a beautiful young woman, was she not?' Following his interview with the judge, a more sober looking Wombwell beamed amiably round the court. At any rate, compared with his examination of John Beardsley yesterday, he appeared to feel himself on safer ground questioning the deceased's brother.

'Yes, she was very beautiful,' confirmed Malcolm.

'And can you tell the court when you last saw her?'

'Like my father said I last saw Lydia on the day of her engagement party.'

'No, no,' cut in Bloom. 'You can only speak for yourself.'

'Then I saw her on the day of her engagement party,' repeated Malcolm. Sullen, handsome Malcolm standing, I imagined, with feet planted firmly apart in the witness box. He looked like a Wolds' tree prepared to withstand any storm thrown at him. Of all the Marquess' progeny, apart from Lydia herself, this was by far the finest physical specimen.

'You were very close, you and your sister, were you not?' asked Wombwell.

'Of course.'

'I expect there were few secrets between you?'

'Few.'

'Did you know Lydia was expecting a child?'

'Yes.'

'How did you feel about that?'

'My opinion hardly mattered. It was how she felt about it that was all important.'

'And how did she feel about it?' asked Wombwell.

'I couldn't rightly say,' shrugged Malcolm.

But hang on, I thought. Did Malcolm know about the affair between the Marquess and his mother? Did Malcolm know his sister was pregnant with her half-brother's child? Did he realise there was another bastard child on the way, an Ashberry bastard as he himself was? How could he bear the thought of Lydia unknowingly marrying her half-brother while carrying her half-brother's child? If he did know, could he live with that secret? The thought of Lydia marrying into the Ashberry clan whose head, Frederick Ashberry, had cuckolded Reginald Bowden – Reginald whom he, Malcolm, had always mistakenly believed was his real father. And if he did know how he must have hated the Ashberry clan, when they had enjoyed all the best things in life while he always had to make do.

'Thank you, Mr Bowden,' Wombwell was saying.

'Mr Bowden, were you aware of the Marquess of Hambleton's plans for a quarry on land you farmed?' I asked.

'I was. You could hardly keep a thing like that secret.'

'Did Lydia know?'

'Yes.'

'Did she tell you if her fiancé, the defendant, knew of his father's plans?'

'She didn't say.'

'But you were extremely close for brother and sister, weren't you, Mr Bowden? Lydia was your "soulmate", was she not?' I asked. I had not forgotten my and Winifred's encounter with Malcolm at Rievaulx Abbey.

'She was everything to me,' agreed Malcolm.

'Would you describe yourselves as inseparable?'

'We were.'

'So how did you feel about her expecting a baby to someone you considered unworthy of her?'

'I hadn't a notion if Ashberry was worthy of Lydia or not then. He was rich, I knew that.'

'Do you suspect it was the defendant's wealth that was the overriding attraction for Lydia too?'

'Lydia was justly using her condition as a lever to get her man to the altar. It has been done by women throughout history.'

'Her man being?'

'Her fiancé, Andrew Ashberry of course. Who else's kid would she be expecting?'

'I don't know, that is why I am asking you, Mr Bowden.'

'Lydia told me herself that the child was Ashberry's,' he snapped.

'How did you react to that?'

'I wasn't right pleased at first, to tell you the truth, but regarded it as Lydia's business whom she chose to marry.'

'Let me get this straight, you weren't happy with Lydia marrying Andrew Ashberry let alone carrying his child?'

'No, I wasn't.'

'But less than a moment ago, you told my learned friend for the prosecution that you weren't sure how you felt about your sister's pregnancy.'

'The man's an obvious fairy,' muttered Malcolm.

'Mr Bowden!' warned Bloom, quicker off the mark this time than he had been with Beardsley.

'You only have to look at him, him and his fancy man.' Malcolm would not be silenced, now he had an audience it was all spilling out. 'He always had more time for Louis Chatterton than our Lydia.'

'Mr Bowden, I'll not warn you again,' growled Bloom. 'Although I understand you are under a great deal of strain having lost your sister in the most horrific circumstances, I'll not allow you to use this court to air unsubstantiated allegations against the prisoner or his companions.'

'Tell me, was it you who bought your sister, your "soulmate",' I emphasised a second time, 'the diamond cross pendant found on her body?'

'No.'

'Do you know who did?'

'No, I presumed it was a gift from Andrew Ashberry.'

'Lydia told him it was a gift from you.'

'That's ridiculous. Where would I get the money to buy such a thing?'

'Did you feel Lydia was bringing shame on your family?' I asked.

'You could say that,' mumbled Malcolm.

'Please speak clearly. Answer "yes" or "no" or say if you don't understand the question.' Thelonious Bloom hadn't finished with the misanthropic young farmer yet.

'Yes.' Malcolm sulked again.

'You do realise you have just put forward the perfect motive for murder?' I suggested. The court held it breath.

'Puh! For family honour, Bowden family honour?' exploded Malcolm. 'You can think what you like, Mr Cairn, proving it is an entirely different matter.'

'What you are doing, Mr Bowden, is demonstrating to this court and the gentlemen of the jury that you are a man with an extremely quick temper.'

'Am I?' ridiculed Malcolm.

'Did you kill Lydia because she was carrying the defendant's child?' I asked above the room's rising hubbub.

'Would I kill just for that?'

'That is a question only you can answer, Mr Bowden.'

'Why would I kill my own sister?'

'"Yes" or "no",' insisted Bloom.

'Of course not,' spat out Malcolm.

'I might wish to recall this witness too at a later date, if your lordship pleases.'

'You are going to have a whole army of the recalled, I can see, Mr Cairn. So be it, though it is rather irregular this court's priority is to get to the truth,' sighed Bloom, before turning back to Malcolm. 'Maybe if there is a next time, Mr Bowden, you will have learnt to compose yourself and be less hostile to the court.'

I looked to the jury, to the public gallery to see how Malcolm Bowden's testimony had been received. My slow intake of breath switched to a gasp. I could hardly believe what I was seeing. Almost losing my balance I staggered a foot or two forward. Winifred was up there in the gallery staring down on me like some ethereal goddess. So she had come back from Paris. She was here.

'Are you all right, James?' Leacock tugged me down by my sleeve.

'Yes, yes, I'm fine,' I told him.

'I swear by Almighty God that the evidence I shall give ... ' Inglis hesitated to adjust his monocle. His moustache twitched as he struggled to find his bearings in the courtroom.

'You are James Brown Inglis and you have a jewellery shop in this city's Coney Street, do you not?' asked Reed.

'Yes, I do.'

'Can you tell the gentlemen of the jury and the court what happened one Wednesday afternoon back in 1901?'

Like a police officer Inglis reached out a black leather notebook from his coat pocket, saying, 'Yes, I can exactly.'

'Have these diary entries been submitted as evidence?' asked Bloom.

'Indeed they have, my lord,' replied Reed, instructing the usher to supply the judge with a copy of the relevant material. 'Good, good, I see you are a man who keeps a diary,' approved junior counsel for the prosecution, turning his attention back to Inglis.

'It was during the afternoon of the sixth of November, when a Mr Louis Chatterton came into my shop to sell me an extremely valuable engagement ring. I immediately recognised it as the same ring I had sold to the Earl of Fadmoor only a couple of months before.'

'And did you know Mr Chatterton was a legitimate friend of the prisoner's?'

'Yes, I had seen them together about York numerous times. And, indeed, on this occasion I saw that the Earl was waiting outside for Mr Chatterton.'

'But he chose not to come into your shop himself?'

'That's correct.'

'Did you not think this was rather strange behaviour?'

'I did.'

'Were you surprised that the prisoner was attempting to sell back his fiancée's ring through the services of Mr Chatterton?'

'Yes, very. I had read that the Earl's fiancée had been missing for little more than five weeks.'

'Rather precipitous, would you say?'

'Yes, personally, I thought so.'

'Thank you, Mr Inglis.' Reed flicked back his gown like a tail.

'Mr Inglis, did anything else unusual happen during that afternoon in November, 1901?' asked Leacock.

'Shortly after Mr Chatterton left another young man came in questioning me about the same transaction.'

'About Lydia Bowden's engagement ring?'

'Yes, that's right.'

'And was this person known to you?'

'No, I had never seen him before in my life. However, would you believe, I am sure I've just crossed paths with him on the floor of this courtroom.'

'Do you mean the previous witness?'

'I do.'

'Is he in this room now?'

Placing his monocle carefully against his eye, Inglis looked around the room before replying 'no'.

'I believe Mr Inglis is referring to Malcolm Bowden, the deceased's brother, my lord,' said Leacock.

'I believe you are right,' replied Bloom. 'Should you feel this has relevance to the defence's case then you are free to seek clarification.'

'I shall bear that in mind, my lord,' replied Leacock, before turning to the usher and requesting Exhibit Seventeen. 'Mr Inglis, do you recognise this diamond cross pendant?' Leacock was going alone here as he dangled Lydia's necklace on its long chain from his fingers.

'I can't quite see,' complained Inglis, peering forward.

'Please,' Leacock nodded to the usher to present the witness with the exhibit for closer scrutiny.

'Yes, I do recognise it,' confirmed Inglis. 'It's a particularly lovely piece this.'

'And was it once part of your stock too.'

'Yes.'

'And might I enquire who bought it from you?'

'Yes, the Earl's younger brother, Gerard Ashberry.'

'When did he buy the pendant from you?'

'Shortly before the Earl bought his fiancée the ring.'

'Days, weeks, before?'

'No more than a week or two. I can check accurately for you if you like,' offered Inglis, reaching for his diary again.

'No, please don't trouble, the fact that it was bought shortly before the defendant purchased the ring will do.'

'I must say I was somewhat bemused by the whole business,' admitted Inglis.

'Why was that?' asked Leacock.

'Lord Gerard had insisted that under no circumstances was I to tell anyone that he had been a customer.'

'In short, he had sworn you to secrecy.'

'Yes, he had. And then when the Earl of Fadmoor bought the ring, I merely assumed Lord Gerard had intended to surprise his future sister-in-law with an engagement gift of his own.'

'Or even some other young lady?'

'Possibly so.'

'But the pendant was bought ahead of the ring,' stressed Leacock.

'Yes, sir.'

The tall distinguished figure of Timon White next stood in the witness box.

'You are an inspector in the North Riding Constabulary, are you not?' Reed began his examination.

'I am, sir.'

'Can you tell the court how you first became involved in Miss Lydia Bowden's disappearance?'

'Well,' exhaled White thoughtfully. White, it seemed, didn't need a little black book. 'Initially, the police believed she had just gone off, wedding nerves or something of that sort. It wasn't until Mr Robert Brown, the Ashberrys' solicitor, received a rather sinister anonymous note over three years later that my boss, Major Bower, asked me to reopen the case.'

'Which you did?'

'Yes, I found out that soon after his fiancée, Miss Bowden, had disappeared, the prisoner sold back her engagement ring to Mr Inglis in York. The deceased's brother, Malcolm Bowden, had followed the prisoner to the jeweller's premises.'

'So it was Mr Bowden who first told you of the prisoner's visit to Mr Inglis?'

'Yes, however Mr Bowden informed me that it was the prisoner's associate, Mr Louis Chatterton, who actually negotiated the sale of the ring while the prisoner remained outside the shop.'

'A rather cloak and dagger operation then?'

'Yes, somewhat,' granted White. 'When questioned the prisoner said that he had found the ring in his dead brother's, Lord Gerard Ashberry's pocket. He said that is why he'd wanted to get rid of it quickly and secretly.'

'But why secretly? Why should it have been in Gerard Ashberry's pocket following his shooting accident?' asked an unconvinced Reed.

'Baffled me too,' admitted White.

'Did you find the prisoner's behaviour very suspicious?'

'Extremely.'

'Please tell the court what happened next.'

'A few months after this it came to light that Miss Bowden's pet dog had been found dead above one of the Ashberry Pits. I immediately arranged to have the pits examined.'

'I believe, counsel for the defence, was involved in the recovery of Miss Bowden's remains, isn't that so?' smarmed Reed.

'Yes, Mr Cairn's climbing expertise was fundamental in retrieving Miss Bowden's body.'

'Can you tell us why you finally decided to arrest the prisoner?' continued Reed, niceties over.

'It was the cufflink, bearing the two interlocking A's, found in the deceased's grasp at post-mortem that provided me with the critical proof I needed.'

'Any questions Mr Cairn, Mr Leacock?' enquired his lordship.

We shook our heads like synchronised puppets.

* * * * *

After the afternoon session had closed, I looked everywhere in the building for Winifred but again she had disappeared, was gone. I had no idea where she was staying now. I consoled myself over a bottle of wine at my favourite public house with Leacock. The Black Swan in Peasholme Green had a fine fire burning on that January night but was almost empty of customers. There was no one in earshot to hear as I complimented Leacock on his cross-examination of Mr James Brown Inglis.

'How did you guess that the pendant and ring came from his shop?' I asked.

'Instinct, old boy,' he laughed. 'There was something about the style of both pieces of jewellery that would appeal to a certain taste.'

'A rich taste. A Mr James Brown Inglis' taste,' I suggested.

'No, no, I meant they are more in keeping with the Aesthetic period.'

'I didn't know you were an expert on women's jewellery, Thomas.'

'There is a lot you don't know about me, James,' replied Leacock, giving me one of his famous private smiles.

'What do you make of Gerard Ashberry buying his future sister-in-law such an expensive diamond cross pendant, and then insisting that the jeweller didn't tell any one?'

'Particularly his brother, one assumes.'

'Yes, quite so.'

'Were both brothers in love with the same girl, do you think?' offered Leacock, draining the last dregs of wine in one.

'I don't know yet but I intend to find out.'

'I am sure you will, James, but what about this for a scenario? – what if the child Lydia was expecting wasn't Andrew's at all but Gerard's?'

'That has also crossed my mind.'

'Just suppose,' continued Leacock, his imagination now well-lubricated by wine, 'Soldier Gerard returns from the war cynical and brutalised. He becomes obsessed with Lydia, the pure country girl. He forces himself upon her. To cover up the scandal of his brother's rape and his own sexual inversion, Andrew agrees to marry Lydia be it in name only. There is an additional complication because Lydia actually falls in love with the father of her coming child, the not-so-gallant officer.'

'The *late* Gerard Ashberry,' I point out.

'Yes, yes, I am coming to that,' enthused Leacock. I feared his imagination was on the cusp of really running riot now. 'Malcolm Bowden kills Gerard after arranging to meet him under false pretences in the Doric Temple. Somehow he has found out that Gerard raped his sister and she is expecting his child, not Andrew's.'

'Well, Lydia could have told Malcolm the truth herself. They were very close. But having a theory is one thing, proving it is another. Another glass for the road, Thomas?' I offered.

'No, no, I've only just got started,' objected Leacock. 'Then someone comes along to the Temple and interrupts ...' And so Leacock's hypotheses went on and on late into the night.

Chapter Thirty-One

'My lord, I would like to call the prisoner.' No opening speech from me, I had waived my right to an opening speech, I was indicating to the jury that the burden of proof rested with the prosecution in this case.

Andrew Ashberry was sworn in. He looked ill. His usually clean-shaven, cherubic cheeks looked in need of a razor. He was ashen as his hand trembled on the Bible.

'You are The Right Honourable Andrew Earl of Fadmoor?' I asked, immediately giving Andrew his formal title before the court.

'I am.'

'Did you know of your father's and John Beardsley's intention to drive your future in-laws from their farm and land in order to develop a stone quarry?'

'My lord, my learned friend is using unnecessarily emotive language,' objected Wombwell.

'Please rephrase your question, Mr Cairn,' his lordship asked me.

'Were you aware of your father's plans to quarry on land farmed by the Bowdens?'

'No, I was not.'

'Now much has been made by the prosecution of your arrangement to sell your fiancée's engagement ring back to Mr Inglis so soon after her disappearance. Can you tell the court and gentlemen of the jury the reason for your haste?'

'That's easy. I just wanted to get rid of the thing.'

'That ring was a link between Gerard and Lydia being in the Doric Temple together around the time of his death, am I correct in thinking?'

'Yes, I suppose it was,' Andrew reluctantly acknowledged.

'Your brother was dead and Lydia was missing. You were frightened of that ring and its implications, weren't you?'

'Yes, yes I was.'

'The reason for this will be made clear to the court in due course. However, Lord Fadmoor, can you confirm that you made a statement to the police saying that you found the ring in your dead brother's, Gerard's pocket?'

'Yes, I did.'

'This statement was untrue, was it not?'

'Yes.'

'You told a blatant lie to protect someone else, isn't that so?'

'Yes.'

'Hurrah, Cairn is doing our job for us,' sniped Wombwell at my hip.

'Did you know who gave Lydia the diamond cross pendant necklace?' I asked Andrew.

'Lydia told me that her brother, Malcolm, had given her it.'

'Not that your brother, Gerard, had?'

'No, I'm certain she said Malcolm had.'

'And there is no chance that you misheard or were mistaken?'

'None whatsoever.'

'So, your fiancée was less than honest with you?'

'So it seems,' agreed Andrew wearily.

'Do you think there was a possibility that Lydia was carrying Gerard's child?'

Andrew hesitated, shifting his weight from one foot to the other in the box.

'Please answer counsel's question,' instructed Bloom. 'And remember that you are under oath.'

'Yes, I was led to believe that Gerard had got Lydia pregnant.'

'Before you announced your engagement, I take it?'

'Yes, some weeks before.'

'Yet, you still went ahead with your plans to marry a woman carrying another man's child, indeed your brother's child?'

'Yes.'

'Why was that, Lord Fadmoor?'

'Because I liked Lydia very much and I felt sorry for her.'

'Isn't the truth of it that your late brother raped Lydia Bowden?'

'No, no. My brother had been badly disturbed by war and was capable of doing many things but not that, never that. Shortly after returning from Mafeking, Gerard had an affair with Lydia. Far from raping her, Lydia was captivated by my dashing younger brother. Unfortunately, his love and commitment fell far short of hers.'

'Did he request that she have an abortion?'

'Yes, but she flatly refused.'

'So to avoid a scandal you offered to marry her yourself, isn't that so?' I asked.

'Yes, I did.'

Here was a readymade wife and possible heir to the Ashberry dynasty without Andrew having to fulfil any abhorrent conjugal rights, I suddenly realised about to take my seat. Lydia would have made an extremely attractive mother – Gerard didn't want her – here was a perfect solution.

'Just one last question, My Lord,' I announced, unfurling to my full height again. 'Did you have any knowledge or involvement in the death of Lydia Bowden?'

'No, I did not,' said Andrew.

Wombwell was on his big flat feet to cross-examine again.

'But you have already admitted to my learned friend for the defence, your own counsel, that you lied to the police. How can the court believe anything you say?'

'You have my word as a …'

'A liar, sir.'

'Mr Wombwell,' warned Bloom.

'How very honourable of you, Lord Fadmoor, offering to marry a young woman spoilt by your brother. If everything was so open and harmonious between you and your brother, why did Lord Gerard Ashberry go to such lengths to conceal that he had purchased the cross pendant from Mr James Brown Inglis? A pendant later to be given to Miss Bowden.'

'Perhaps he wanted it to be a surprise,' retorted Andrew lamely.

'A surprise for you, My Lord,' chuckled Wombwell. 'Tell me, are you familiar with the Ashberry Windypits?'

'Slightly.'

'Do you agree that you wouldn't expect to find a body down one of those pits in a thousand years? Indeed, it is only recently that bodies of ancients have been recovered from such places.'

Before Andrew had a chance to answer, I was on my feet. 'With respect I put this to the court, why would the Earl of Fadmoor incriminate himself by placing Miss Bowden's body so near to home?'

'Maybe it just happened that way, in that particular location, my lord,' offered Wombwell to the judge.

'Please answer counsel's for the prosecution's original question,' Bloom instructed Andrew.

'It is true that it is an extremely isolated and difficult location,' he admitted.

'Might I ask where did you go during the lunchtime of the shoot on the twenty-eighth of September, 1901?'

'I've no idea.'

'According to the written testimony of your Head Keeper, Charlie Parkes, you disappeared with your brother, Gerard, for some time. Gerard failed to reappear for the afternoon shoot and wasn't seen again until he was found dead in the Doric Temple that evening, isn't that so?'

'I expect you are accusing me of murdering my own brother now,' muttered Andrew.

'Please answer the question,' instructed Bloom again.

'It was so long ago, I can't exactly remember, my lord. But I think I might have gone back to the Hall.'

'Do you think anyone will be able to confirm your presence there?' asked the judge.

'My architect, Louis Chatterton, might,' suggested Andrew.

'Then perhaps, Mr Cairn, you should call this Mr Chatterton to see if his memory is better that the prisoner's,' advised Bloom.

'I certainly will, my lord.'

Due to all the new evidence coming in, I was being forced to arrange and rearrange my own witness list by the minute. I nodded back to Trotter to seek Chatterton out. I even looked up to the public gallery to see if he was there. He wasn't but Winifred was. She was back again as if she had never left yesterday's afternoon session. This time though, I was surprised to see that she was accompanied by her young half-brother, Cedric. I now felt really empowered, inspired.

'I suggest, Lord Fadmoor, that you didn't in fact know of your intended's pregnancy until after the engagement party,' continued Wombwell. 'Perhaps your brother, Gerard, decided to inform you of the situation or maybe Miss Bowden told you herself. Who actually did tell you that Miss Bowden was with child?'

'Gerard was the first to tell me.'

'When exactly?'

'As I've already stated many times, it was some weeks before I asked Lydia to marry me.'

'I must say I find your motivation bewildering, Lord Fadmoor. A man of your rank and position would have the pick of most debutantes. I expect you did all this to preserve the family name?'

'Yes, such things are important to us.'

'"Us" being?'

'The family of course.'

'No, no, I suggest you mean the gentry, the aristocracy, don't you?'

'We do try to preserve certain values,' countered Andrew.

'Well, Lord Fadmoor, I wish all noble households, nay royal households, put the same emphasis on moral values,' grunted Wombwell. His quip rumbled appreciatively across the floor of the court.

'Wombwell has done a good job there,' muttered Leacock. 'He's made Andrew sound like an arrogant prig and associated him in the jury's mind with the King.'

'Andrew's hardly in the same league as Edward VII,' I whispered back. 'But maybe it was a mistake to put him in the box.'

Decrepit William Smethers next took centre stage. As always he was bound to the floor of things – a caricature of the ancient manservant. Bending even further over the good book, I saw that his grey hair retained the same middle parting that once must have parted a glossy sea of black.

'Mr Smethers you are a senior servant at Ashberry Hall, are you not?' I asked.

'I am the butler.'

'Tell me, were you surprised when Lord Fadmoor got engaged to Lydia Bowden?'

'Yes, I was.'

'Can you tell the court and gentlemen of the jury why that was?'

'Because I always thought she was more enamoured with Lord Gerard.'

'Did you ever see any animosity between the two brothers over Miss Bowden?'

'No, never.'

'Did you notice any animosity between Lord Gerard and Lydia Bowden?'

'Only in the days leading up to her engagement party.'

'In what way?'

'I heard him telling her she shouldn't go ahead with it.'

'Go ahead with what?'

'The engagement, the marriage I expect.'

'My lord, this is hearsay,' pointed out Wombwell – Wombwell too late on the draw.

'I instruct the jury to disregard the last statement made by the witness as it is an assumption not fact,' said Bloom.

'But you formed the impression that Gerard Ashberry was unhappy with Lydia's engagement to his brother?' I continued undaunted.

'Yes, I certainly felt that to be the case.'

'And Lord Frederick Ashberry?'

'The Marquess was dead set against the match, that was apparent for the whole world to see.'

'Thank you, Mr Smethers.'

'Any questions for this witness?' Bloom raised an eye at Wombwell.

'No questions,' said Wombwell, with a dismissive shake of the head.

More decorative than ever, Charnley Lodge was sworn in. He explained why Beardsley sacked him. They disagreed over the ethical cost of the quarry to the tenant farmers. Beardsley was being paid by Frederick Ashberry to use his influence to push the plans through the local council.

'Beardsley was an embarrassing womaniser into the bargain. He made frequent overtures to Miss Bowden in my presence.'

'Are you telling the court that he openly flirted with Miss Bowden?'

'That's right.'

'Even when she was spoken for?'

'Even when *he* was spoken for.'

'What exactly do you mean by that?' I was forced to ask.

'Mr Beardsley was engaged himself to another lady in York.'

I glimpsed up to the gallery. I could not read her expression. My only comfort was Cedric was with her that day. Thankfully, for me, there was no unpleasant reminder there either: in appearance Winifred's brother definitely took after their late mother rather than his father.

'But would it be fair to say he regarded a country girl as easy game?' I continued, clearing my throat.

'Yes, I think he did.'

'Even though Lydia Bowden was the Earl of Fadmoor's intended?'

'Irrespective of any future alliance.'

'Did Miss Bowden respond to Mr Beardsley's attempt at seduction?'

'Wait a minute, my lord,' complained Wombwell. 'My learned friend has leaped from a little harmless flirtation to seduction.'

'Perhaps you could rephrase the question, Mr Cairn,' suggested Bloom.

'Did Miss Bowden respond to Mr Beardsley's "harmless flirtation"?' I smirked.

'Not that I could see.'

'Do you think there is any possibility that Mr Beardsley could have been the father of Miss Bowden's unborn child?'

'My lord, my learned friend is asking the unanswerable,' appealed an incandescent Wombwell. 'John Beardsley is a Member of Parliament for this city and as such deserves more respect in this courtroom. He is not the man on trial here.'

'My lord, might I in turn remind counsel for the prosecution that all men and women, irrespective of their position in society, deserve respect.'

Someone in the public gallery slow clapped my words until it built up into an ovation.

'Silence!' screamed Bloom. 'This is not a place of entertainment. In spite of being in full agreement with Mr Cairn regarding his views on respect, that notwithstanding I do not think the witness is in a position to ascertain whether Mr Beardsley was responsible or not for Miss Bowden's fecund state and I uphold Mr Wombwell's objection.'

'No more questions, my lord.' I had had my day – my revenge – regarding Beardsley. I looked up to the public gallery for affirmation. Winifred's and Cedric's seats were empty.

Chapter Thirty-Two

Trotter told me during lunch that he had located Louis Chatterton wringing his hands outside the courtroom while Andrew had been giving his evidence. Chatterton told Trotter he could not bear to listen in case it had all gone wrong. He agreed to make himself available as a witness that afternoon.

'You are Louis Chatterton and you are an architect and designer based in this city, are you not?' I asked.

'I am.'

'Would you be good enough to tell the court and gentlemen of the jury what you were doing in the September of 1901?'

'Yes, that's easy, I was planning some restoration work at Ashberry Hall.'

'And who at the Hall was overseeing these plans of yours?'

'Andrew Ashberry. It was Andrew's pet project.'

'Not the Marquess' then?'

'No, the Marquess was more interested in schemes that made money.'

'And his son on spending it,' stage-whispered Wombwell.

'Like the quarry?' I maliciously asked.

'Yes, like the quarry,' agreed Chatterton.

'So you knew about this quarry proposal?'

'No, not until recently.'

'Did you attend the partridge shoot the day after the Earl's and Miss Bowden's engagement party?'

'No, I don't like field sports.'

'Can you remember what you were doing on that day?'

'If it was a Saturday, I expect I would be still working on my designs at the Hall.'

'Good, good, then perhaps Mr Chatterton you could help clear up a certain matter.'

'Of course, I'm only too eager to oblige in anyway I can.'

'Did you see the Earl at anytime during that Saturday, the Saturday of the shoot?'

'Yes, we breakfasted together.'

'When did you see him next?'

'I'm not sure. I can't remember too clearly.'

My heart fell.

'Did you see him before dinner, before Lord Gerard's body was discovered in the Doric Temple?' I persisted. 'Please take your time.'

'Come to think of it I believe I did. Andrew came into the Hall complaining to me that the shoot was a party of amateurs who couldn't keep up the pace of flushing out the birds.'

'Are you able to recall when this happened exactly?' I asked with dinted pride.

'Not exactly. What I do remember is Andrew complaining that he had just left Gerard, and Gerard was refusing to return to the shoot.'

'The afternoon shoot?'

'That's correct.'

'So, this must have been around lunchtime?'

'I expect it was. The only reason I have any recollection of this conversation is because of what happened later in the day.'

'Lord Gerard's death?'

'That's right.'

'Did the Earl say if Gerard had given any reason for not returning to the shoot?'

'No, but the strange thing is he suspected Gerard might be meeting someone.'

'Who? Do you know?'

'Andrew suspected it might have been Lydia. Then when Lydia went missing ...'

'Can you remember if you remained at the Hall following your conversation with Lord Fadmoor?'

'No, no, I recall what happened now, I walked back to the shoot with Andrew just to take the air.'

'So, you were with him almost the entire lunchtime?'

'Yes. Indeed I remember speaking to you, Mr Cairn, outside the shooting lodge.'

'I expect counsel for the defence was one of the *amateur* sportsmen referred to,' heehawed Bloom.

'I cannot tell a lie, my lord, I certainly would never regard myself as a professional gun. I have no more questions for this witness.' As I sat down, Wombwell was up like a bandalore.

'Mr Chatterton, do you believe everything the prisoner tells you?' he sneered.

Chatterton visibly flinched at the word "prisoner".

'Well, I ...'

'Do you not think that the prisoner could have simply invented this tale about Lord Gerard meeting someone to give himself an alibi?'

'No,' replied Chatterton, quickly collecting himself.

'My lord,' I said, getting to my feet. 'At your suggestion we have called Mr Chatterton here today to verify that Lord Fadmoor visited the Hall that lunchtime. Mr Chatterton has on his own volition further testified that he accompanied Lord Fadmoor back to the shoot. That being the case, the Earl would have had no time to meet or waylay Miss Bowden between the morning's and the afternoon's drives.'

'Mr Wombwell?' The raised judicial eyebrow again.

'I merely question how reliable this witness' memory is,' contested Wombwell.

'Not the reliability of the witness himself?' asked Bloom.

'Well, since your lordship asks, certain allegations have been made regarding this witness' relationship to the prisoner.'

'And I have told the jury to discount them as they are without foundation.'

'Do you not think, Mr Chatterton, that the prisoner could have told you that his brother, Gerard, was meeting Lydia Bowden when he himself was?' continued Wombwell.

'No, I don't believe that to be the case,' replied Chatterton, his voice rising an octave.

'My lord,' I appealed, 'my learned friend has already asked this question.'

'I have no more questions,' announced Wombwell smartly.

'Permit me to call, my lord, Friederich Wilhelm Eurich to discuss the complex pathology in this case,' I requested equally smartly.

'Please,' motioned Bloom.

'You are Doctor Friederich Wilhelm Eurich and you are a general practitioner, bacteriologist, honorary physician to Bradford Hospitals and work in the forensic department at Leeds Medical School, is that correct?'

'Yes, sir, that is correct.'

'Previously, I see here,' I shuffled through my papers, 'you worked as a neurologist at the Lancashire County Asylum. A man of many parts, would I be right in saying?'

'I have always tried to juggle many balls in the air,' smiled Eurich.

'One of those balls is pioneering work in Bradford into cutaneous anthrax, otherwise known as woolsorter's disease, is that not so?'

'That is correct.'

'I also see here that following the submission of your original MD thesis, you were awarded a prestigious gold medal.'

'They cannot have had too many candidates that year,' laughed Eurich. How I had misjudged this man. Everything about him was measured and modest. He was already winning over the court.

'You are something of an expert in psychological diseases, is that fair to say?'

'Yes.'

'Your expertise in both bacteriology and psychological medicine is the reason you have been called here today, Doctor Eurich. It has been put forward by counsel for the prosecution that a reason for Miss Bowden's murder could have been that she suffered from syphilis, a disease that killed her mother. I understand you were invited by the pathologist in this case, Doctor Tate, to take some samples from Miss Bowden's mummified corpse to see if you could ascertain if this was true. Would you be kind enough to inform the court of your findings?'

'It was only last year that Fritz Schaudinn and Erich Hoffmann discovered that syphilis, colloquially known as the "Great Pox", is caused by a bacterium called *Treponema pallidum*. As a bacteriologist this discovery was of tremendous interest, and you can imagine my excitement when I was invited by Doctor Tate to see if I could locate any traces of *Treponema pallidum* in the deceased.'

'And could you?' I asked.

'No, I found none.'

'Were there any other tests you could do to prove or disprove that Miss Bowden suffered from the disease?'

'Indeed, I performed a physical examination. I found no abnormal notches or peg-shaped teeth, known as Hutchinson's teeth, in the deceased's remains. Her nose appeared to be fine and perfectly shaped. There was no sign that the bridge of her nose had collapsed, the saddle nose is often a reliable indication of congenital syphilis. I attempted to see if there was any clouding of the cornea known as interstitial keratitis but, due to natural deterioration and the mummification process itself, it was impossible to reach any conclusion on that. Nor were there any signs of bone lesions indicative of tertiary syphilis.'

'In short, Doctor Eurich, did you find anything to show that Miss Bowden suffered from the same disease that killed her mother?'

'No, I did not.'

Keen-as-mustard Reed on his toes again.

'Doctor Eurich, you couldn't be sure one way or the other, isn't that the truth of it?' he weighed in aggressively.

'No, I can't agree with you there.'

'Why can't you agree with me there?'

'Because I set about a process of elimination.'

'Ah, "elimination", now we have it. You don't really expect the court to believe that these bacterial deposits, known as *Treponema pallidum*, would have survived in the organs and orifices of a body for nearly four years, do you?'

'No, perhaps not, as I have already testified I found none.'

'Because *you* found none that doesn't mean none existed.'

'My lord, I must protest, my learned friend is bullying the witness,' I objected.

'But your witness is an expert in his field, indeed in many fields, as you yourself eagerly pointed out. I think he should answer the question,' confirmed Bloom.

'Though I found no bacterial evidence to say the victim suffered from syphilis, I found plenty of physical evidence to dispute that she had ever contracted the disease, my lord,' Eurich turned slightly to address Bloom directly.

'My lord,' I piped up again. 'It was the prosecution who put forward the hypothesis that Lydia Bowden could have been killed because she was pregnant and suffering from this ghastly venereal disease. I think that

Doctor Eurich has demonstrated that she bore no signs of syphilis in death and so certainly would not have shown them in life.'

'No more questions, my lord,' put in Reed, disappointed.

'"The victim", I like that,' whispered Leacock. 'Your Doctor Eurich is nobody's fool.'

'Certainly not Reed's,' I replied. 'And next comes my ace witness.'

Initially Stephen Ashberry seemed perfectly normal as he mounted the steps into the witness box, indeed superficially his attitude appeared extremely genial as he surveyed the floor of the court.

'Lord Stephen Ashberry, you are the brother of the defendant in this case?'

'I am.'

'Can you tell the court and gentlemen of the jury what you overheard and witnessed around lunchtime on Saturday, the twenty-eighth of September, 1901?'

'I was walking along the terrace garden when I heard raised voices coming from the Doric Temple. I was surprised because I thought everyone was at the shoot so I decided to investigate.'

'Could you tell who the voices belonged to?'

'Yes, one was definitely my brother Gerard's the other was female.'

'And what was this heated exchange about?'

'Something to do with a child.'

'Did you become aware of who the female might be?'

'Yes, as I got closer I realised it was Lydia. Gerard was telling her she couldn't continue with her pregnancy or her engagement to our eldest brother, Andrew.'

'Did he give a reason?'

'Yes, although I couldn't quite believe what he was saying.'

'Please continue.'

'Gerard said that she was really our half-sister. Our father had admitted it to him the previous night. Our father had instructed him to tell her.'

'The Marquess of Hambleton had admitted to being the father of you all?'

'Yes, he told Gerard that Mary Bowden was putting pressure on him to reveal the truth and stop the marriage.'

I suddenly became aware of Andrew gulping for breath in the dock. He looked about to faint again. This was obviously a shock for him. He seemingly had had no idea of his impending incestuous marriage to Lydia. Another glass of water was sent for.

'Then what did you hear?' I asked Stephen.

'"You are lying," Lydia told Gerard, adding, "you lie about everything." "I am not lying when I tell you, your mother gave our father syphilis," said Gerard. "Syphilis which was later passed onto our dear mother, Lady Hambleton, when she was pregnant with Stephen. That is why Stephen is in such a mess, is such a mess," he told Lydia.' There was a catch in Stephen's voice as he related this to the court. 'Lydia objected and told my brother that our father must have contracted the disease from one of his London whores – the whores being the reason her mother terminated their affair all those years ago. Gerard was having none of this, insisting her mother was the source of infection. He suggested her mother must have contracted it from one of her many lovers. Lydia responded by asking if he really believed her mother, a simple country woman, had the opportunity for numerous associations with syphilitic men. And if that was the case why wasn't she or her brother Malcolm affected likewise. "It only takes the one time," my brother told her. "Yes, and that one time was with your father," she retorted. "*Our* father now, remember," said my brother, always one to have the last word.'

'Please tell the court what happened next, Lord Stephen.'

'I saw Malcolm Bowden strolling across the lawn towards the Temple with his dog. I was forced to press myself between a bush and the Temple wall. "He is saying terrible things," Lydia screamed to Malcolm. "Gerard says the Marquess is my father." "It's true," Malcolm told her. "You are their half-sister. I learnt it from our mother yesterday when she realised the truth was the only way of stopping the wedding." "I don't believe any of you," screamed Lydia again. "It is true," Malcolm assured her. "Does Andrew know about his relationship to me?" asked Lydia. No one answered. "God! How can I knowingly marry my own half-brother?" Lydia began sobbing hysterically. "You are responsible for all this, you monster," Malcolm yelled at Gerard. "I told her to get rid of it weeks ago," replied Gerard, adding, "anyway, how do I know that the brat she is carrying is really mine?" "Because you bloody well raped her." Malcolm's voice rose in anger. Gerard jeered back, "She wanted it. She'll never get it from my big brother, and certainly not now." There was a light tinkling sound on the floor and I guessed Lydia had flung her engagement ring at Gerard. Then the dog began barking. Thinking this was the end of the quarrel, I began to make my escape. Behind me I heard an explosion that forced me to cover my ears. Then a dull thud. Then silence, complete silence. And all I was left with, my lasting memory of my elder brother was that he had referred to me as being "a mess".'

'Forgive me, Lord Stephen, but your appearance has changed over the years. Why is that?' I asked.

'I have congenital syphilis,' came Stephen's unemotional reply.

'And do you think you contracted this disease from your mother or father?'

'My lord, any answer the witness gives would be purely speculative,' shambled up Wombwell. 'And would have no direct relevance on this case.'

'Of course my learned friend is correct and I immediately retract the question.' I bowed my apology. I had made my point without waiting for admonishment from on high or Stephen Ashberry's answer.

'Very impressive, Lord Stephen. You have given an almost word for word rendition of the conversations in the Doric Temple. How can you remember so precisely what was said after so many years have passed?' cross-examined Wombwell.

'It was the day my brother Gerard died, I was hardly likely to forget what happened on that day.'

'But *word for word*?' repeated Wombwell.

'I have that sort of memory,' shrugged Stephen. 'Pa always said I should have been an actor.'

'Might I ask why you haven't come forward with this vital piece of evidence before?'

'Pa felt it was better I didn't at the time. Gerard's death was found to be accidental and Andrew hadn't been accused of murdering Lydia then.'

'Do you do everything your father says, Lord Stephen?'

'Just about.' Stephen gave one of his rather unnerving staring smiles.

'Please tell the court how old you are.'

'I am twenty-two.'

'So, you are twenty-two years younger than your elder brother, the Earl?'

'Yes, I am,' sighed Stephen. 'As always the runt, the afterthought.'

'Forgive me, but very much an afterthought,' said Wombwell, rustling through his notes. 'I see you are just a couple of years younger than the deceased's brother, Malcolm Bowden.'

'Oh him, I don't like him,' said Stephen.

'And why is that?'

'Oh, no special reason,' deflected Stephen.

'My lord, I wonder if you would be kind enough to permit me to ask one or two more questions of Lord Stephen?' I asked, drawing to my full height like a headmaster.

'Please be my guest,' replied Bloom.

'Lord Stephen, following the incident in the Doric Temple, after you had initially made your escape, did you go back to check on your elder brother's wellbeing?'

'I can't remember,' replied Stephen.

'You can't remember but you can remember everything else, "word for word" as my learned friend put it.'

'I might have done.'

'You cannot be such a heartless chap as to just walk away from your possibly injured brother, can you?'

'You're right, I did go back into the Temple.'

'And what did you find there?'

'Blood. Gerard was laying in a pool of blood.'

'Was he obviously dead?'

'Yes, obviously. His chest was gaping open.'

'Tell me, Lord Stephen, did you take anything from the Temple, any evidence of what had transpired there?'

'Not that I can recall.'

'I want you to think about this carefully as the court and gentlemen of the jury are well aware that you have a phenomenal memory,' I flattered.

'Might have done,' repeated Stephen. He paused thoughtfully for a few seconds. 'Yes, I remember now, the ring, I picked up Lydia's engagement ring off the floor.'

'What did you do then?'

'Wrapped it in my handkerchief and put it in my pocket.'

'Why did you take the ring?'

'It was pretty.'

'And what did you do with it next?'

'Washed it.'

'"Washed it"?'

'Yes, it was covered in Gerard's blood,' explained Stephen.

The court gasped. This was a cool customer indeed.

'What did you do next?' I asked.

'Put it in my bedroom drawer.'

'When did you realise it was missing?'

'Sometime the next morning after the undertaker had taken Gerard's body away.'

'Thank you, Lord Stephen, no more questions.' I now had absolute confirmation that what Andrew and Louis Chatterton had finally told me was the truth. The ring hadn't been in Gerard's pocket at all but in Stephen's bedroom drawer. Andrew had made the entire tale up to conceal the actions of his youngest brother, perhaps believing this troubled egotistical young man had played a part in Gerard's murder.

Chapter Thirty-Three

'Your friend's back,' said Trotter, nudging me in the ribs and pointing up towards Winifred in the public gallery. Winifred returned a rather condescending, or was it satirical smile in my direction. I didn't care, she was back. It was the fourth day – perhaps the last day – of the Ashberry trial and I intended to give my best performance.

The unbelievably named rustic Jess Onion stood to attention as he was sworn in. Slowly spoken, an obdurate countryman, his leather gaiters squeaked as they rubbed together in the witness box. No doubt underneath the bluff Mr Onion was extremely nervous.

'Mr Onion do you live in a forester's cottage near the geological features known as the Ashberry Pits?' I began.

'Keeper's cottage,' corrected Onion. 'I am a keeper, not a forester.'

'Apologies for my inaccuracy, Mr Onion,' I bowed. Onion brusquely shrugged off my city ignorance. 'Mr Onion were you familiar with Farmer Bowden's dog, Rain?'

'My lord, really.' I could hear Wombwell scraping to his feet across from me.

Bloom raised a judicial hand to silence him. 'No, Mr Wombwell, I am as curious as the rest of the court to find out where Mr Cairn is going with this.'

'Did you know Farmer Bowden's dog, Rain?' I asked Onion again.

'Yes, sir. Though it were more Lydia's and Malcolm's dog than Reg Bowden's.'

'Was it really?'

'Yes, sir.'

'And what type of dog was it?'

'A collie bitch, begging your pardon.'

A small enclave in the court sniggered.

'A Border Collie bitch, isn't that right?'

'Yes, sir.'

'My lord, counsel for the defence is now giving us all a lesson on dog breeds,' Wombwell again.

'Please, Mr Wombwell, I have already told you that I am curious where this is leading,' said Bloom.

'Would you recognise Rain from other collies?' I asked Onion.

'Yes, sir, she had a black patch over one eye, a white patch over t'other. Very unusual she was.'

'And do you frequent the Hare Inn at Scawton, Mr Onion?'

'I do.'

'Did you tell the landlord there that you had often heard Rain howling up by the Ashberry Pits?'

'I did, sir.'

'At night?'

'Yes, usually at night.'

'Was this before or after Lydia Bowden went missing?'

'After, I believe.'

'"After"?'

'Yes, although Malcolm and Lydia often walked up Ashberry Hill with Rain. With or without them, perhaps the dog grew to like the place.'

'Umm, "with or without them".'

'Yes, sir.'

'Malcolm and Lydia, you say?'

'Yes, sir.'

'I really feel it is important to clarify this point. You are sure you heard the dog, Rain, howling up by the Windypits *after* Miss Bowden went missing?'

'I'm sure, sir.'

'I have no more questions for this witness, my lord,' I said resuming my seat.

'Mr Reed?' ventured Bloom. Junior counsel for the prosecution was already eager and waiting.

'Mr Onion, on how many occasions did you say you heard the dog howling up by the Windypits?' asked Reed.

'Must 'ave been five or six times.'

'Didn't you investigate?'

'It was on pitch black winter nights.'

'I bet that didn't stop you making your way to the public house though, did it?' muttered Reed.

'Mr Reed,' censured Bloom.

'To tell you the truth, I thought little on it until a Rievaulx fella found her,' said Onion.

'Found who?' asked Reed.

'Why the dog of course,' replied Onion.

'How could you be so sure it was the same dog that had been howling above the Windypits?' snorted Reed.

'Please, sir, I am a countryman. I can tell one creature from another, one dog from another. Besides Rain was eventually found above one of them pits. Stiff with death and t' cold.'

'I have no more questions for this witness.' said Reed, bowing out as gracefully as he could with such a heavy heart.

I nodded to Onion as he passed in front of me. He had held.

There had to be a connection with the shooting of Gerard Ashberry and Lydia's death – there just had to be – but had Gerard really shot himself? I had seen signs of combat fatigue in Gerard myself during my weekend at Ashberry Hall all those years ago, or was there another sinister explanation? Only Malcolm Bowden was left alive to answer this. It suddenly struck me that the guilty often answer direct questions with another question: like "why would I kill my own sister?".

Malcolm Bowden had once told me "Live for the day and bugger the rest of 'em." When I looked at the younger Bowden across the courtroom in the witness box, I was haunted by the insane screams I had heard as I left Bootham Park Hospital. Was this Malcolm's real fear? – that he would finish up like his mother, that Lydia would finish up like their mother, her unborn child likewise. And who was the cause of all Malcolm's pain? – the Marquess, who, on top of threatening his sanity, now threatened his livelihood.

'You are a man filled with resentments, aren't you, Mr Bowden?'

'Sorry?'

'Before your sister went missing you had a sickly mother at home, a somewhat intransigent father and a difficult tenant living. If this wasn't enough to contend with you felt your sister was running wild, running free with the Ashberrys, is that not so?'

'Just about sums it up,' came Malcolm's surly reply.

'"Yes" or "no",' insisted Bloom.

'Yees.' Squeezed out between clenched teeth.

'But above all you resented the Marquess of Hambleton stealing the man you thought you were, a son of the soil, did you not?'

'Sorry?' Again Malcolm looked bewildered.

'Because you weren't really farmer Bowden's son but Frederick Ashberry's illegitimate son, were you not?'

'Who cares?' hissed Malcolm.

'Answer counsel's question,' instructed Bloom.

'I'm not really sure who my father is anymore.'

'How and when did you learn about the true state of things?'

'Ma told me the day of Lydia's engagement party. She said Lydia could never marry Andrew Ashberry as they were related.'

'She told you this on the day before Lydia went missing?'

'That's right.'

'You knew nothing about it until then?'

'Nothing. She asked me to try and put a stop to the wedding.'

'By telling Lydia the truth?'

'That's right.'

'And did you?'

'No, I never got round to it. Gerard had already told her by the time I reached the Temple.'

'How did you come to be at the Doric Temple that day?'

'Lydia had sent word from the big 'ouse that Gerard had arranged to meet her there at lunchtime. She didn't want to see him on her own.'

'I expect this revelation about the Marquess being your father made you feel very angry, did it not?' I asked. Malcolm merely shook his head. Not waiting for a reply, I pressed on. 'You and Lydia had always had so little when your paternal half-brothers enjoyed so much.'

'Didn't they just.'

'Please answer "yes" or "no",' insisted Bloom wearily again.

'Yees.'

'So Lydia was an agnate sibling of the man she intended to marry?'

'A what?'

'A consanguine sister.'

Malcolm looked lost. I didn't mind this: I wanted him to feel lost, out of his depth so I could gently haul him in.

'In law we usually use the term "consanguine" instead of "agnate" meaning blood-related,' explained Bloom.

'Lydia was a paternal half-sister of the Ashberry boys,' I simplified further. 'I expect your mother informed you about Lydia when she told you of your own status, did she not?'

'Puh! What status? My mother never discussed or cared about *my* bloody status.'

'Mr Bowden,' warned Bloom.

'What? Mary Bowden never discussed the subject of your personal paternity?' I was incredulous.

'I don't think she thought it was important. The fact that my sister was about to marry her half-brother was the most pressing matter to her at the time.'

'Were you invited to your sister's engagement party at the Hall, Mr Bowden?' I asked.

'No I was not. I wouldn't have gone if I had been.'

'The Marquess planned to open a quarry on land farmed by you and your surrogate father, did he not?'

'Surrogate, what?'

'Land farmed by you and Reginald Bowden.'

'Yes, he did.'

'So not only had the Marquess deprived you of legitimacy, he was now attempting to destroy your future in farming?'

'That's right.'

'And your beloved sister knew nothing of her true relationship to Lord Fadmoor, not until the incident in the Doric Temple, I take it?'

'No, not as far as I know.'

'You have told the court earlier that you knew Lydia was pregnant. When did she exactly tell you about her condition?'

'Early in the new year.'

'Early in the new year when Gerard Ashberry would still have been with his regiment, is that not so?'

'Yes.'

'Well, how can that be, Mr Bowden? Your sister was only three months pregnant when she went missing on the twenty-eighth of September, 1901, near the end of the year.' I waited to let both the court and Malcolm digest this. 'You further told this court in your original evidence that Lydia told you Lord Fadmoor was the father of her child, did you not?'

'Yes.' Said with head down.

'I think you are lying, Mr Bowden.'

'Think what you like.' Said in an undertone.

'Lord Stephen Ashberry doesn't like you very much, does he?'

'It's mutual.' The head lifted, the piercing blue eyes glared angrily across the court at me.

'Why doesn't he like you?' I persisted.

'Because I stopped him hanging one of our dogs up from a beam in the barn.'

'Which dog? Rain?'

'No, no, a mangy mongrel we had long before Rain. Stephen and I were little lads at the time.'

'The court has just heard from Lord Stephen that he overheard an argument between Lydia and his brother, Gerard, in the Doric Temple, where Gerard told Lydia her mother was responsible for giving the Marquess a venereal disease ...'

'Utter rubbish!' screamed Malcolm.

'During that same conversation, Gerard asked Lydia how could he be sure that the child she was carrying was really his. Did you know, Mr Bowden, that your sister wasn't carrying Andrew's child but Gerard's?'

'Does it matter?' snarled Malcolm. 'One way or the other it would be an Ashberry child.'

'A child without a legitimate father?'

'Yes.'

'A child like you without status?'

'Possibly so.'

'A child implanted in the womb of the sister you loved so much by a man who had so little regard for her?'

'He was a bastard.'

In the circumstances an unfortunate choice of word, I noted.

'I believe you did know that your sister was expecting Gerard's child and not Andrew's. I also believe you knew that after Lydia had refused to have the child aborted, the two Ashberry brothers came up with their marriage plan, is that not so?'

'Yes, but that was before they were aware that Lydia was closely related to them.'

'I further suggest that it wasn't Lydia but you who arranged the meeting between the three of you in the Doric Temple during that lunchtime.'

'Why would I do that?'

'To confront Gerard over the rape of your sister.'

'He wasn't the sort to give a damn about that.'

'No, but the fact that Lydia was his half-sister was a further reason for her terminating the pregnancy. You wanted Gerard to add his weight to your campaign.'

'What campaign? What twaddle, I hated the man.'

'In the same way you hated the thought of your sister giving birth to his child, is that not so?'

'If it was his child,' persisted Malcolm.

'So did you confront him?'

'No.'

'Stephen Ashberry has already testified that he overheard you arguing with Gerard and calling him a monster.'

'He was.'

'Then Stephen Ashberry heard a shot and a thud.'

'You can't really believe that I'd kill a man in cold blood.'

'Perhaps not in *cold blood*. Afterwards you continued to beg Lydia to get rid of the child, didn't you?'

'No, I did not.' Said quietly.

'She refused?'

'No, she did not.'

'The atmosphere between the two of you must have been highly charged as you made your way back home to Broadshaw Farm. You had just killed the father of your sister's child. Perhaps Lydia threatened to tell the authorities, that is when you strangled her and later transported her body by cart up to the Ashberry Pits.'

'I loved my sister. Why would I do such a terrible thing? I've nothing more ...' Malcolm began to weep.

'Leave him be,' someone screamed from the public gallery. 'Let my lad be.'

I looked up and saw Reginald Bowden – his face beetroot red – on his feet and shaking his fist not far behind the seated Winifred and Cedric.

'My lord, I know this is highly irregular and I didn't initially feel it would be necessary, but I would like to recall Reginald Bowden in the interests of justice.'

Reginald Bowden stooped over the Bible, already a broken man.

Like a cautious robin, alert to the kestrel, my eyes darted around the court before I'd risk the drop for that final magic crumb. Mr Wombwell remained seated.

'Mr Bowden, the usher will present you with pen and paper,' I told Reginald. 'Would you be kind enough to write out the word *filicide*?' I had to carefully spell out each character for him. The usher returned the paper to me: Mr Bowden's *f* had a certain tight control to it. The usher next passed the paper and Mr Brown's anonymous "Well Wisher" note across to his lordship for comparison. 'I am no handwriting expert, my lord, but I would suggest that the *filicide* on that "Well Wisher" note was written in the hand of Mr Bowden senior.'

His lordship lifted up the paper and then the note before bringing first one and then the other closer to his nose.

'I agree, counsel, the two examples certainly look the same to me. We can of course have them examined by an expert.'

Bowden had turned an even deeper red and had begun to sweat.

'He told me ...' he stuttered.

'Who told you what?' I asked.

'No one.' Reginald compressed his lips together.

'You do realise, Mr Bowden, that you have perjured yourself and are already in a great deal of trouble,' Bloom reminded him.

'I allus do everything with 'im in mind,' muttered the farmer with hanging head.

'For whom? What are you talking about, man?' asked Bloom, beginning to lose his patience.

'Malcolm. Lydia said Malcolm had ruined her life and marriage prospects.'

'How?' I asked.

'She was her mother's daughter right enough.'

'How?' I insisted.

'She was going to tell lies about our Malcolm shooting Lord Ashberry.'

'Lord Gerard Ashberry?'

'That's right.'

'Why would she lie about that?'

'Because she was mad like her mother. Never like me, never mine.'

'You obviously have a great sense of loyalty towards Malcolm though, do you not?' I asked. Reginald did not answer. 'If only you had felt as much loyalty for your daughter, Lydia.'

'See it as you wish.'

'But then, I forget, Lydia was never your real daughter, was she?'

'She was always whatever she wanted to be.'

'It was Malcolm whom you believed to be your true son, isn't that so?'

'More than believed. The one time that bitch let me near her in years it happened, the miracle happened,' snarled Reginald. The cuckold genie had finally sprung from the box full of vitriol.

'So what you're telling us is that Malcolm and Lydia were what is known as uterine siblings, siblings sharing the same mother but not the same father. Perhaps it was that slight difference that made them so close, so attracted to each other,' I suggested.

'I don't know about that. She was going to tell on him, my boy.'

'By "she", you mean Lydia again, don't you?'

'Yes.'

'What was she going to say exactly?' I asked. Reginald Bowden just shook his head slowly from side to side. 'She was going to confess to the police what happened in the Doric Temple, wasn't she?'

'I ...'

'During the struggle between Gerard Ashberry and your Malcolm.'

'The shotgun just went off, Mr Cairn, you have to believe that.'

'Are you telling the court that the shooting of Gerard Ashberry was an accident?'

'Yes, and Malcolm *is* my son. He's all I've got left.'

'So, are the court and gentlemen of the jury right in drawing the conclusion that you murdered Lydia Bowden to protect your son?'

'I'll say no more until I have legal representation,' replied a suddenly more astute Reginald Bowden.

'But it wasn't really Lydia you were choking to death, Mr Bowden, was it? Lydia was just an unfortunate representation of your unfaithful wife. You were actually killing all those years of your own suffocating humiliation,' I flopped back down onto the bench, adrenaline still pumping through every vein, my legs shaking.

Mr Justice Bloom nodded gravely to a policeman stationed near the door. Out of my eye corner, I saw Andrew Ashberry slump back in the dock as Reginald Bowden was taken. Whether from shock, disbelief or relief I wasn't sure.

'Was that your final re-examination, Mr Cairn?' asked Bloom.

I struggled back onto my feet. 'Yes, sorry, my lord, that concludes the case for the defence.'

'I think we will take this opportunity to adjourn for lunch, so we can all get our breath back. Before the afternoon session I would like a word with both Mr Wombwell and Mr Cairn in my chambers before they embark on their closing speeches.'

Chapter Thirty-Four

Wombwell lumbered onto his feet, determined to see things through to the bitter end.

'May it please your lordship, gentlemen of the jury, I am sure that every one of you must be relieved that we are coming to the end of this trial, although I am equally sure that no one in this court will regret taking part and doing his duty in the name of justice,' he began, rubbing his index finger across his nose. 'I, too, am very much relieved it is nearing the end. As an advocate at the bar there is nothing so distasteful, so stressful as having to cross-examine a man charged with murder. Whatever that man's previous station was in life – and there is no disputing that this case has aroused tremendous interest because of who the prisoner is – nevertheless, he must suffer the same consequences for his actions as the common man. Whether an earl or a plumber we are all subject to the laws of this land and are equally answerable, equally responsible.'

Someone high up on the tier of public benches liked this, applauded this.

'We have learnt that the prisoner is not above lying to the police regarding his fiancée's engagement ring, which he falsely claimed he had found in his deceased brother's pocket. A man capable of telling one lie is capable of telling many.'

Again applause from the same quarter. Bloom scowled his disapproval.

'We have heard,' continued Wombwell encouraged, 'a well-argued case from my learned friends opposite, they have put forward an excellent defence, there is no disputing that. But, alas, what they have singularly failed to do is give a convincing explanation of how a gold cufflink bearing the interlocking initials AA came to be in the grasp of the dead woman, Miss Lydia Bowden. We should not forget that she was the victim in this milieu of lies and deception. Miss Bowden was robbed of her young life at the hands of another. Because of that one cufflink, linking the prisoner to her at the time of her death, we still maintain that there is a case to answer for that man in the dock over there.' Wombwell jabbed that same rubbing nose index finger across at Andrew.

There was a surprised clearing of throats and an uncomfortable shuffling of pants on the bench seats opposite. And, that was that, Wombwell had simply gone through the motions. He had no more to add to his closing speech.

'Mr Cairn?' His lordship gave me the challenging raised eyebrow.

'My lord, gentlemen of the jury, I feel it has become apparent towards the end of this trial that Lydia Bowden's death is connected to the shooting of Lord Gerard Ashberry. Although the coroner at the time felt Lord Gerard was shot accidentally, both Gerard and Lydia died on the same day only a few miles apart, and no one is in any doubt that Lydia's death was anything other than murder. I would suggest this cannot be just an extraordinary coincidence.'

Muffled approval from the gallery.

'The clues to this mystery are buried deeply in the relationship of the Ashberry siblings to the Bowdens. Malcolm Bowden enjoyed a close relationship with his sister, Lydia, while perhaps eventually believing that he too was the Marquess of Hambleton's son. This has proved not to be the case as testified by his real father, Reginald Bowden. Lydia was in fact Malcolm's maternal half-sister. Malcolm Bowden and Stephen Ashberry, you may have noticed, are separated by just one or two years. On his own volition, Stephen Ashberry has openly admitted that he has congenital syphilis. Malcolm shows no signs of the disease and neither did Lydia according to Doctor Eurich. There is no substantial evidence to prove Lydia had syphilis or that it could have been a motive for her murder. I suggest that the Marquess contracted that disease just as his affair with Mary Bowden was coming to an abrupt end. I further suggest that, although he remains asymptomatic, it was the Marquess of Hambleton who passed the disease onto Mrs Bowden and his late wife, the Marchioness, Lord Stephen's mother. Stephen alone, being younger than his brothers and half-sister, contracted this terrible disease.'

I glanced to where Frederick Ashberry had been sitting throughout his son's trial. He glared back at me – puce with rage and embarrassment – served him right, I didn't care and looked away.

'Lord Stephen Ashberry has admitted that he took Miss Bowden's engagement ring from the Doric Temple following Lord Gerard's death. I do know that at first the Earl of Fadmoor put about a story that he had found the ring in his deceased brother's pocket. He made this story up believing his youngest brother might be implicated in murder. Might I point out to the jury that rightly or wrongly there is a degree of protection here, hardly in accordance with the actions of a callous man capable of murdering either his fiancée or his brother. In the same way I do not believe that Malcolm Bowden murdered his sister, although I do believe he was involved in a fight with Lord Gerard Ashberry which resulted in the peer's death. I feel the prosecution in this case has failed to provide a sound motive for my client wanting Lydia dead,' I told the court. 'I believe the discovered cufflink was too obvious a clue, too blatant. I believe that cufflink was planted in Lydia's grasp to incriminate Andrew Ashberry and deflect attention from the real perpetrator.'

'Do you believe there is a possibility that perpetrator is the victim's surrogate father who is now in custody for perjury?' interrupted Bloom.

'I do, my lord. Please allow me to run through the scenario of events as I see them happening on that Saturday afternoon in late September, 1901. Malcolm Bowden struggles with Gerard Ashberry in the Doric Temple and the gun goes off killing Gerard.'

'As corroborated by Lord Stephen Ashberry,' put in Bloom again.

'That is correct, my lord. Mr Bowden then runs off home in a state of shock. Lydia, slowed by her inadequate footwear, follows on with the dog, Rain. Rain, who had accompanied Malcolm to the meeting in the Temple. Hearing his terrified son's story, Farmer Bowden takes off from his cottage to meet Lydia believing her to be the only witness to the tragedy. He begs her to keep silent. She refuses saying Malcolm has ruined her life. Farmer Bowden has already admitted she said this to him. Perhaps it is then that she shows him the gold cufflinks with interlocking A's, telling him that she still intends giving them to Andrew. Rain, the collie, perhaps senses the tension between father and step-daughter on their walk back to Broadshaw Farm. All of a sudden the disturbed dog bolts up the hillside. They shout for her but she does not return. They have no other option than to follow her up in the direction of Ashberry Windypits. All the while, Farmer Bowden is begging Lydia to spare *his* boy. She will not listen to him so he begins to formulate a plan here in this isolated spot. He grew to hate her mother. This young woman is the embodiment of the woman who cuckolded him, unmanned him. How can he allow her to take the one thing that is his, that he loves above the farm, above everything else – his son? How can he allow her to carry an Ashberry child? He explodes, striking out at Lydia. She hits her head on a felled tree stump. There is no stopping him, now he has started. He must finish off the job. Astride her he presses his strong hands round her neck. He finds the cufflinks in her coat pocket, takes one to discard later, pressing the other into her hand before closing it. Then, almost with care, he drops her body down one of the nearby Windypits. He has no conscience about incriminating Andrew Ashberry – the heir of his hated enemy – someone he has heard rumoured is homosexual. Farmer Bowden has owned up to being the author of the "Well Wisher" note to Mr Robert Brown, will he confess to Lydia's murder? We shall have to wait and see but I am sure the man accused over there in the dock is innocent of the charge brought against him. True it is, I met beautiful Lydia Bowden once at her engagement party, and then saw with my own eyes the graphic details of her demise when her remains were discovered down Ashberry Pit. A sight that will haunt me for the rest of my life. And I, like any other reasonable man, am keen to find the perpetrator of this terrible crime. At the same time, however, I know that in accordance with the laws of any civilised society we have to find the true guilty party. I believe with both my heart and mind that The Right Honourable Andrew Earl of Fadmoor is incapable of such a vile act and, we have shown, that in all probability the blame lies in entirely another direction. I ask you to find Lord Fadmoor not guilty of this abhorrent indictment brought against him.'

Almost without pause Thelonious Bloom began his charge to the jury.

'Gentlemen of the jury, it is my duty to put all the facts before you. Miss Lydia Bowden, the prisoner's fiancée, went missing on Saturday, twenty-eighth of September, 1901. Her body wasn't recovered until the first of July, 1905, three years and nine months later, down one of the Ashberry Windypits near her home and Ashberry Hall, Helmsley. According to the pathologist, Doctor Richard Tate, who conducted the post-mortem she died from asphyxiation due to manual strangulation. You must be sure beyond all reasonable doubt that the prisoner was the one who strangled her. Permit me to remind you that although counsel for the defence has given a reasoned argument that the murder of Miss Lydia Bowden was connected to the death of the prisoner's brother, Lord Gerard Ashberry, the prisoner is solely on trial for the murder of Miss Bowden. However, I am forced to point out that the evidence of the Crown's witnesses, Malcolm and Reginald Bowden, must be regarded as severely flawed and worthless. Indeed, I suspect that only the evidence given by Mr Reginald Bowden during his final cross-examination might be considered to have any merit to it at all.'

Again muffled approval but this time from the more informed floor of the court.

'Let me end as I began by saying, if there be any doubt in it, the prisoner must have the benefit of that doubt. If there be none, let your verdict be equally clear and let justice be carried out. Will you consider your verdict?'

'Do you think they will be out long?' Leacock asked me.

'Who knows with juries,' I replied.

'But surely they can't find against us?'

'Who knows with juries,' I repeated, suddenly feeling extremely fatigued. 'They can throw up some big surprises.'

Almost an hour later we had word that the court was to reconvene.

'Only an hour,' exclaimed Leacock in panic.

'Means nothing,' said the voice of experience from behind.

'Trotter's right,' agreed Brown.

I said nothing – looking over as Andrew Ashberry returned to the dock – feeling as if it was I who was about to learn if I would live or die.

I knew that the black square of cloth, known as the black cap, would be waiting somewhere on the judge's bench. Should a guilty verdict be announced: sentencing Thelonious Bloom would place the cloth, one of the four corners facing outward, on top of his wig uttering the words "and may the Lord have mercy upon your soul". A supportive "amen" would follow from the court chaplain.

'They're coming in,' said Leacock.

I tried to read the faces of the twelve good men and true as they took their seats. They looked grim and impassive. If I had been a betting man, I would not have put any money on an acquittal judging from their expressions.

'Members of the jury, are you all agreed upon your verdict?' asked the clerk of assize.

'Yes,' replied the foreman.

'Do you find Andrew Ashberry guilty of murder, or not guilty?'

'Not guilty,' rang out in the absolute silence.

'You find Andrew Ashberry not guilty of murder, and that is the verdict of you all?'

'Yes.' The foreman turned to address Bloom directly. 'However we would like to address some misgivings regarding this trial to your lordship.'

'Please proceed,' Bloom told him.

'We feel there are witnesses, who have appeared at this trial, with greater knowledge of the events leading to the death of Miss Bowden than the Earl of Fadmoor ever had.'

'The court gratefully takes on board your caveats, and let me assure you the matter is already in hand,' Bloom told them; giving a ceremonial bow as he left the court, left the black cap discarded behind.

The close of day, the scraping of wood on floor like the ending of a long school day. Wombwell gave me a begrudging nod – that was the only acknowledgement I got from him or his team – they had insisted on continuing the trial, despite Bloom questioning the validity of their case after Reginald Bowden had admitted writing the anonymous note and god knows what else.

Thomas Leacock was overjoyed: he had not defended such a big case in a long time.

Trotter was brimming with pride, Brown with tears. Andrew Ashberry had relaxed into a place beyond relief. Manly embraces all round. But it wasn't until I made my way through the forest of courtroom furniture that the serious personal business began in the corridor outside.

Winifred was waiting there with her brother. Cedric nodded polite recognition. He had grown into an extremely handsome young man.

'Well, Mr Cairn, you really are quite a man with words,' said Winifred.

'Even though they mount up to merely talk and theatricals,' I barbed back.

'No, no, you chose exactly the right words this time. In fact I have never heard such an eloquent defence.'

'So, I am not too bad then?'

'No, not *too* bad.'

'Does this sound like an appropriately worded invitation? Winifred Holbrook will you and your brother do me the honour of dinner tonight?' Before the assembled gathering, still begowned, I took her hand.

Chapter Thirty-Five

Two weeks later, Timon White called to see me in Bootham Chambers.

'I thought you might be interested in the aftermath of the Ashberry trial,' he said.

'Of course I am. You have my undivided attention. Tea,' I offered. White shook his head.

'No time for tea, but thanks.' He smiled a set of perfect teeth.

'So, the aftermath?'

'Reginald Bowden is under arrest for perjury. Malcolm Bowden likewise is being held at Northallerton Gaol for perjury and the manslaughter of Gerard Ashberry.'

'Manslaughter?'

'Yes, Malcolm says after Lydia threw the Earl's ring at Gerard, Gerard pointed his gun at both of them. A struggle ensued and the gun went off.'

'Do you believe him?'

'Well, it does rather fit in with earwigging Stephen's version of events. And it was Gerard's gun. Malcolm came to that meeting in the Doric Temple unarmed.'

'And has Reginald been charged with the murder of Lydia yet?'

'Although you painted a vivid picture in court of what could have happened, and possibly did happen, we need more than supposition, we need more hard and factual evidence to make a charge of murder stick.'

'I see,' I said, disappointed. Although was I really disappointed? The hanging of any man or woman is a grim business and from conception poor old Reggie had been dealt an appalling hand in life.'

'You do realise, Mr Cairn, that your scenario of events leading up to the killing of Lydia Bowden could have just as easily applied to Malcolm. Speaking to a number of witnesses around and about Scawton, and as you yourself intimated in court, we've been led to believe that Malcolm enjoyed an unusually intense relationship with his sister.'

'Are you suggesting Malcolm might have murdered Lydia because she was carrying another man's child? That he killed her out of fraternal spite and jealousy?'

'Consider, Mr Cairn, we do not know unequivocally whose child Miss Bowden was carrying.'

'You don't think ... We're not speaking of incest here?'

'I wouldn't go as far as saying that but they were observed on numerous occasions sharing a physical closeness above that normally expected between brother and sister. Perhaps it was Malcolm, not Reginald, who chased after the dog up to the Windypits with Lydia. Perhaps he couldn't bear the thought of his sister carrying an Ashberry child or indeed any other man's child – a bastard child like he wrongly assumed himself to be.'

'Do you believe Reginald was prepared to sacrifice himself for his son?'

'You heard him at the trial "Leave him be. Let my lad be".'

'By the same argument both men could have been culpable. Could have worked together.'

'That might have happened too. Malcolm could have told his father that he had killed Lydia, and the old man helped him conceal his crime by disposing of her body down the Windypit.'

'Or vice versa.'

'Just so. Despite his neglected appearance, Reginald is still as strong and capable as Malcolm.'

'So I understand.'

'Tougher and meaner if anything.'

'I've heard that too.'

'Both men are extremely quick tempered.'

'I've seen that too.'

'Of course you have in court.'

'Will we ever know the truth of it?'

'Not unless one of them breaks down and gives the other away.'

'That's highly unlikely.'

'I do believe I've taken up enough of your time, Mr Cairn,' smiled Timon White, adjusting his peaked cap at a roguish angle. 'One way or the other the Bowdens are in custody and face hefty prison sentences. Indeed, Reginald might not live to see his freedom and Malcolm is facing an even heavier sentence.'

'And is this the justice Lydia Bowden deserves?'

'It is the only justice we've got. I suppose these things have a funny way of working out. I am what might be called a pragmatist in these matters, Mr Cairn.'

'So am I,' I agreed.

'Remember any time you want a climbing partner. Mont Blanc is awaiting us.' White's – aptly named – perfect set of teeth smiled again.

I thought about the surprising outcome to the Ashberry affair for a long time after he had gone. I knew he was right – a more just conclusion couldn't have been written.

* * * * *

After the trial Winifred became my constant companion and resided with me in my Gillygate townhouse. Better me, than living above the card slapping Ursula Howell. There was no more talk of Paris – a lot of talk about fated love – yet Winifred still would not agree to marry me. Maybe that was because she would never agree to honour and obey any man. Perhaps she had too much of her real father's fiery, poetical Fenian in her for that. Perhaps she had been put off any aspirations of wedded bliss by her mother's unfortunate second marriage to the pessimistic and politically extreme Cedric Holbrook. However, without actually tying the knot – without even realising it – we were both enjoying wedded bliss. I felt finally there was an unbreakable lifetime's bond between us. Equality, I knew by then this was the way things were heading and I was happy enough with that. I was prepared to live in sin. How could I expect anything else when the love of my life was a woman of suffrage?

With the arrival of Winifred, my maid Kate remained in position. She had, I believe, found a new man friend who worked in the railway office, and was obviously more comfortable working for me with another woman in the house. In turn, she and Winifred became great friends.

So, while fiercely maintaining her independent status, Winifred did agree to a honeymoon of sorts. We decided to take a year out from our respective careers and like John Ruskin take the Grand Tour.

August 1906 saw us in Italy. We drank in Tuscan warmth, energy, novelty and vividness until we rolled intoxicated to the next walled town. I kept my promise and took Winifred to Florence. We marvelled at Jacopo Pontormo's painting of the *Deposition from the Cross* standing alone before it in the church of Santa Felicita. Winifred said the whole experience made her feel lightheaded. We watched the sluggish afternoon flow of the Arno River from the Ponte Vecchio, our legs lazy with walking and wine.

But perhaps the highlight of our tour was a statue of a young woman reading a book in Florence's Uffizi Gallery. Her absorbed expression was timeless. We couldn't tell if she was Greek, Roman or medieval because the long gown she wore was dateless too. We had already gauped at the wrinkled veined suffering of the brilliant Michelangelo Buonarotti but this modest masterpiece was serenity itself.

'She's so real,' said Winifred transfixed.

'It's as if she is made of flesh and blood, not stone,' I agreed.

'Well, hello ... hello ... hello,' echoed a voice down the gallery. We almost jumped out of our skins.

'Do you think they have followed us all the way over here?' whispered Winifred. We stood there in astonishment as Andrew Ashberry and Louis Chatterton walked towards us – arms linked – well, this was Italy after all.

'This is an unbelievable coincidence,' said Andrew, kissing Winifred's cheek. 'Louis and I were only just talking about you the other day, James.'

'That's right,' agreed his companion.

'Just before we left England, we think we've solved the mystery of the sophisticated Well Wisher note supposedly written by Reginald Bowden to Mr Brown,' announced Andrew.

'But it wasn't "supposedly written by Reginald Bowden", it was written in his hand,' I objected.

'Indeed it was,' acknowledged Andrew. 'Written by him but dictated by someone else.'

'Oh, who?'

'Listen to this, one of our estate workers reported seeing a dandy leaving Broadshaw Farm around the time the note was penned. He told us the Bowdens' visitor struck him as odd because of his attire. He said the man was wearing a blue satin waistcoat covered in embroidered butterflies.'

'My god!' I exclaimed. 'Not Charnley Lodge?'

'The same,' confirmed Andrew.

'The worker had never seen a man dressed in such a fashion before in his life, and certainly not coming out of Reginald Bowden's door,' put in Chatterton.

'Regarding that note, I remember Reginald saying something in court to the effect "he told me", I expect he meant Lodge told him to write the note. I always wondered about that "he told me", and how a man like Reginald had come to use "filicide", when he couldn't even spell the word.'

'As you know Charnley Lodge had his own axe to grind against my father and Beardsley for sacking him,' said Andrew.

'It all makes sense now,' I replied, smiling down on the nodding in agreement head of Winifred. 'So Charley Lodge of all people was the editor of that note.'

Then Andrew did an extraordinary thing. Something that threw us all into a gaping silence. He took the diamond cross pendant from his wallet, the pendant once worn by Lydia, and fastened it round the neck of the statue of the woman reading a book.

'You can't leave it there. It's priceless,' I objected.

'What is? The statue or the pendant?' asked Andrew.

'Both,' chorused Winifred and Chatterton.

'Suits her though, doesn't it? She can keep it. The Uffizi can regard it as a donation from Gerard. I no longer have use for it,' replied Andrew, turning on his heels.

Author's Note

Yorkshire is a county of ruined Gothic abbeys – the skeletons in Henry VIII's cupboard – but all retaining their dramatic outlines against changing skies. No more beautiful than the Cistercian Rievaulx set in remote Ryedale. I could not imagine a more evocative place to set a novel. Then again there's Florence ...

Years after James Cairn experienced the incident in the Uffizi, Bowden father and son remained imprisoned by bars and their own consciences within Northallerton Gaol's grey walls.

Malcolm served his sentence for the manslaughter of Lord Gerard Ashberry. He became an avid poetry reader and expert on the rural poems of John Clare. Reginald Bowden died of heart failure only days before his release. It was rumoured that he made a death bed confession that it was indeed he, not his son, who had murdered Lydia to silence her.

Inspector Timon White left the North Riding of Yorkshire Constabulary and headed south to London to become a leading light in New Scotland Yard, built on the Victorian Embankment. The new police headquarters was clad with granite quarried by prisoners on Dartmoor. It was one of the first public buildings to be lit by electricity. About to house guardians of the law, New Scotland Yard had a rather ill-omened beginning: a dismembered female torso was found during its construction. This unsolved murder became known as the Whitehall Mystery.

The Right Honourable John Beardsley eventually lost his Tory parliamentary seat as the Liberal Party enjoyed its final great hurrah in government. First under Sir Henry Campbell-Bannerman, and following his death under Herbert Asquith. But it wasn't the rise in fortune of the Liberals that cost Beardsley his place in the Commons, no more a scandal of his own making: something to do with the buying and selling of gold bullion following information procured from a banker's wife.

Catherine Tiplady's young amore, the mole catcher James Wright, was killed in a farm accident. Was this fate's way of evening things up too? I'm not sure but that's what happened.

Charnley Lodge, who escaped his input into the Ashberry affair, became a successful bookmaker. Digby West, occasionally placed one or two unsuccessful bets with him. Lodge was no longer a square peg in a round hole: the racecourse was where those waistcoats belonged.

Speaking of Digby West, the confirmed bachelor, James and Winifred were guests at his wedding as he placed his safest bet in years on a Northamptonshire lass.

From here on the annals of fact and fiction change into historical reality.

The Russian Revolution of 1905 sowed the seeds of the February Revolution of 1917. The terrible events of Bloody Sunday, the massacre in St Petersburg's Palace Square, triggered a line of protests throughout the country. The rest of Europe, the old order, watched on fearing where war or revolution would strike next.

Despite prevalent anti-Semitism among the medical profession in England, in 1908 Friederich Wilhelm Eurich took over from H. J. Campbell and became Professor of Forensic Medicine at Leeds. However, he remained rather an unsung hero regarding his bacterial research for the Bradford Anthrax Investigation Board. Risking his own health, Eurich was a pioneer in the eradication of anthrax from fleeces used in Bradford mills – work that helped save thousands of workers from the disease in Yorkshire's wool industry.

The jeweller James Brown Inglis had married Anne Coates of Market Weighton c.1885. First noted as being a Heraldic Engraver of 4 Spurriergate, York, in 1887. He was registered as a jeweller at 4 Coney Street, York, in 1896. He was elected a York Councillor 1904 – 1910, Sheriff 1911 – 1912 and Alderman 1914. His wife, Anne, died on 24th January 1919. He became Governor of the Merchant Adventurers' Company 1920 – 1921 and Lord Mayor in 1922. He took a second wife, Sarah Freeman, in April 1923.

A final act: Thomas MacCarte the lion tamer, alias Massarti, following his terrible death was buried in Bolton's Tonge Cemetery in the January of 1872.

Inspector Timon White's boss, the Chief Constable of the North Riding Constabulary was indeed the colourful dapper Major Robert Lister Bower, reputed to be the most handsome man in the British Army during his service career. It is believed that Edgar Wallace's *Sanders of the River* was based on Bower and his exploits in Africa in the late nineteenth century.

Acknowledgements

I owe an immense debt of gratitude to Jeremy Mills; his Publishing Manager, Hazel Goodes, and graphic designer, Dawn Cockcroft, for giving this book life.

Thanks also must go to Professor Ian Scowen during his time as head of chemical and forensic sciences at Bradford University. His help in my understanding of the effect of strychnine poisoning was invaluable.

I give acknowledgement to Eric Ambler and all employees at Leeds Town Hall for their kindness in furnishing me with information about the Victorian Bridewell and law courts there. The nearby Victorian Tiled Hall Café is to be highly recommended too.

Last and certainly not least I owe so much to my husband, Paul, in both his help with the editorial process and ceaseless encouragement.

Author Profile

Educated in Leeds, Amanda Taylor did some magazine work and won a National Poetry Prize. She played squash for Yorkshire for nine years. Despite living in the middle of a grouse moor, about as far away as you can get from the sea, Amanda completed a successful relay swim of the English Channel and maintains that working out her plots helps the tedium of all those training miles. This is her third novel in the Cairn Mystery Trilogy.

Visit her website: **www.amandataylorauthor.com**

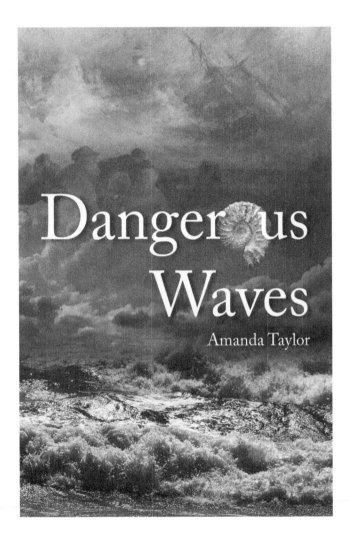

'... a tremendous mystery with twists and turns that keep you gripped until the final page. I couldn't put it down.'
— **Kay Mellor**

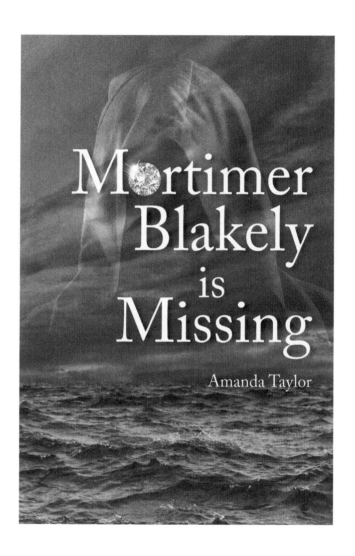

Mortimer
Blakely
is
Missing

Amanda Taylor

'*Mortimer Blakely is Missing* is a wonderful read. It is compelling story: gripping, original, accomplished and challenging.'

Gervase Phinn

Lightning Source UK Ltd.
Milton Keynes UK
UKOW06f0237120216

268239UK00008B/63/P